The Shaman's Bride

by

Laura Strickland

The Viking Brides, Book 2

The Shaman's Bride

Cover Art by *Diana Carlile*

The Wild Rose Press, Inc.
PO Box 708
Adams Basin, NY 14410-0708
Visit us at www.thewildrosepress.com

Publishing History
First Edition, 2022
Trade Paperback ISBN 978-1-5092-3968-9
Digital ISBN 978-1-5092-3969-6

The Viking Brides, Book 2
Published in the United States of America

A curse escaped her lips, and the person with whom she'd collided gave a grunt. His hands caught at her, closing on her arms in a steadying grip, and keeping her from falling.

For an instant they stood so, tightly linked, Gyda, half blinded by the dark of the hut. She felt—

A hard rush of emotions, like a punch to the gut. Warmth came first, stealing through his fingers, quickly followed by a tumble of images. The fall of light on water. The glowing coals of a near-dead fire, a heap of furs upon which two bodies lay, locked in passion. Blood, blood, and more blood.

She stumbled back through the doorway into the sunlight, trying to escape the images—to escape him. He came with her, his fingers still wrapped around her arms, and the clear light washed over them.

"Mistress Gyda, are you all right?"

The shaman. It was Gunnar's shaman—Lodvar. Gyda narrowed her eyes against the glare and regarded him. The emotions connected to those images continued to assault her, making it difficult to think clearly.

He felt the way music sounded—the way the notes vibrated from Modir's harp when she played, or when the women sang all together while at work on the shore. Beautiful, harmonious, powerful yet oddly still. All these things did she feel from him, combined with a flare of attraction so fierce and lustful it stole her breath away and knocked her back on her heels.

Chapter One

Sorvagur, The Faroe Islands—Summer 930

Gyda Tolljursdottir whirled in place, her feet performing a complicated dance beneath her, and raised the sword. Her hair, loosened during the combat, swirled out around her like an ash-blonde shawl, and the breath surged in her lungs. Locking eyes with her opponent, she bared her teeth in a smile. Sweat stood out on his skin. Did he look worried? Better yet, might she take him down this time? Her tingling muscles argued so, and her heart, singing within her, rose like one of her father's long ships cresting a wave.

She engaged her opponent's blade, and his eyes narrowed. Bright hazel eyes, they were, and as familiar to her as her own. At the moment they brimmed with annoyance, and she warned herself, *Here it comes. He will try to finish me now.*

Sure enough, his blade soared up in a swooping arc. Gyda ducked, and as she did, the call hit her. She froze, and felt the edge of her brother's blade catch in her hair.

"By Odin's eye!" Magnus bellowed, and reined in his ire. "What are you trying to do, Gyda? Make a murderer of me?"

Still motionless and in a half crouch, Gyda turned her eyes to the sea. Her brother's voice, sharp with questioning, faded away from her.

The warning came from there, from the sea. It raced through the clear blue, early summer sky the way a hawk might, swooping toward its prey. Awareness of some terrible danger. *Darkness rode the waters.*

Out of sight it was, too far away to be seen by the eye. But if she held her breath and listened, *listened* with the inner knowing that sometimes came to life, she just might be able to hear—

"Gyda. Gyda!"

A different call, this was. It sounded like a gull, and it effectively shattered Gyda's concentration. Was that what she'd heard? Only her mother's voice?

Quite probably, for here came the woman herself, rife with aggravation and puffing from the climb up the cliff path from the shore. This place, with its broad view of the ocean, that stretched for an unbroken distance southward to the Alban islands, made a favorite place for the young men of the settlement to practice at arms, especially on such a still and temperate day as this one. It must not have taken much thought for Gyda's mother, Eadha, to locate her.

Ach, but Gyda wasn't in the mood to be harangued by *Modir*, especially here before her brother Magnus's companions, whom she'd hoped to impress. She could already hear them muttering to one another. And was that a muffled snigger or two she caught?

Eadha Magnusson, as everyone in Gyda's world knew, ran the settlement of Sorvagur, even though Gyda's father, Tolljur Magnusson, held the title of Jarl. Tolljur, who had been a berserker and warrior without match back in Iceland, backed down for only one person in his life, and that person now approached

Gyda with blazing hazel eyes identical to Magnus's.

"Gyda," she called again, and it effectively blotted out that other call, the one that had soared over the water and echoed of danger. "Did you not promise to help the rest of us down on the shore? And yet I find you here with a weapon in your hand. Once again!"

Gyda lowered the blade, which she'd had to borrow from Magnus, since no one felt it fitting for a young woman to possess a sword of her own. She hoped to earn the right to carry it someday, as a shieldmaiden, but that eventuality found no favor with either of her parents.

"You do not know what you are talking about," Modir said when Gyda had asked for permission to fight. And *Fadir*, with the troubled look that sometimes invaded his gray eyes, laid his broad hand on her head, just as he had when she was a child, and told her, "There is no need for you to place yourself in harm's way, *Dottir*. Leave that to your *brodir*, and me."

A familiar wave of frustration rose inside her as she turned and faced her mother. Did they not see she was no longer a child but a woman, grown? Indeed, should she not be wed and bedded by now, and mistress of her own house? If she chose one of the young men at this moment standing around her, instead of a sword, would she then garner some respect?

"Come away," Modir snapped, just as she might address a servant. "We are already halfway through the morning's work, and you are needed."

Gyda's nose wrinkled involuntarily. Cleaning fish, the women of the settlement were, down at the harbor. Of all the women's chores Gyda encountered on a regular basis—and there existed an unending number of them—she detested that the most. The sheer, backbreaking labor of it, the way the scales stuck to her hands. The odor that seemed to get all the way into the back of her throat and wouldn't go away for days.

Magnus snatched the sword out of her hand and gave her shoulder a push. "Go on."

"I am not finished here," Gyda protested, with all the dignity she could muster.

"You are needed." Magnus grinned, mischief flaring in his eyes. "By the *women*."

This time all the young men shared a chuckle. Gyda lifted her head and clamped down hard on her ire. A warrior, as Fadir always said, did not lose control of his—or her, so Gyda supposed—anger. Not even when being upbraided like a five-year-old.

"*Ja*, but…" She took time to rake her brother with a glare before directing her gaze at the others loitering nearby like so many dolts, causing them to fall silent. "I will be back. And then I will beat the leggings off all you lot, eh?"

They laughed, and the moment passed. Gyda wiped her sweaty hands on her skirt and stepped up to Modir, who immediately turned back toward the shore.

"You did promise me your help, Gyda. And I want to get through this task before the rain moves in."

Ja, Gyda had promised, in a moment of weakness—or guilt—and fair was fair. She supposed Modir did not enjoy the task any more than she did. Modir would rather be playing on her harp, working at stitching Fadir's new tunic or, more likely, talking with him. All Gyda's life, her parents' close relationship had provided an example, and one difficult to follow. Some time ago Gyda had decided if she could not find a man to love the way Modir loved Fadir, she would take no man at all.

So here she was, with no man at all, on her way to perform a chore she detested.

As they headed down the path that led to the shore, Modir sighed. "It is not that I am unsympathetic, Gyda. I would be the last one to tell you to abandon your dreams. But you know your father will never allow you to go viking. You waste your time. And I do need the help."

"Ja." Gyda breathed the word, half under her breath. Here, heading down the steep path with the sea stretching out in front of them, all deep blue layers that stretched to infinity, the calling struck her again. *Darkness.* Danger rode those waters, just beyond the horizon. If she could only hear…

Stumbling to a halt, she strained once more to listen. She heard the women working down on the shore, talking to one another and laughing. She could hear Magnus's voice also, up behind her where he'd resumed drilling the men. She heard the gulls, circling above the tempting array of fish guts that marked the shore. And…

"Gyda," Modir protested in annoyance.

Gyda reached out and clutched Modir's arm. "Wait."

Eadha's eyes met hers and widened. "Dottir, what is it?"

A storm? Did one of the gales that sometimes savaged the Faroes lurk beyond sight? Yet the sea lay so still with the sun shining on it, like glass. And what she sensed did not feel like weather, but—

"Gyda," Modir interrupted the fragile thought yet

again. Modir should understand. Did she not have a connection with Fadir that, in the past, had allowed her to travel to him, unseen? And did the ancient gift of the Sight not travel along her bloodline, back in the Alban Isles?

Here in Sorvagur, that Alban blood ran mingled with Norse, the mothers and fathers of Gyda's generation having come from two very different sources. This, though, was a place of peace. Or so it had been...

Modir's gaze quickened. "Trouble?" she asked simply.

Gyda once more stretched her senses wide, sending them out over the water—seeking—until they encountered—ja, darkness. Her nostrils flared like those of a pony that had run too far, and she blinked rapidly. "Trouble," she confirmed. Suddenly, words not her own came from her. "There is danger. It rides the breasts of the waves. It brings us great harm."

Modir grasped Gyda's arm in turn. "We must bring this to your father. He oversees the plowing." She always knew just where he was, even if they'd not seen each other since breakfast. "Let us go to him." Modir's emotions rushed at Gyda: distress. Dread. Like many of the other women working on the shore below, Modir had been through much in the past—removed by force from the home she loved, held in captivity and slavery—before relocation here to this place of sometime peace.

But, as Fadir often said, one must battle for peace in order to keep it.

"What is amiss?" Modir's good friend, Brida, called up, seeing them stopped on the path.

"Trouble." Modir waved an arm. "From the sea."

All the women paused in their task and gazed out across the broad breast of the ocean.

Brida called back, "I see nothing."

Modir wasted no time making a reply. Releasing Gyda's arm, she turned and scrambled back up the path, moving like a goat. Gyda hurried after her.

Fadir and others of the men had begun clearing a new field this morning, readying it for planting. The season came late here, and they must take advantage while they could. Modir, with Gyda in her wake, swept through the clifftop area where the younger men still practiced at arms and hurried on without pausing.

When they reached the far field, they saw the men spread out across it, collecting what Fadir called the eternal stones. No matter how many got plucked from the thin soil, more seemed to sprout like weeds.

It made for a marginal existence, yet Fader remained reluctant to go raiding like others of his blood. It had happened only a time or two in the past, mostly in retaliation for raids that had been launched against them.

Once, when Gyda was still young, there had even been a raid upon Husavik, from whence Fadir came, in response to an attack by the leader there, a man called Jarl Gunnar. The bloody time, Modir called it. But Gyda remembered it as a time of plenty, for their warriors had proved victorious and the community had food and other goods to spare.

As her brother, Magnus, often asked Fadir, why not go raiding? "Is it not in our blood? Are you not a warrior?" he would propose.

A farmer, now. Gyda could see him, amid perhaps

a score of other men, spread out with their backs bowed, laboring. She picked out her father's head with ease—not the tallest among the men, but his ashen head, streaked with silver, matched her own.

He might not like the task before him, but he always applied himself with determination, resolved to leave the path of the berserker behind. Gyda had seen him slip into his berserker's rage only once or twice, when the settlement came under attack.

He stretched now and turned as if he felt Modir's presence. Eyes on her, he waited for her to reach him.

She ran the last few steps.

"What is it, Eadha, Wife? What has happened?"

"Nothing, Husband. Not yet." Modir directed a glance at Gyda, one that bade her join them.

They made a small huddle there in the sunny field, beneath the big, wide sky.

So far away from any trouble did this place feel, Gyda questioned what she'd felt, over again. Like a woman in a dimly lit hut, she groped for the sensation of danger.

Ja, it existed still, a dark, miasmic blot.

"Dottir?"

Gyda gazed into her father's gray eyes. "Danger comes," she told him. "From just out of sight, beyond the horizon."

Chapter Two

In the past, Gyda had witnessed her father in any
number of moods, brought about by a plethora of
situations. A formidable man marked by the scars of
many past battles, and with the deep gouges
representing the bear's claim upon him, scoring both
cheeks, his demeanor often proved measured and grave.
But his eyes could shine with love when he gazed upon
his wife. And he could break up into laughter when at
play with Gyda or Magnus.

Gyda liked best to see him that way, relaxed and
silly. But now, Modir spoke rapidly in his ear, and
when Gyda joined them, he turned a look on her, heavy
and grim.

"A Vision, is it?" he asked her directly.

"Nei, Fadir, just a flash—a sensing. I nearly missed
it."

"Danger, you say?" He frowned, and the light in
his eyes flickered, as when a shadow passes through a
patch of sunlight.

He glanced around at the bright field and the men
gathered, then away toward the harbor, where the
women had been working. "Here? In my place?"

Ja, he felt responsible for everyone and everything
here. Gyda knew that. He had founded this place more
than a score of years ago, he and those who'd followed
him from Iceland. A heavy weight to bear.

"Dottir, are you certain?"

Again, Gyda met his gaze. "Ja, Fadir. I wish it were not so."

He grunted and shifted the hoe in his hand, making of it instantly a weapon. The other men—those who'd followed him from Husavik and their sons—observed the gesture. None failed to understand it.

They might be farmers, at least nominally. But the warrior did not lie any farther beneath the surface than the stones beneath this thin sod.

Magnus loped up, barely breaking a sweat from his effort—perhaps he had sensed the discord also. Tall and slender, supple with whipcord strength in his long body, he topped his father by a bit. Whereas Gyda favored Tolljur, and could never be mistaken for anything but his daughter, Magnus favored Modir with a glint of red in his wild mane, now bound out of his way. A trace of reddish beard ran along his jaw, and his skin showed a pattern of freckles beneath the tan.

"What is it? Fadir?"

Tolljur laid a hand on his son's shoulder, the touch lending both support and caution. "Son, we must see to our defenses."

****

Word spread throughout the settlement the way a fire might, with astonishing speed. Even before Magnus reached the shore, the men had begun to gather on the highest point of the clifftop, where they gazed out to sea.

Such a splendid vantage should give generous warning of attack, almost as much as Gyda's senses.

"I must go see Kaddi," Tolljur said.

The aged shaman, Fadir's guide and caregiver back

in the days when he entered battle as a berserker at the head of a warrior throng, clung to life but lightly, and rarely left his bed these days. The young girls of Sorvagur took turns tending him, bringing him his meals and sweeping out his hut. Deeply beloved, he would be missed if and when he passed to the next world.

The very idea made Gyda's heart ache. She stopped in to see the old man nearly every day and brought him treats whenever she could.

"I will come with you," she told Fadir now.

He shot her a look and nodded. Kaddi's hut lay at the center of the settlement, in a place of protection. One of Gyda's friends, named Aya, stepped out when they approached, and greeted them fondly.

"Jarl Tolljur, and Gyda. How are you this fine day?"

"We need words with Master Kaddi. How fares he?"

Aya looked hesitant. "A bit distracted, to tell the truth."

"Ja," Tolljur grunted. "Dottir, come."

The interior of the small hut was dim and quiet. The old man lay in his bed against the wall, his wizened fingers clamped on his blanket. When they entered, his one remaining eye, now turned milky, sought their faces. Like Fadir Odin, he'd sacrificed the other eye years ago in the pursuit of wisdom.

"Ah," he greeted them. "I knew you would come. Who has Seen?"

A check in Fadir's step allowed Gyda to move forward. She went to her knees at the side of the bed and touched the old man's hand.

"Not a Vision, Master Kaddi. But—but a warning."

"Ah." He attempted to focus on her, and touched her face in turn. "Beautiful lass. You look like your aunt did, long ago. Tolljur, does she not look like your *søstir*?"

"She does, and named for her." Tolljur came and squatted down also.

"But I think," Kaddi mused, "you have the spirit of your modir's people, inside." He tapped his own chest, above the heart.

Gyda nodded. Modir had told her that back in the Alban islands, from whence she'd come, the Second Sight was a common gift. Such abilities traveled through the blood.

Modir had once wished to follow the holy path— the same Kaddi traveled—and become a priestess. That had been before her capture, and claiming by Fadir.

"Master Kaddi, a great darkness lies out upon the breast of the water, beyond the horizon. I have not Seen but felt this. I fear—I fear it brings us harm."

"Ach." Kaddi's milky eye focused on Fadir.

"Have you felt this thing also?" Fadir asked directly. "Can you tell if the danger is real?"

"If the lass says it, then it is so."

"Ja." Fadir shifted unhappily. "But—who is it brings this harm to us?"

"Once," Kaddi said, "I would have been able to tell you. I would speak to Fadir Odin, and cast the runes."

"I know. Can you not do so now?"

Gyda whispered, "We will bring your stones here to you, whatever you need."

The old man closed his eye. The hut became so still, the sunlight pouring in through the open door gained sentience. It touched Kaddi's silver head and, for an instant, Gyda felt sure the great god had come.

Belief in such beings, as her mother had taught her, must be absolute. Without belief, no help would come.

With his eye still closed, Kaddi bade, "Bring me my rune stones."

"Bring them," Fadir told Gyda in turn.

She scrambled up. She knew where the stones rested, in a finely woven bag, on the shelf. When she took them up, her hand brushed the bundle of herbs beside them, and their scent rose, swift and pungent.

A voice whispered in her head. *Remember.*

But she had little to remember, other than this place where she'd been born and lived all her life.

She laid the bag in the old man's lap. He untied it with stiff fingers and reached inside. He spoke a prayer, almost under his breath. *Great Odin, guide me as ever you have done. Lead me. Help me see.*

He reached out and seized Gyda's wrist. "You— you, warrior lass. You will help me see."

"Ja, Master Kaddi."

He drew forth a rune and placed it on the blanket. Gyda named it for him, and the others that followed, one by one.

He spoke in a drone, "An old enemy, become new. It is a puzzle. Except it is not." He focused his foggy gaze once more on Fadir. "You and I both know, son, from whence this peril comes. It rushes over the water from Husavik."

****

Fadir and Modir, along with other senior members of the settlement, talked long into the night. The younger men, Magnus among them, kept watch from the cliffs and, unable to sleep, Gyda wandered among them.

She found her brother gazing steadfastly off into the night, peace riding his shoulders. Once, so Modir said, Fadir had feared the birth of a son, believing that just as he'd inherited the berserker's curse from his father, a boy child might receive it from him. Despite being named for that very man, though, Magnus had shown few tendencies. He took most strongly after Modir's forebears and, so she said, strongly resembled her father, who had been a chief and a warrior, back in the Alban isles.

Indeed, even at the age of a score and two, Magnus made a fierce warrior, with all Fadir's abilities—save the one. Yet he rarely lost his temper and seldom slipped into what might be considered a rage of any kind.

"All quiet?" Gyda asked, as she had the others she passed.

"Ja." He gave her a mischievous smile. "Of course, I possess but ordinary senses. Why do you not employ yours?"

"I do not know that I want to." Gyda shivered. "Once was enough." She reached out and clasped her brother's hand. They were close, having been born barely a year apart. "I felt a great darkness, Magnus."

"You think it's Fadir's old enemies? From Husavik?"

"So Kaddi says."

Magnus grunted. "Then it will come to battle. Fadir will die defending this place. And I with him."

"And I," Gyda agreed softly.

Magnus turned his head to her. "Fadir will never

agree to let you fight."

"If the invaders are one bit as evil as they feel, he will have no choice. You know I am able to use a sword."

"You are getting better."

"Good enough. If it comes to a life-or-death defense—"

Magnus shook his head. "Sparring with us, ja, you can hold your own. We have no wish to harm you. But against seasoned warriors, the ilk of those who used to fight with Fadir—"

Gyda's heart fell on a surge of disappointment. Had he been playing with her during the training, her fine brother? Letting her think she possessed skills she had not? Tartly, she said, "Danger makes for a sharp sword."

"Or a severed head. No matter, Fadir adores you. He will never permit it."

"Ach, and does he love you so much less than me, that he will let you risk yourself?"

"He has no choice. I am his son."

"That is very unfair."

Magnus chuckled softly. "Sometimes you sound too much like Modir."

Gyda gazed away over the water into the dark that hovered at the horizon. She didn't even need to try, now, in order to sense it. Like a miasma, a sickness, the danger moved ever closer.

"Fadir," she told her brother, "may soon have no choice, no choice but to let me fight."

Chapter Three

With the arrival of dawn came Gyda's best friend, Astrid, who found her still stationed on the clifftop with Magnus, both of them keeping watch.

Astrid, daughter of Modir's friend and fellow captive Rona and the Norse warrior she'd wed, had chestnut brown hair and her father's fair complexion, along with his startlingly blue eyes. She came with her skirts kilted high and a basket over her arm.

"Can you see anything?" she called.

Magnus turned his head. Gyda suspected—though he'd not admitted—he had an eye for Astrid. She knew for a fact that Astrid favored her brother, though so far each had been too uncertain to let the other know.

"They are out there," Magnus said. "Hanging just over the horizon. They won't come in far enough to let us see them."

Astrid shot a look at Gyda, who nodded. The danger now hummed through her, like the vibration of an approaching storm.

"They will come with the next dark," Magnus said. He smiled at his sister. "Try to take us by surprise, not knowing we have our own herald."

Astrid directed a look down to the harbor, where Fadir's two dragon boats rested at anchor. "Will we mount a defense?"

"Ha, sure. The elders discuss this even now."

"I remember—" Astrid broke off. They all remembered battles from when they were small. Fire and darkness, terror and violence. The first time Gyda saw her father slip into his berserker's trance had changed her life, and altered her relationship with the man she'd known always to be gentle and restrained. He had met the invaders on the shore and been unstoppable during the fight that followed. With his warriors at his back, he'd driven the invaders away.

For many years, they'd not returned. If this threat came to a fight, would Fadir once more transform into the berserker? If Gyda understood correctly, he could not keep from it, under duress. That troubled her deeply, for Fadir was no longer the young man he had been.

She might lose him. The terrible thought caused a catch in her heart. She was, and always had been, her father's lass. Ja, he loved Magnus also, as only a strong man could love. But she, Gyda, was his first born, and they shared an almost magical bond.

She simply could not bear to lose him.

Besides, if he fell, so would the settlement. And then what?

She'd listened to her mother's stories of captivity. Modir and most the other women who'd come away from Husavik had once been slaves.

Gyda could not imagine trading her life of freedom—ja, even privilege—here, for one of slavery in Iceland.

"How many boats do you think they have?" Astrid looked from Magnus to Gyda.

Gyda closed her eyes and sent her consciousness out over the water, still as calm as a scrying glass. Ja, they hung just out of sight, even as Magnus said. Sometimes she wondered if her brother did not also have a touch of the Sight.

"One. There is but one dragon boat." She could feel the men teeming there. Avarice. Hatred. Aggression.

"One may be enough."

"Nei," Magnus said immediately. "We will defend this blessed place—out of love, if nothing else."

Astrid turned her gaze on him, and Gyda could see the adoration in her eyes.

Ja, Modir often called this a blessed place, even a holy place, where they had been able to come together and build a measure of safety.

Astrid sighed. "I brought breakfast. Are you hungry?"

Magnus flashed a smile. "Always."

She blushed and fished in her basket. "Bread and cheese."

"Thank you, Mistress."

Ja, Gyda thought, a possible romance between these two. If they had not waited too long.

****

After the elders emerged from their meeting at Tolljur's house, the entire settlement gathered on the top of the cliff. Two of the strongest young men went to Kaddi's hut and carried him out, wrapped up in his blankets.

Tolljur, who rarely spoke in public, made a speech.

"Danger approaches—invaders. One long ship, so my dottir says, but as you know, a single dragon boat may be well loaded with men and weapons, and can bring disaster.

"We will defend our home." He let those words hang in the air while he gazed from face to face, and to the green land beyond. "Because it is our home. Those of you who have fought with me before know—I will not yield."

The men cheered. Gyda wondered what they found, other than the courage inherent in those words, to praise. If this fight came, some of them would not survive. As Fadir had, she looked into the faces—all known, and many dearly loved. She could not bear the thought of losing any of them.

Because she'd sensed that darkness hanging over the water, life would change. Nothing would ever be the same.

The men moved on to practical matters. Those of the older generation had long been warriors. The younger were well trained. A watch would be organized, weapons readied. Each of them had a role to play.

Gyda should have felt reassured by it all. Instead, a near-paralyzing sensation gripped her heart. "What is it?" Modir clasped her arm as they walked back to the house.

"If not for me—for what I sensed—we would not face all this trouble."

"Dottir, that is not so. Without you, we would have no warning."

At midday, cries came from the cliffs. Everyone within hearing distance ran, the men clutching their weapons.

"What do you see?" Fadir called to the girl stationed there.

"A dragon ship. Look!"

"Ah!" Fadir exclaimed.

The ship had, indeed, decided to show itself. It lay along the deep blue line of the horizon, perfectly motionless, and barely visible from this distance.

"Only the one," Modir panted.

Fadir narrowed his eyes. "Ja. But why would he show himself now?" Better, he left unsaid, to launch an attack after dark.

"Foolish," Magnus whispered, and young Astrid asked, "Does he know we can see him?"

"He knows. Any Viking worth the name can calculate his distances."

"Then what—"

Fadir merely shook his head.

No one on the clifftop moved, while the long ship came in. It moved very slowly, barely perceptibly, at first but by mid-afternoon the watchers could see the carvings on the prow and the shields hung over the side. Rowers brought it in over that deceptively calm sea.

"Is it a war ship?" someone asked.

Fadir shook his head. "Impossible to tell." He added under his breath, so Gyda, who stood beside him, could hear, "Must be. What else?"

What, indeed? Frustration and anxiety increased as they waited to see. Young mothers stood with their babes clutched in their arms. When Fadir gave the signal, they would flee inland, but they did not like abandoning their homes and their husbands.

Modir paced, unable to keep still, but Fadir stood like a rock, the sun beating down on his ashen head and bringing out the sweat on his shoulders, unmoving.

At last a message came from Kaddi. By then—late afternoon—nearly everyone in the settlement swarmed the cliff, with only Kaddi himself and a few others left at home.

One of the girls who helped look after the old man came running to Fadir. "My master has cast the stones! He says the portents are not for war."

Fadir appeared shocked, and a murmur ran through the crowd.

Gyda stepped forward and touched her father's arm. "Fadir, I would yet argue caution."

His gray eyes met hers. "Would you doubt Master Kaddi?"

"No, never. But I felt what lies out there on the water."

"Ja, Dottir. Do you feel it still?"

She shook her head. "I cannot."

He made a decision. "Bring your weapons," he called to the men. The strange ship—looking large and very fine—had nearly slipped into the harbor where lay his two boats at anchor.

"We will go down and meet him, this man who comes."

Chapter Four

The men moved in a throng, silently and purposefully, down from the cliff to the sheltered harbor. The older generation, those who'd come to these isles with Tolljur Magnusson, were warriors born and bred. These days they might play at being farmers, but weapons still came easily to their hands.

The younger men, mostly the sons of freed Alban women, had been trained well by their fathers, and went as eagerly.

Many of the women returned to the settlement. Only Modir lingered, still eyeing the incoming ship. Gyda joined her.

"Will they fight as soon as they hit the shore?" If so, the cliff made a prime vantage point.

Modir shook her head, a faraway look in her eyes. Did she remember old battles, such as the one in which she'd been captured?

"Modir—I could fight."

Modir turned her head, and Gyda received the full impact of her gaze. Wide her eyes were, and full of light—so like Magnus's eyes it was uncanny. "Do not be foolish."

"It is not foolish. You know I have been training with the sword. Magnus and some of his friends work with me."

"Aye, and that is well enough, if you seek to amuse

yourself."

"Amuse!"

"This is in deadly earnest." Modir's eyes moved to the path, where men still moved down to the harbor with Tolljur at their head. She whispered, "I cannot bear to lose him. *Lugh, please.*"

Lugh, as Gyda knew, was the Alban god Modir followed, whose protection had accompanied her from the far distant isle where she'd been born and raised. Not so different, perhaps, from Odin.

"If you fear for Fadir—"

"I always fear for him. You have no idea what war can bring."

"—then let me go down there and stand with him, fight to help defend our home."

"Nay. You should help me organize the women and children in case we need to move them all inland."

Yet Eadha stood unmoving, watching—watching the bright scene as the ship came in, and the group of men, fully armed, waited.

Like a scene from a dream it was, or a Vision, as the long ship, its dragon head gazing serenely at the shore, slipped into place beside Fadir's two vessels, and the men aboard dropped anchor. Gyda heard them calling and answering orders, their voices sharp in the still air.

A figure climbed to perch beside the bow, one hand resting on the dragon's carved neck, leaning outward. Tall he was, with a head of hair like spun gold, broad of shoulder and lean of hip. A vigorous form, though from the distance Gyda could not guess his age. He wore a sword but made no move to reach for the hilt. Surely if these invaders meant to attack, they'd already be over the side of the ship and running through the water.

He called something, though Gyda could not hear what. Fader started forward.

"Nay," Modir said. "It is a trap."

Without hesitation, Gyda turned and pelted for the shore.

Fleet of foot when need be, she could often best Magnus in a race, and she went now prodded by fear. She had no weapon, aside from the small knife she always carried in her pocket, and that more utilitarian than aught else. A lass never knew when she might need a knife. She would fight with it, if she had to.

Quick she might be, but before she reached the shore, the invaders had disembarked over the sides of their vessel and splashed through the water.

The leader came with his hand extended to Fadir. Gyda caught only the end of their exchange.

"—come in peace. I am Gunnar Fritisson, and I lead these men."

****

Gunnar Fritisson. Surely Gyda had heard that name before, if only in pieces. Gunnar had been the name of the jarl at Husavik, whom Fadir followed back in Iceland. The man with whom he had broken when he left. Friti had been that man's son, a treacherous backstabber, denounced even by his own father.

And this man, as Gyda saw when she reached her brother, could not be much older than she, as were the bulk of the men he had brought with him.

They gained the shore one by one, wearing their weapons yet with none in their hands. They cast their eyes interestedly over the green rise of land, and at the cliffs and the settlement.

Under her breath, she asked Magnus, "What does this mean?"

"He says they do not bring battle. I do not like it."

Neither did Gyda. Such words did not fit with the emotions she'd sensed coming to her over the water.

"I must tell Fadir—do not trust him."

Gyda started forward, and Magnus warned, "Wait."

He caught at her arm, but she slipped through his fingers and took a place at Fadir's side, where she found herself facing Gunnar Fritisson.

He had an interesting face, strong in the bone and pleasing in its proportions. A deep tan—proof of time spent on the ocean or out in the field—colored his forehead and shoulders. In contrast, his hair looked startlingly light. His eyes might have been the bluest Gyda had ever seen.

They smiled when he focused on her face, and his voice turned warm.

"And who is this?"

"My daughter, Gyda." Gyda had never heard her father use so cold a tone. Nor had she seen him look at anyone the way he now looked at Gunnar Fritisson. Like he wanted to take the younger man apart with his bare hands.

Gunnar gestured to the others of his party, a throng nearly a score in number. "Jarl Tolljur, we have broken with the settlement back in Husavik. We wish to join you here, instead."

****

"I do not trust him," Fadir stormed, pacing beside the fire in their dwelling. "He is Friti Gunnarsson's son. And Annaborg's." He fairly spat that name.

25

Gyda had heard of these folks before; they came from a past she'd never known. The names had the power to affect both her parents deeply. Fadir's distress was palpable, and found its reflection in Modir's eyes.

"Why would he come here?" Modir wondered aloud. "And bring so many with him?"

"He says his grandfather, Gunnar, has died, and his father has seized power in Husavik."

"But how could Friti seize power? Gunnar shunned him for his misdeeds. When we left—"

"Ja, but Gunnar had no other sons, at least not legitimate ones. And, disgraced or not, blood will tell."

"I have to say, Tolljur, it is a likely story."

"Too likely, and the young man tells it far too glibly, and with a smile on his accursed lips."

Gyda relaxed a bit. She need not worry about Fadir proving incautious. His suspicion matched her own.

"Then," Magnus, also present, suggested, "tell him to go. Bid him get back on that fine ship of his and sail away from our shores."

"I will. First, I supposed I should hear him out. I want to know why he and his company choose to come here, of all places in the world."

"Hear him out," Magnus growled, "and bid him go."

Modir blew out a breath. "At least, this is better than a battle and blood spilled on the shore."

"Is it?" Ruefully, Fadir shook his head. "In battle, I know where I am. Wife, I am not the man for words and negotiations."

"Well then, Husband—'tis well you have me."

Gyda went out just before nightfall and peered down at the harbor and at the boat that lay there at

26

anchor. The strangers had been ordered to stay aboard this night—no offers of hospitality here—and a guard had been set. Despite Gunnar Fritisson's friendly words, treachery could well lie behind his blue eyes.

Someone moved into place at Gyda's shoulder. Magnus? No, Modir.

"What are you doing?" Modir asked.

"I doubted the boat was really there—yet it is."

"Aye." Eadha whispered the word in her own language, some of which Gyda understood. "Dottir, you will keep away from Gunnar Fritisson."

"He is handsome enough." Why had Gyda even said so, save it was the truth?

Modir glanced at her. "Maybe so. But his father was responsible for the death of your aunt—she for whom you are named." Modir sounded unhappy. "She whom, so your father says, you favor so strongly."

"You never knew my aunt?"

Modir shook her head again. "But your father's feelings regarding her death are strong. He will protect you from Gunnar Fritisson, if needs must."

"Ach, Modir." Gyda narrowed her eyes at the dragon ship. "You may reassure him. I am perfectly capable of protecting myself."

Chapter Five

She was here.

Here, in this place of great, steep cliffs, of deep-water fjords, of green turf so bright it hurt the eyes. Like a lodestone, she had pulled him across the ocean, caused him to join with a man he despised, and throw in with this wretched, treacherous scheme.

Had he caught a glimpse of her yet? So strong had been the pull yesterday, there on the rocky shore, it had near blasted his senses. After a lifetime of yearning, he sensed his goal was at last in sight.

To be so close, yet still unable to find her…

He paced to the gunwale of the ship and gazed landward. The scent of the water filled his nose, and the beauty of this place stirred him. He'd not expected it.

Was she who called to him also beautiful? He smiled to himself. It did not matter if she was or was not. The destined home of his heart, he would love her no matter how she appeared.

He already did.

He lifted his head and watched the mist rise from the cliffs into the morning sky. A cauldron of enchantment was this bay. It spoke to him even as did the elusive woman who'd spoken to his heart, to his mind, all his life.

It felt as if he recognized something here. But for all that, he had not recognized her yesterday.

Gunnar strolled up to take the place beside him. "Well, Lodvar, what are the portents?"

The sarcasm in Gunnar's voice argued a level of mockery. Why did he ask, if he didn't believe? Why had he brought Lodvar along, if he gave so little credence to the guidance a shaman might provide?

Ach, but it would be a rash man indeed who spat in the eye of the gods. And Gunnar tended to cover all eventualities, if he could.

"All remains favorable," he answered evenly.

"You have cast the stones?"

"To be sure." Lodvar shot his jarl a close look. Not a hard man to measure, Gunnar Fritisson, for all his inclination toward deception. "I cast them each morning, in order to read the day."

"Ja, Lodvar Haraldsson, and what will this day bring to me?"

"Communication."

"Ach, it does not take a Seer to forecast that. I must convince this old man, this former berserker, that I can be of benefit to him."

"He does not look so old."

"He is of my fadir's generation." Gunnar snorted. "Though not your fadir's. Yours is an old man."

Lodvar shrugged. His father had been held in high esteem by the old jarl, Gunnar's grandfather, also called Gunnar. In fact, Lodvar's mother, an Alban slave called Catrin, had been awarded to Harald by the jarl for services rendered. Harald had lost no time in getting her with child. Lodvar had been born a slave, but his father's favor had brought him opportunities. As had the talents with which he'd been born—the ability to communicate with the gods, to interpret their messages.

To foresee the future.

Harald—toward whom Lodvar had mixed feelings—had given him an education. That had allowed Lodvar to take care of his mother.

He hoped she would be all right without him, back in Husavik. Things had changed drastically since the death of the old jarl, and not for the better.

"Will I be able to deal with him, this Tolljur Magnusson?"

Lodvar shrugged. He did not wish to be bothered with Gunnar's concerns, not at this moment. He wanted to concentrate on the fact that after a lifetime's longing, he'd nearly reached his goal, his heart's-ease.

She was here. But which of the women he had seen?

"Better to persuade him than fight against him," he told Gunnar steadily.

The new jarl's son did not like the implied slur to his judgment or to his prowess. "You think I could not best him in battle?"

Lodvar met Gunnar's gaze, deceptively wide and inherently dangerous. "I did not say that. But he is a berserker, and such men are to be treated carefully."

"Ja."

"Such men are worthy of respect."

"As am I. Son and grandson of jarls, am I not? And clever with my tongue or a sword."

Clever was Gunnar Fritisson, ja, the way Loki was clever. And Gunnar's father had only become jarl at the moment of his own father's death—a questionable event in and of itself.

Gunnar touched the ship's rail lightly. "I will talk that old berserker round. And you, Lodvar, will help me, if you know what is good for you." He gave his companion a blinding smile. "Or should I say, if you know what is good for your mother, back home?"

****

"Fadir, I wish to sit in on the meeting."

"What?" Fadir turned his head and looked at Gyda. He appeared distracted, his gray eyes gone foggy and opaque. Had he even heard what Gyda said?

Apparently so, for after an instant he replied, "You? Why?"

"I would take the measure of these men. I do not trust them, not given what I felt out on that water before they came in."

"I do not trust them either," Modir put in. They'd just finished breakfast around their own fire, and Modir busied herself clearing away the remains of the meal. "You know who he is, Tolljur. The son of Friti and Anaborg. It would be mad to trust him."

"Who is Anaborg, exactly?" Gyda asked. She'd heard the name in the past, when her parents spoke of Husavik, but never with any details attached.

Her parents exchanged a look before Modir bit her lip. "No one of consequence."

"Come! How am I to help, if I do not understand all the implications?" Gyda shot a look at her brother, who sat listening quietly, as was his way.

Somewhat surprisingly, it was Fadir who answered. "Anaborg Helmsdottir was a young woman of Husavik, a vixen, a deceptive she-wolf who once tried to kill your mother. Quite mad, by the time we left."

Gyda stared. "Tried to kill—"

"And nearly succeeded. So *nei*, we will not trust

31

this young man. But we will meet with him. And listen."

"While we sharpen our swords," Magnus put in.

"It is always wise to keep a sharp sword." Fadir hesitated. "He wants something, this Gunnar Fritisson. We need to determine what."

Gyda asked, "Will you bring Kaddi down for the meeting?"

"Not yet. I think we will keep Kaddi as a secret weapon. This—this will be just a casual meeting, ja? All polite and easy." Fadir did focus on Gyda then. "And you can help. He will not suspect that the pretty lass offering him refreshment can also peer into his heart, eh?"

"If I can." Gyda felt suddenly uncertain.

"You can," Modir declared. "And you will."

****

Fadir might be Jarl of Sorvagur, but he lived like the others of the settlement, in a plain dwelling. Comfortable it was, but no declaration of wealth.

Gunnar Fritisson strode in as if he owned the place, moving the way a trained warrior did, with assured confidence, and glanced about as if weighing that wealth. He did not look impressed. Gyda wondered what the dwellings in Husavik might be like.

Three other men accompanied him, one at his shoulder and two more trailing him in the manner of guards. Indeed, when Fadir invited them to sit, the two remained standing instead, stationed near the door. They wore their weapons, but had none of them drawn.

No matter, Gyda thought. Fadir and Magnus were also armed, and she had her own knife in her belt. No doubt Modir also carried a concealed weapon. If it came to a fight, it would be short and sharp.

Even more than weapons, Gunnar Fritisson brought an aura into the dwelling. Intensely masculine, it threatened to overwhelm Gyda's senses, and begged her to focus on him, excluding the others.

No denying that he was an attractive man. Near in height to Magnus, who overtopped Fadir a bit, he had a powerful build, with those broad shoulders and muscular legs.

He wore his hair loose—unusual enough for a man—perhaps because he knew what an impression its color made. While fair-headed men were common in Gyda's world, such locks of flaxen gold stood out, as did his face, which might have been pretty had it not been quite so hard and rugged.

She wondered if he took after his mother, Anaborg, the she-wolf.

He smiled as he took the seat Fadir offered, beside the hearth. His brilliant blue gaze next swept Gyda up and down, displaying flattering interest, before he nodded at Modir.

"Mistress."

The impact of his presence almost caused Gyda to overlook the man at his shoulder—almost. Yet, once she turned her gaze on him, she found him impressive in his own right.

Brown hair, he had—an ordinary, medium brown—but dressed in a far from ordinary fashion. Indeed, he wore part of it loose, like Gunnar, but the rest had been captured into a series of braids, each adorned with white feathers. The feathers made her think of old Kaddi, who possessed a raven-feather cloak and wore it on occasions when he wanted to demonstrate his power.

Did this man also possess power? Hard to tell, with Gunnar's energy overshadowing the room.

The brown-haired man cast Gyda a look as inquiring as her own. Did his eyes match his hair, or were they hazel? Nei, an unusual shade of tawny gold.

"Thank you for meeting with us," Gunnar said. "This is my advisor, Lodvar Haraldsson. I trust you have no objection to his presence?"

Modir turned to the young man, and her eyes widened. "Surely—surely we have met before?"

Chapter Six

Two women in the chamber, Lodvar thought, while his inner senses clamored for his attention. Two women—might one of them be she whom he had sought so long? He frowned as he met the gaze of the woman who had addressed him. Near his mother's age, she had a stark, well-hewn look about her and a brown birthmark on her cheek. Her hair carried a reddish gleam in the firelight. Most certainly, she did not look Norse.

Could she be the one he was meant to find? The thought caused him a jolt of disappointment. Surely not.

Yet she suggested he felt familiar to her, that they might have met…

"Mistress," he said cautiously, "I do not think so."

"I suppose it would not be possible." Disregarding Gunnar's mild glare of surprise—in his world, females did not speak out of turn—the woman went on, confident in the possession of her right. "Who is your mother, back in Husavik?"

Another surprising question. In Husavik, one's mother did not matter. Only one's sire counted.

"My father was the jarl's man, Harald, and kept the great hall for him."

Now the woman—wife of the berserker jarl, she must be—looked surprised. But she shot a look at Gunnar before placing a hand on Lodvar's arm. "We will speak later."

"This is my wife." Tolljur Magnusson confirmed it. "And my daughter, Gyda."

Daughter? Could she be the one?

Lodvar turned his gaze to the younger woman, even as Gunnar did also, and found he hoped so.

Hoped so.

For Gyda was a beauty. Indeed, difficult to believe such a flower had come from that stark woman and this bear of a man. Tall she was for a woman, yet delicately made, with a body equal parts strength and grace. Ashen hair tumbled in a spill of waves down her back, and something in her fair, oval face caught at the heart.

Lodvar met her eyes—pale gray like her father's and set wide in that exquisite face, and longing rose violently in his chest.

Against all reason, he wanted it. He wanted her to be the one.

"Mistress Gyda." Gunnar gave her his most charming smile. "Had I known such beauty lay here at Sorvagur, I would have made the voyage sooner."

The berserker growled. Protective he would be of his women, ja. Gunnar would need to go carefully if he wished to win this woman's favor.

"Sit," Tolljur Magnusson said, "and tell me why you have come."

Gunnar sat where invited, beside the fire, and donned his most earnest look. He could play very well at sincerity when he chose, and now frowned as if searching out his words most carefully.

"The situation in Husavik is not good, since the death of my grandfather, Jarl Gunnar. You know something of how things were there?" He directed a look at their host.

Tolljur joined him beside the fire. "I do."

"My father has long stood disgraced in my grandfather's eyes. Denied the place of jarl after him. Yet my grandfather has no other son." He corrected himself. "No legitimate son. And when my grandfather died unexpectedly—" He hesitated. "My father seized power."

Gunnar raised those earnest eyes to Tolljur's face. "I have broken with him. I, and my men, can stay in Husavik no longer. We have come to you—seeking refuge."

Tolljur and his wife exchanged a single look before Tolljur cleared his throat. "And what should make you ask for refuge here, of all places?"

"There are several reasons. You have a good location, on the trade route eastward. There is already a fine, established settlement. And I thought you might be in need of warriors."

"Did you?" Tolljur's expression gave away nothing.

"Besides, is this not a place of safety? Did not you and all your folk come here seeking refuge?"

"More than a score of years ago. Tell me, Gunnar Fritisson, were you close to your grandfather?"

"I was." Gunnar summoned an expression of grief. "Despite the rift between him and my father, he did acknowledge me, and saw me well-trained both at arms and diplomacy."

"I am surprised he did not, then, name you as his successor."

"Ja, Tolljur Magnusson, so he did. My father refuses to acknowledge my claim."

"And your mother?" Mistress Eadha spoke again, causing Gunnar to shoot her another well-disguised look of disapproval. "Does she not back your claim?"

"Mistress, my mother is mad, and has been these many years. To do Fadir justice, he has looked after her well all the while, but she is able to take no part in our dispute."

"And I ask once more, why come to me?" Tolljur spread his hands. Broad and scarred, they clearly showed the marks of past battles, but not so much as his face, which bore twin rows of deep furrows down each cheek. The mark of the bear, those must be, and terrible to behold.

Only Gunnar, or his father, Friti, would dare to take such a man on. Dared Lodvar hope they might fail?

Gunnar leaned forward, his earnest expression very much in evidence. "Jarl Tolljur, I need your help."

The berserker huffed. Wry humor, and a measure of incredulity, flavored the sound. "Why should I help you?"

"Because"—Gunnar widened his eyes—"you need my help in turn. My father, so it seems, has an old score to settle with you. And now that he is Jarl, and has the means, he's vowed to come here and destroy you all."

****

"Well, Lodvar, and how do you think that went?"

Gunnar asked the question like a man who already knew the answer. It had, indeed, been a stellar performance on his part, back at Tolljur Magnusson's house. And, while Gunnar rarely entertained doubts about his victories, he did enjoy crowing about them.

As they made their way back to the long ship,

trailed by the two guards—mostly for effect, Lodvar wagered—Gunnar just had to boast. "Do you think he believed me, the great berserker?"

"Hard to tell." Willing to give Gunnar little approval, Lodvar spoke in measured tones. "The woman is shrewd."

"The woman?" Fool that he was, Gunnar dismissed Mistress Eadha out of hand. "She does not matter."

"She does, and will speak in her husband's ear. He will listen."

"Which just shows how weak he is. Just as Fadir said." Gunnar shrugged. "Why should Tolljur Magnusson's wife fail to believe me? There is enough truth in the tale."

"Perhaps." Lodvar hesitated. "The woman has some power." There had been a goodly measure of it there in the room. Lodvar did not believe it stemmed from the berserker, from the younger woman, or Tolljur's son, though he could be wrong.

"We are protected." Gunnar gave Lodvar a hard stare. "You see to that." Gunnar thought for a moment, his insistence visible in his eyes. "You must make sure of it."

"How?"

"That woman—Tolljur's wife—she wishes to speak with you of her days in Husavik. You can win her good favor and opinion."

And, Lodvar thought, not for the first time, why should he help to further Gunnar's interests? Had he not already betrayed his conscience enough?

Gunnar gave him a smile, the one others rarely saw from him—sly and dangerous. "I know you will help me. For your mother's sake, if for no other reason."

That put a check in Lodvar's step, nearly making him trip on the steep path down to the harbor. With him away, his mother was at the mercy of Friti Gunnarsson, back in Husavik. Carefully, he said, "I will speak with Mistress Eadha, ja."

"And win her around?"

"I will try."

"Good. Good. All is well with us, ja?" Gunnar flung a heavy arm around Lodvar's shoulders. Lodvar endured the assault, even though Gunnar's touch made his skin crawl.

"And you will speak to your gods, asking them to assure our success?"

Lodvar said nothing, and Gunnar's thoughts, moving like swift water, flowed on. "The dottir is beautiful, though, is she not?"

"She is."

"Gyda. She must have suitors, a woman like that." Gunnar's smile broadened. "But none, ever, the like of me."

****

"Do you believe him?"

Fadir asked the question while pacing the room, all his steadfast composure flown. As soon as Gunnar and his men left the room, he'd come to life, with a rush of energy.

"Nei," Modir and Gyda reacted in chorus. Magnus had followed the visitors out, making sure they went on their way.

Tolljur treated his wife and daughter in turn to sharp glances. "Then what is he about?"

"The gods only know." Modir scowled. "Think on his parents—Friti Gunnarsson and that woman Anaborg

Helmsdottir. How could he be aught but deceptive?"

Fadir shrugged uncomfortably. "You cannot blame a young man for his parents."

"I can," Modir snapped, "when his mother is Anaborg."

Fadir shivered. "He says she is still mad. After all these years."

"Aye. I am surprised Friti did not strangle her in the night, long ago." Modir laid her hand on Fadir's arm. "We cannot trust him. But the other—" Modir's eyes took on a faraway look. "Do you suppose he is Catrin's son? He has the look of her, especially about the eyes. I need to speak with him, alone if I can. See what I might discover."

Fadir switched his gaze to Gyda. "What of you, Dottir? Could you sense any threat, as you did before they landed?"

Gyda hesitated. "Not so strong as I did before. But there is still something, Fadir, if well disguised. Do not mistake. Both those young men are dangerous to all of us."

Chapter Seven

The clang of weapons and the echo of raised voices resounded on the shore, disturbing the peace of the afternoon. Lodvar, transported by his thoughts for a few moments while at his prayers, came to earth with a decided bump of annoyance and alarm.

Had Gunnar and his crew fallen into battle with their hosts? But nei, for he heard laughter mixed in with what sounded like good-natured shouting.

He rose from the deck of the dragon ship and discovered most of the crew had gone ashore while he remained at his prayers. On the strip of beach that fronted the impossibly green cliffs, they sparred with the young men of Tolljur's settlement.

No way now to discover who'd started it. Predictably, Gunnar stood at the forefront, facing off against a young man who, even from a distance, Lodvar recognized as Magnus, the berserker's son. They fought with their swords, hacking at one another with true Viking abandon.

Not that Magnus Tolljursson looked particularly Norse. He had, rather, the look of his mother about him, and Lodvar knew enough of that to dub him an Alban half-breed. Like Lodvar himself, he carried a measure of Gaelic blood.

Whatever the blood that filled Magnus Tolljursson, it had warriors behind it. The man moved with powerful grace, and he came at Gunnar with confident aggression. Not many fighters managed that, and Lodvar watched with interest.

Would Magnus be the man to take Gunnar down?

Ja, all in good nature this was meant to be. But Gunnar did not like getting the worst of anything, and Lodvar saw him take light.

Careful, he told Magnus silently.

Gunnar's men from the long ship had all gone ashore and stood watching the contest. Likewise, the young men of the settlement were at Magnus's back. They saw two strong rams contesting for territory.

Abruptly, Gunnar raised his sword and delivered a blow that had nothing playful about it. Breath caught, Lodvar went over the side and waded ashore.

By the time he arrived at the scene, all play had dissipated. The two young men fought in earnest, and the onlookers had fallen mostly silent.

The fool, Lodvar thought. He will wreck his own plan. Better to let Magnus win, feed his sense of confidence.

The sun, beating down from a cloudless sky, had heated the air, as had the combat. Both young men sweated, and drew in deep full-lung breaths.

Whatever Magnus's heritage might be, he'd been trained at arms by an elite Norse warrior, and fought like one. As Lodvar watched, he met Gunnar's wave of aggression blow for blow and turned it back upon him.

Gunnar's handsome face altered in an ugly snarl. Lodvar had watched him fight before, had seen him gut a man without hesitation, had seen him perform hideous atrocities in battle, and after.

Worse, probably, than any berserker.

The mood on the shore had become so grim and quiet, Lodvar heard quite clearly when a woman's voice called out from the top of the cliff. He jerked his gaze up and, just as he did, Gunnar pulled one of his trick moves, kicking Magnus's legs out from under and falling upon him with raised sword.

The figure on the cliff flew down. Well, nei, she didn't fly but might as well have, so fast did she run along the steep path to reach the shore. Her hair, half braided, streamed out behind her.

And her spirit assailed Lodvar's senses.

He knew her then. In one blinding moment of clearsightedness, he did.

The berserker's daughter.

The woman he'd lived so long to find.

She came screaming like a Valkyrie over the battlefield, and she turned every head—even that of Gunnar, who had his blade to her brother's throat.

"You shall not!" She bellowed as she came. "Face me. Face me!"

Gunnar, to give him credit, stared and backed off. What man would not? Magnificent she looked, in her beauty and her rage.

"Mistress," Gunnar declared, "I will not face you. You are a woman."

"Ja? And are you afraid to face a woman?"

The taunt might anger another man. Gunnar merely smiled. "Fear you? I think not." He gestured with his sword. "Better to ask your brother about fear, who lets a woman come to his rescue."

By now, Magnus had sprung to his feet, his face ruddy. He did not rise to the jibe, though, and backed off a step.

Would he let the maiden have her combat? Ach, but she could never best Gunnar, of all men.

Yet Gunnar could not think to harm her—his host's daughter. Not when he wanted to win the berserker's good will.

"You cheated," she accused Gunnar, and gestured at her brother's legs with the weapon she held—a knife. "What manner of honor is that?"

"It is not cheating if it helps me win."

And there, Lodvar thought, was Gunnar, expressed in a single sentence.

Gyda Tolljursdottir scowled at him. "That may be so in *Husavik*." She fairly spat the word. "But not here, on our shores. You will go by our rules, or you will get back on your long boat and leave."

Gunnar did not like that. Lodvar could tell by the way his brows flew up and all trace of humor fled his face. A woman did not give orders, nei, especially not to him.

But he kept his composure, lowered his sword to his side, and sketched a graceful bow.

"Mistress Gyda, you are far too beautiful to risk yourself in combat."

True enough, though Lodvar saw she liked that even less than Gunnar appreciated her invitation to leave.

She sneered at Gunnar—there, before all his men. No woman ever gazed with such denigration at a man generally considered as fair to look upon as Baldur.

Somehow, Lodvar tore his gaze from her and focused on Magnus. What manner of man, indeed, was he who let his sister rush into combat on his behalf and said nothing?

One of confidence, it seemed. For Magnus had put his sword into its scabbard, and appeared entirely self-possessed. And now he reached for his sister, fingers catching at hers with gentle familiarity.

"Come away, Gyda. We see of what he is made."

We see of what he is made? What did Magnus Tolljursson mean by that?

Whatever the meaning, Gunnar did not like it. He drew himself up. "Nei, look here. That was but a friendly bout, was it not? Between jarls' sons."

"True." Magnus lifted his head. His hair flared with red in the sun. "And we have your measure."

The girl spat, "In an honorable bout, while sparring, we do not pull dirty tricks."

"So," Magnus offered, "did our father teach me."

"Your father is a berserker. His very presence on the field of battle is a form of trickery."

The woman went cold at the implied slur, while iron settled in Magnus Tolljursson's eyes.

Magnus stepped forward. "Maybe you and I, Gunnar Fritisson, need to match one another in true combat. No playing. And all the trickery you wish."

"Nah, nah." Gunnar lifted his hand. "You take my words the wrong way. I mean no offense. Your father is a great man. And a legend back in Husavik." He managed a smile. "Is that not why I have come?"

"I know not why you have come," Mistress Gyda responded. "It is certain you will have to earn Fadir's trust."

With a flare of his own, Gunnar told her, "Your welcome to a visitor, Mistress, leaves something to be desired."

"Ja, well, this visitor was not invited, and should

watch his step. Come, brother."

Hands still linked, she and Magnus led the way from the shore, the other young men melting away like snowflakes on a hot stone.

Gunnar, watching them go, appeared baffled. Ja, Lodvar acknowledged—coming from Husavik, he had little concept of true honor. Though, Lodvar had to admit, the old jarl had possessed a measure of it, enough to make him condemn and virtually ostracize his own son for his misdeeds.

But the old jarl was dead, and mayhem now ruled Husavik—the kind of mayhem Loki might invoke.

Gunnar turned and raked Lodvar with a look. "Touchy, these berserker offspring," he remarked.

"You have angered her. Was that wise?"

Gunnar tossed his fair head. "She can be won round, like any woman. She needs some discipline, and to learn to hold her tongue—unless it is wanted."

She is not that kind of woman, nor ever will be. Lodvar did not speak the words aloud, though he felt them to the roots of his soul. For he knew her, had followed the traces of her being—first encountered during spiritual journeying—all the way through time, and across an ocean.

"Be careful," he said instead. "She has influence with her brother, and will have the same with her father."

"You are right." Gunnar slapped Lodvar's shoulder as he used to do when they were younger—right before beating him soundly, and for no other reason than that Lodvar had been born a slave. "Beautiful she is, and it occurs to me there may be more than one way of taking over this settlement."

Lodvar made no reply. Yet, within, his determination strengthened. He must warn Gyda Tolljursdottir. He must seek out and speak with this woman of his heart.

Chapter Eight

"My father, Friti Gunnarsson, intends to attack your settlement. More, he intends to destroy you. I thought you—being a man of legend as you are—deserved fair warning."

Gyda narrowed her eyes as she took in Gunnar's words. The five of them—Fadir, Magnus, Gyda and Gunnar, along with his companion, called Lodvar—sat around the fire in Fadir's dwelling, deep in discussion. To be sure, Modir was there also, ostensibly preparing fare to offer the guests. Gyda knew how hard Modir listened.

Fadir appeared impassive. Well, he usually appeared so, no matter what turmoil might grip him internally. Gyda could not imagine him inclined to trust anything Gunnar Fritisson said.

After their encounter on the shore, she was willing to trust nothing about the warrior from Husavik. Despite how handsome he might be. And no one could deny he was handsome. In repose, as she'd first marked, his face might be accused of beauty. But it possessed such strength and animation that, especially combined with his masculine form, one could never doubt he was all male.

But ja, any woman might wish for such flowing golden locks and eyes so wide and blue.

He glittered and gleamed, precisely like a sharp,

drawn blade.

In contrast, his companion made a dark sheath to that blade, composed and almost too still. An advisor, Gunnar had called him, and ja, judging by his clothing, he was a man of some importance, for he wore a robe of fine, dark blue and several sigils Gyda recognized as denoting power and protection. She wondered again if he were a man of Kaddi's ilk.

Devoid of his grand clothing—a fine thought for her to entertain—he might be almost too ordinary. Long hair of medium brown, neither remarkably dark nor light, a narrow face with well-marked cheekbones and slightly slanted brows. Only those eyes—burning steady and golden—gave him any claim to the extraordinary.

His eyes rested far too often on her, Gyda. She found it disconcerting when she needed to concentrate on—and dissect—everything Gunnar said.

Fadir spoke, and she tore her gaze away from Lodvar's.

"If what you say is true, I should think your loyalty to your father would prevent you bringing any such warning to me."

Gunnar looked thoughtful. "I told you, my father and I have broken ways. I will be frank with you, Jarl Tolljur. The break was a long time coming. Fadir and I were never on good terms. Growing up, I was much closer to my grandfather than my father, who stood disgraced in Grandfather's eyes." Gunnar raised those wide blue eyes to Fadir's face. "I believe you know why."

"Ja. I know." Fadir and Friti Gunnarsson were old enemies. Friti had once attempted to kill Fadir by poisoning the draught he took while recovering from his berserker's trance. That act of treachery had been the last straw and had turned Jarl Gunnar against his son completely.

"I thought perhaps, after we left Husavik, your father returned to Jarl Gunnar's good favor."

Gunnar shook his head weightily. "He did try. He never succeeded, despite naming me, his first-born, after the man who had disowned him."

"I see." Fadir exchanged a glance with Modir, who'd stopped moving about the room and stood listening openly.

"My grandfather intended I should be jarl after him. To be sure, we did not know he was dying. I thought to have him in my life many more years yet. Since his death was unexpected, I find it also suspicious."

"You suppose your father had something to do with it?"

"I cannot say for certain. I do know that, following Grandfather's death, my father made haste to state his claim to the title of jarl, dismissing my grandfather's wishes and promises to me."

Fadir waved a scarred hand. "A difficult situation, Gunnar Fritisson. But nothing, I still say, that should bring you here to me."

"Jarl Tolljur, have you ever heard the saying, the enemy of my enemy is my friend?"

"Of course."

Gunnar leaned forward earnestly. "My father, sad to say, has become my enemy. I want the place I was promised, in Husavik. And he is your enemy also—for, Jarl Tolljur, my father will come here, with all his warriors behind him, and attack you."

No one in the chamber moved—not Fadir, whose expression remained impassive, nor Magnus, who regarded Gunnar from beneath lowered brows. Not Modir, who stood with her arms akimbo, nor the young man called Lodvar, who looked at no one.

Fader scoffed, "You think I am afraid of him?"

"I think, Jarl Tolljur, you should be."

"He has come before, seeking to destroy us. We sent him away again."

"Now, he has all Grandfather's resources behind him, and vengeance in his heart. Jarl Tolljur, I want my inheritance—but I will need your help to win it. You help me to do that, and I will help you fight off my father and defeat him once and for all. Then there will exist between Husavik and Sorvagur ties of friendship and harmony."

Again, Fadir and Modir exchanged a glance. Sometimes, Gyda suspected they communicated without speaking aloud. And again, the young man, Lodvar, raised his gaze to Gyda's face. It almost felt as if he sought to tell her something, also.

"Why," Fadir asked with deliberation, "should I take on a battle when I now have none?"

"Because, as I say, battle is coming to you. You will not need to go to Husavik with your sword and shield, if my father attacks you here."

"If," Fadir repeated. "No offense, young man, but you seek my help and thus might say anything."

That made Lodvar glance at Gunnar crosswise, a measuring look.

Indeed, Gunnar might have flushed with anger. Instead, he spread his hands. "You need not believe me,

Jarl Tolljur. Yet I think you know my father—the darkness and cruelty that occupy his heart and mind. Ask yourself if this thing might not be true."

Darkness. Gyda recalled the sensation that had seized her when she gazed out over the water. Like prodding an aching tooth, she explored, trying to discover if she could sense it now.

Nei. But deception existed here in this room. Gunnar did not tell the truth, at least not all the truth.

Fadir said, "Let me give some thought to what you have told me, Gunnar Fritisson."

Gunnar inclined his fair head. "My grandfather respected you, Tolljur Magnusson, as he did your father before you. I understand they were great friends."

"My father traveled to Husavik with Jarl Gunnar, from Norway. And ja, they were close at one time."

"Then let us reforge that friendship." Gunnar glanced at Gyda. "There are ways to bind such an alliance."

Fadir stiffened, and the stare he gave Gunnar contained no trace of friendliness. He repeated only, "Let me think on it."

Gunnar did not appear satisfied, but nodded. "I appreciate whatever consideration you offer me. I urge you, only, do not take too long. When we left Husavik, my father already prepared his ships for departure. And you know what they say, Jarl Tolljur—the world is small, to a man with anger in his heart."

Chapter Nine

"A moment, young man, if you will."

The woman's rather strident voice halted Lodvar on his way out of the jarl's dwelling. Both he and Gunnar turned.

Mistress Eadha ignored Gunnar, though. She had her gaze pinned compellingly on Lodvar. He shot Gunnar a look and stepped back through the doorway even as Gunnar moved off.

Mistress Eadha smiled. Nei, she was not a beautiful woman—not like her daughter—but strength lay in her face, and something familiar filled her eyes.

What did he sense about her? A likeness with his own mother, who had also come from the Alban isles? A place called Lewis, that he'd never seen but which, nevertheless, lingered in his blood.

He inclined his head. "Mistress."

"Could you spare me a moment, please?" Command rather than supplication colored the appeal. This woman, with her formidable husband, commanded the settlement, and the men here deferred to their women.

"Of course, Mistress."

She smiled, and it softened and warmed her face. "Thank you, Lodvar Haraldsson. Let us walk."

Out across the green sward they went. Tall for a woman, she matched his strides, and the sun lit her hair to red. After a moment, she said, "I think I know your mother."

"You do," Lodvar agreed. "Her name is Catrin, and she spoke often of you while I was growing."

Mistress Eadha's compelling, hazel gaze fixed on him. "Catrin! I did suppose it was so, when you named your father. How is she? Please tell me she has kept well."

Lodvar hesitated. What to say? His modir's life could not be described as happy, by any means. "Things improved for her when my father took her to wife. It gave her a measure of status, after being a slave."

"Ah." Grief sounded in Mistress Eadha's voice. "I wanted so badly to bring her away with me, when we left Husavik. She was carrying you then, and your father would not agree to it, no matter what Tolljur offered him in exchange for her."

"In exchange?" Lodvar repeated.

The look she shot at him turned apologetic. "Tolljur would have purchased her—it was the only way, you understand, and is what we did with so many others of the Alban women who were slaves. She was my friend, back in Lewis, growing up. She it was who helped make my life bearable when I first arrived in Husavik. And she's the only one I was not able to bring awa' with me." Her voice broke. "Her life cannot have been easy, nor yours."

"Nei." Lodvar could only agree. Why speak of the constant slurs, the indignities, the degradation? This woman knew. "She has faced some challenges with her health these last years. But Harald eventually built his own house, and now she is mistress of that."

"Had she other children?"

Lodvar shook his head.

"Just you, then? What a joy you must be to her." She inspected him with a crosswise look. "You have the look of her, much more than of your father."

"You remember him?"

"Indeed, I do." Mistress Eadha kept her voice carefully blank, but Lodvar heard the disgust. "I am glad to hear he did the right thing, in the end."

"He is very old now. Possibly dying." Lodvar shared the information emotionlessly. "I think he wanted to make certain she stayed and cared for him in the end. It was no—" He sought for the word.

"Kindness?" Mistress Eadha suggested softly.

"Kindness." There had been very little of that, in Lodvar's life. At least, not from anyone save Modir.

"I would love to see her again," Mistress Eadha said, heartfelt. "But I am that grateful for having met you—a part of her, and all." They had reached the headland. She paused and faced him. The wind, blowing inshore, stirred her hair and light filled her eyes. "You appear to have done well for yourself. Right-hand man to Gunnar Fritisson."

Lodvar said nothing. He should warn her—do not trust Gunnar. He is not what he pretends. She deserved warning, if only by virtue of being Modir's friend. Yet Modir remained at Husavik, at the jarl's mercy.

"I have been fortunate. I displayed, early, talents that gave me value in the jarl's eyes."

She laid her fingers on his arm. "You follow the gods?"

"And speak with them."

"You must meet Kaddi while you are here."

Lodvar smiled. "That would be an honor. I have heard much of him."

"He is aged now. Fragile. But I have studied with him for many years. He taught me much of what I know."

"Ja, Mistress." Lodvar hesitated. His mother had said of this woman that she could hear others' thoughts. He wondered if she could hear his now. With a slight bow, he said, "I look forward to spending time with both of you."

"I will take you to him, and soon. You must understand, his mind is not what it was. He waits daily for his god to come and collect him."

"His passing will be a great loss to all of you."

"I do not know how I will endure it. He has been like a grandfather to me."

"We endure as we must." He could tell her a few things about endurance. About listening to his father take his pleasure upon Modir, back when they all still lived in the great hall. About the few times Harald had—against Modir's will—lent her to his good friends, and Lodvar had been unable to prevent it.

Modir, having passed first bloom and suffering from debilitating aches in the joints, was no longer subjected to that. But she still lay in danger, and Lodvar must do all he could to protect her.

Mistress Eadha gave him a speaking look. Perhaps she truly could hear his thoughts. "I would that I could visit with your mother, if only for a short while."

"It would hearten her much."

"Instead, I will visit with you while you are here, and you shall take my best wishes to her when you return to Husavik. Did you know she stood up for me at my wedding, when I married Tolljur?"

"She never said."

"It is so. One of the few friends I had there, then." She began walking again, back toward the settlement. "Tell me, has Husavik changed much?"

Lodvar contemplated the question, wondering if he might warn this woman of the impending danger that existed, without actually speaking the words. If she could hear his thoughts, she might guess.

But then, even his thoughts might endanger Modir. "Nothing has changed, Mistress. Husavik is a place of secrets."

"Still?"

"Ja, still." He spoke the word with emphasis. Did she understand?

Just outside the settlement, she turned to face him once more. "'Twas always, aye, a place of secrets. And"—her eyes sought his—"of treachery."

"Mistress, as I say, *nothing* has changed."

****

"What did she say to you, that ugly woman?" Gunnar, lounging in his usual place aboard the long boat, asked the question as soon as Lodvar arrived.

"She is scarcely ugly," Lodvar protested, before he thought better of it.

Gunnar screwed up his face. "You think not, with that great mark on her cheek? She is not the beauty her daughter is. That one! Such eyes, such breasts. I wonder how many men she has had."

None. Lodvar could not tell how he knew that, he just did. Gyda's spirit had called to his across the distances. He was destined to be hers, even more than she to be his.

He leaned his stick against the mast and unfastened his cloak, even while his loathing for his companion rose.

"I wonder," Gunnar mused, "if she is still good and tight. I will find out."

"Will you?" Lodvar hoped the loathing did not show.

"Ja. I have decided it will be well for me to wed the berserker's daughter. You can see that he holds her in affection. Possessing her will give me power over him."

Possessing her?

"And if she is not willing to accept you, this Gyda Tolljursdottir?"

"She will." Gunnar smiled. "Can I not be charming? Do not all the women follow me with their eyes?"

They did, up to a point—until they discovered what lay beneath the golden locks and smiling face.

"Besides"—Gunnar shrugged—"it is not up to her. A marriage alliance is forged between men."

"Perhaps not, here. They seem to afford their women a goodly measure of power."

"Ja." A grin spread across Gunnar's face. "Did you see her fly at me with that weapon, in defense of her brother? There is passion there, Lodvar. Breaking her will be sheer pleasure."

Breaking her. Ach, and the berserker's lass needed fair warning.

From him? Perhaps, but not directly, not if he wanted to keep Modir safe. Nei, he would have to pass her the warning through another. And he thought he just might know the way.

Chapter Ten

"It is an honor to meet you." Lodvar bowed his head in deference to the old man perched inside the wooden bed. Outside, the sun shone steady and bright, but very little radiance reached the interior of the hut, which lay steeped in gloom. Small the place was and fragrant with the scents of magic. Herbs and precious resins, and the unmistakable residue of spells cast.

Power dwelt here, a great deal of it.

The spirit which commanded that power, however, found itself in a failing vessel, indeed. The old man had lost an eye sometime in the past. Lodvar doubted he could see much with the one he had left. And age held him in its grip. Lodvar didn't think he'd ever seen anyone so old.

Mistress Eadha had brought him here at his request. He'd expected the fabled shaman to make an impression. Being close to him, though, felt humbling.

Kaddi smiled. "Mistress Eadha says you follow the same path as me. It is well. Our world needs those who will speak to and seek guidance from the gods."

"I do follow a path," Lodvar admitted. "I cannot say whether it matches yours, honored one."

Kaddi's smile widened. He had no teeth, and his face told a tale in wrinkles. He glanced at Mistress Eadha.

"You may leave us, girl."

She did not like that. She felt protective of the old man—well, no doubt they all did. Kaddi was a treasure, one they might not possess for much longer.

"Are you sure—?"

"He will not harm me." Kaddi gestured at Lodvar with confidence.

"I will not," Lodvar assured her also. "You may trust me."

She gave him a stare that looked into and through him.

"We will talk about things we have in common," Kaddi said. "Girl, let us do so in peace."

Without another word, she rose and went out.

The old man settled more comfortably in his bed. "There will be refreshments close at hand. I cannot see them there, but those who care for me leave them, always. I cannot see you well either, young man, but I can feel you. And I recognize what I feel."

"I recognize the power within you also, Master."

"You will be wondering about my eye. Everyone always wonders. I sacrificed it long ago in exchange for wisdom, emulating Fadir Odin."

"Was the wisdom you received worth the price?"

Kaddi chuckled. "Only another shaman would ask me that."

"It is a high price."

"Ja. And that question is one I have contemplated often. Was it worth the pain? I have concluded that wisdom is always worth the price asked, and paid."

"I am glad to hear it."

The old man waved a bony hand. "As you know, there is a cost for everything. We sacrifice on a daily basis—for knowledge, for pleasure—for love."

"Love?"

"That most of all. Tell me, young man, how does your power manifest?"

"I am led. I am *called*. I receive knowing."

"Visions?"

"Not usually, nei, Master. It is more like—like hearing a song inside my head, my heart. It persists until I can bear it no longer and must follow."

"Ach, interesting. And have you followed such a calling in coming here?"

Lodvar hesitated. "I have."

"To what purpose?"

Love. But Lodvar could not speak that aloud. "I am not yet certain."

Kaddi sat back a bit and nodded. "Mistress Eadha has told me who you are. I recall your mother. She stood up at Mistress Eadha's wedding."

"She was a slave then."

"Has your father, Harald, not provided for her by now?"

"He married her three years ago."

"Then she will be wife, and slave no longer."

"She is still slave." In every way that mattered. "As am I."

"Ah, young man, you have reached a worthy place, an honored one. Surely you have broken the chains into which you were born."

"In Husavik, those chains endure."

"A shaman must be certain of his own worth, if he is to achieve anything. You may have begun life as a slave—you now belong to the gods. There is no higher status to achieve."

Lodvar felt it then, the kindness that lay beneath

the old man's confidence.

"It is good of you to say so, Master Kaddi."

"It is truth. But I have learned a curious thing about truth. It is truth only to the extent that you believe it. A man may be persuaded to believe anything."

Kaddi's one eye, opposite the empty pocked socket, focused on Lodvar. "Even that he deserves love."

"Love." Lodvar repeated the work flatly, though it shook him to the core. Could this old man tell what he sought in coming to Sorvagur?

He smiled tightly. "Love comes seldom, Master Kaddi, to men such as we."

"It is so. I never had a wife, and seldom spent my passion on a woman. Some say it is better so. Hoarding such energies allows us to direct them into holy channels. But I will admit, such is a trial when a man is young."

Lodvar did not know what to say to that. Should he confess to the calling that had haunted him, so strong it might be better labeled a command, and had in fact made him throw in with Gunnar on this venture? Dangerous ground, for one who lived a guarded inner life, to give so much of himself away.

Yet if he wanted to provide Kaddi with a warning—best, perhaps, to broach the matter.

Before he could speak, Kaddi went on, "I knew Jarl Gunnar very well, of course, in days of old. An interesting man. You no doubt know he was once an outcast."

"Ja."

"When he left Norway, he took Tolljur's father, Magnus, with him because Magnus was a berserker, and Gunnar wanted to make his mark on the world. To Magnus's lasting detriment, he agreed to accompany his friend to Iceland.

"Gunnar was not a trustworthy man, but he did believe himself capable of dispensing justice. As I say, a man's beliefs shape him. That made Gunnar turn on his own favored son after Friti schemed to kill Tolljur, and Anaborg—now Friti's wife—struck Mistress Eadha down, trying to murder her."

Lodvar lifted his brows. Young Gunnar's mother, Anaborg, would cause any sensible man caution. She had been mad all Lodvar's life, often raving, and might well meet her neighbors stark naked. She tried to seduce any man she met.

She must have been beautiful, in her youth. Now, she made Lodvar's blood run cold.

Carefully, he told the old man, "Treachery did abound, so it seems, in the Husavik of old. I believe," he emphasized that word, "it still does. And even closer to hand, a smiling face may hide a black heart."

Kaddi's eye widened. He got the message. "I see. Your mother, I comprehend, is still there—ready to Friti Gunnarsson's hands."

"She is."

"So your hands are tied."

Lodvar lifted them. "They are."

"Yet there is a bond between those who, in all earnestness, follow their gods, no matter how those gods be named. When first I met Mistress Eadha, she was stubborn, willful, and a slave."

"Like my mother."

"Like your mother. But I saw—and felt—in her the tug of magic and more than a hint of the Sight. I feel that also in you."

Lodvar bowed his head.

"We must honor that bond between us, young man, whether we be enemies or otherwise."

Lodvar met Kaddi's milky gaze. "Are we enemies?"

"Nei. Nei."

Lodvar released his breath, relieved in the knowledge his message had been received.

"Go now." The old man lifted a hand. "Let me rest, and contemplate all you have—and have not—said."

"Contemplate, Master?"

"Ja—a way out of this tangle, if nothing else."

Chapter Eleven

The beautiful day should have brought Gyda joy, but while hurrying along the worn path to Kaddi's hut, she found little of that emotion in her heart. She followed the trail of her mother who, someone said, had gone off in the company of Gunnar's shaman.

A waste, she called it, of a perfectly good afternoon. Situated as the settlement was on a rock stranded in the midst of the ocean, subject to every storm and shower of rain that blew across the breast of the water, they did not get many afternoons full of warm, radiant sunlight, or a blue sky that, scour it as she might, showed no clouds.

She should be on the shore sparring with her brother, or climbing the rocks searching for birds' eggs. Not running an errand for Brita, who fretted over the feast set for this evening.

When Kaddi's hut came into view, she saw no sign of Modir, nor of the girl currently looking after the old man. Though if Modir lingered inside, perhaps seeking advice from her aged friend, Aya might well have taken the opportunity to be off about some task of her own.

Without hesitation, and confident of her welcome, she lowered her head and barreled through the door. After the bright sunshine, she could initially see little, and reeled in surprise when she crashed violently into someone on his way out.

A curse escaped her lips, and the person with whom she'd collided gave a grunt. His hands caught at her, closing on her arms in a steadying grip, and keeping her from falling.

For an instant they stood so, tightly linked, Gyda, half blinded by the dark of the hut. She felt—

A hard rush of emotions, like a punch to the gut. Warmth came first, stealing through his fingers, quickly followed by a tumble of images. The fall of light on water. The glowing coals of a near-dead fire, a heap of furs upon which two bodies lay, locked in passion. Blood, blood, and more blood.

She stumbled back through the doorway into the sunlight, trying to escape the images—to escape him. He came with her, his fingers still wrapped around her arms, and the clear light washed over them.

"Mistress Gyda, are you all right?"

The shaman. It was Gunnar's shaman—Lodvar. Gyda narrowed her eyes against the glare and regarded him. The emotions connected to those images continued to assault her, making it difficult to think clearly.

He felt the way music sounded—the way the notes vibrated from Modir's harp when she played, or when the women sang all together while at work on the shore. Beautiful, harmonious, powerful yet oddly still. All these things did she feel from him, combined with a flare of attraction so fierce and lustful it stole her breath away and knocked her back on her heels.

"I—" She began to respond to his question and froze. Was she all right? No. Most certainly not. She must run. Flee this, flee him.

Instead, she gazed into his eyes. Such curious eyes he had, tawny gold and framed by brown lashes, much darker than his hair. They were, perhaps, the one remarkable feature in an otherwise ordinary face, at least until he smiled at Gyda, and her world tilted.

Had she ever received such a smile? Warm, like the sunshine that bathed them, and as personal as his touch. Slightly crooked, and utterly beautiful, it seemed to unite them, and swayed Gyda where she stood.

His fingers slid down her arms to her wrists, and tightened. "Here—perhaps you should sit down."

He led her to the bench where Kaddi liked to sit on fine days. Once seated, though, he kept hold of her hands. "Mistress, what is it?"

"I am not sure." She hated displaying weakness and, instead, liked to appear as strong as her brother.

Concern flooded the shaman's eyes. "May I fetch you a draught of water?"

She ignored the offer and, forgetting she'd come searching for her mother, gazed into his face again.

"Who are you?" A foolish question. He'd been introduced to her—Lodvar Haraldsson. She knew who, and what, he was purported to be, but she sensed more, much more.

The smile flickered across his face again, sunlight on water. By all the holy powers, he was a beautiful being, after all.

"I am the son of my jarl's seneschal, got on a slave—one who was once friend to your mother in their own faraway land."

"Catrin? Modir has often spoken of her, and how hard it went leaving her behind in Husavik when she and Fadir left. So…" She examined him still more closely, well aware he still cradled her hands in his. "You are the child she carried at that time?"

"I am."

"And you grew into a holy man."

"I did."

"What a wondrous thing. And what a fortunate life you must have had." He clearly stood in favor with Gunnar, was dressed well, and looked healthy. "I would love to hear about it sometime."

"I would like nothing better than to tell you, Mistress Gyda. And to hear about your life here, growing up."

How curious—how easy she felt with him after that first stab of intense attraction, as if two souls meant to be together in friendship had found one another at last. Friendship, or something more? He made an appealing prospect, sitting there in the warm sun, with his hair spilling over his shoulders and the light chasing through those remarkable eyes.

She might just lean forward and kiss him. Their lips would meet gently, soft and warm, and nothing—nothing to fear in him.

No, of that one thing she felt sure—she need never fear this heart.

Perhaps the connection she felt with him, so instant and so intense, stemmed from the blood. Their mothers came from the same place. Neither of them had seen the Gaels' lands but had been raised in the world of the Norse—he more than she, perhaps, since so many of the women who'd come away from Husavik to the Faroes had been Alban slaves and had held on to their own ways.

Lodvar squeezed Gyda's hands lightly. "Do you feel better now?"

"Better, ja." She drew a breath, gazing into his

eyes. "I came looking for my mother. There is to be a grand feast tonight, and she is needed for the preparations."

"She was here, but left after bringing me to Master Kaddi."

Gyda withdrew her fingers from his. He let them go readily, but it took an effort on her part to break that connection. "I had better go find her." She got to her feet. "Before Brita goes mad entirely."

He rose also, moving with restrained grace. Another spear of desire shot through Gyda's belly. Suddenly she longed to see—and feel—the body beneath that fine blue robe. The idea shocked her so, she had to turn away.

Just as quickly, she swung back again. "Perhaps I shall see you at the feast."

"I hope so, Mistress Gyda. It would be the fondest wish of my heart."

****

"There is to be a grand feast this evening. Tolljur Magnusson honors me." Gunnar lounged in his place near the mast, aboard ship, all coiled energy that did not fool Lodvar. Gunnar possessed the temperament of an adder that pretended to be at ease, while prepared to strike. He smiled the smile Lodvar hated to see. "I think I have won his trust after all."

"Do you?" Lodvar's words carried more of an edge than he intended. His moments with Gyda—in her presence at last after years of yearning—had lifted him like a sweet dream. He hated crashing back down to Gunnar's level.

Gunnar's intense blue gaze fastened to his face. "Did you speak to the old man? Do you suppose he still has influence, or is he just a weak, doddering ancient?"

"He has influence, ja."

"You must win him over, then, soothe any suspicions that may arise in his withered mind. Our scheme will then be well in hand."

Our scheme. Lodvar wanted to say he desired no part in it. Indeed, had he not just delivered a warning to Kaddi, one the elderly shaman might well pass on to Tolljur? And if he did, if Gunnar and his accursed father Friti's plan went up in flames, what would happen then? What, to Lodvar's mother, fast in Friti's hands?

Gunnar and his father were not men to cross. Lodvar could only hope Kaddi possessed the wit to dissemble.

"And what does that look upon your face mean, I wonder, holy man? You are in this with us, are you not?"

"To be sure."

"It is not healthy to betray me."

"Why would I betray you? You think me a fool?"

Gunnar did not answer immediately. He toyed with the weapon he held in his hands—a dirk stolen during one of his raids in Alba. Lodvar had seen what Gunnar could do with that small knife, and flinched at the memory.

"I am not certain, Lodvar Haraldsson, what I think you. There is a defiance in you at times which does not befit a slave."

"I am no longer a slave. The gods speak to me. Fadir Odin does. He shows me the path forward."

"The path to my success. So you do tell me. But is that the truth?"

Ach, what made Gunnar Fritisson and his father so dangerous was the fact that they possessed a certain amount of crude intelligence. It operated, always, to benefit them. That made of it an even more heedless weapon.

In their youth, Gunnar had beleaguered Lodvar, mocked and ridiculed him, trapped and, with the help of his friends, thrashed him soundly. When Harald, his father, protested, Friti had laughed over it. "Your son is a slave. Let him learn his place, so he will respect his betters."

Only the old jarl, Jarl Gunnar, had taken Lodvar's part. "Let the boy be educated. We need the services of a holy man. If Odin speaks to him, it means something."

But Gunnar had gone on to the next world. Back in Husavik, Friti held sway.

And young Gunnar's smile was as sharp as his dirk.

"The gods," Lodvar told him, "do not lie. And it is worth my life to fail in repeating what they say to me."

"Ja, and worth your mother's life for you to fail in your loyalty to me."

Chapter Twelve

Light hung late in the sky at this time of year. When Lodvar, with the rest of Gunnar's party, walked up from the dragon boat, that light seemed to dance in the air like enchantment. Perhaps a measure of magic was loose in this place. And at work between him and Tolljur Magnusson's daughter?

How he longed to see her. The calling that had drawn him to her for so many years now fairly screamed aloud. After touching her, holding her hands, it ran rampant in his heart and mind.

Unstoppable.

He glanced at the man who walked beside him. Gunnar's handsome face looked serene—his very walk declared his confidence. His world was in order, his plans all in hand.

He thought he'd already won.

Had he?

"I hope they have mead in this gods-forsaken place."

"It is a good place," Lodvar returned. "Beautiful."

"What is beauty, save in a woman? And even an ugly slave may be enjoyed in the dark. There is little here to steal. It is a strategic position, though—Fadir is right in that."

Friti Gunnarsson cared nothing for strategy. He wanted revenge upon his old enemy—only that.

"If there is mead, or at least ale, I will wait until Tolljur Magnusson has taken too much, and then propose to him an alliance that will greatly benefit us."

"Have you not already offered him an alliance?"

Gunnar grunted. "I speak of a marriage alliance with his daughter. I would not mind throwing that one down on her back and rutting the whole night long."

Lodvar hoped the clear light did not reveal his anger. "Be careful. Tolljur is berserker—such men are able to hold their liquor."

"I will make sure he drinks plenty."

"And the girl may well have a say in it."

Gunnar turned all-too-perceptive eyes on him. "Is that what Fadir Odin tells you?"

"It is common sense. These men offer their women much leeway."

"Fools." Gunnar spoke the word under his breath. Fortunate, for Tolljur Magnusson came forward then to greet them, his lady at his side.

One could glean very little from Tolljur's expression. A berserker felt no pain in battle and betrayed no evidence of his hurts. This man must be well trained in displaying no weakness or, indeed, his emotions.

His wife, though, showed much in the set of her shoulders, her rebellious jaw, and her narrowed eyes. Pride lay there, and more than a touch of defiance.

"Welcome," Tolljur said. "We have set up outside because I do not have a great hall, and it is a fine night." He raised his hands. "What hall could be more magnificent than these surroundings?"

Lodvar's heart rose in response to the man's love of the place. Ja, these folks might have come from another land, but they cared deeply for this, their home.

Gunnar spoke in response, but Lodvar lost track of what he said, for across the green sward came Gyda, and her appearance nearly rendered him senseless.

Seeing her felt precisely like being dealt a hard blow to the gut. A woman who appeared lovely even when dressed in the humblest of clothing, she'd now made an effort and no doubt wore her finest—a graceful gown of blue several shades lighter than his own robe, and an overdress of creamy white, embroidered all over with flowers and leaves, in golden thread. A necklace of amber encircled her throat, and her hair hung loose in rippling waves over her shoulders and back.

"Welcome," she said. Lodvar supposed she spoke to Gunnar, but she looked at him.

"Dottir," Tolljur said with some pride, "pray show our guests to their places."

Gunnar bowed, charm filling him the way he filled his own clothing. "May I hope for your company during the evening's feast, Mistress?"

"You will sit at the head table with my family. Come."

Gunnar appropriated Gyda's arm. As she turned away, her gaze once more met Lodvar's, for only an instant. What did he see in her eyes? A memory of the brief moments they'd spent in the sun outside Kaddi's hut? Or was that wishful thinking on his part?

Tables had been set up in a pattern on the headland, just above the settlement. Two large fires burned, and torches set about the perimeter would add light, once darkness fell. As they arrived, Gunnar's men were shown to places, dispersed among the folk of the settlement. Gunnar would have to hope they held their tongues once the drink began to flow, for Lodvar could see vats of what must be ale laid by.

He wondered where he would sit. The top table held a limited number of places—Magnus Tolljursson, who rose at their approach, already occupied one of them.

And Kaddi held another. When they reached the table, the old man smiled at Lodvar. He wore an ancient, dusty cloak made of raven's feathers, and made no attempt to rise.

Like a good daughter of the hall, Gyda seated her parents at the center of the board with Gunnar between them. Magnus—well armed—held the place on the other side of his mother.

"Master Lodvar?" Gyda turned to him. For an instant, her gaze met his again. "We are at this end, alongside Master Kaddi."

We?

Ach, the gods smiled upon him, without question. For she showed him to a place near the old man, and sat between. Almost afraid to breathe for his delight, he sat staring at his own hands—feeling her presence beside him, soft and heady as the approaching night.

Gunnar shot him a frustrated look down the board. He'd wanted the place beside the berserker's daughter so he might work his wiles on her.

And ja, Gunnar possessed wiles. Half the women he seduced back home went willingly with him, and did not see they'd been used until later, when he dropped them.

Women began to circulate, filling cups with ale. Lodvar had to make some sort of conversation, speak to this woman who possessed his heart, but awe at her beauty and nearness kept him silent.

"A bonny evening," she spoke in his ear.

He turned to look at her. She sat close—the board was not overly long to accommodate so many. He could feel the warmth of her arm, almost pressed to his.

He lifted a brow. "Bonny?"

She smiled. Small dimples appeared at the corners of her mouth. "A word my mother uses. It means—"

"Beautiful. Like you."

She looked surprised at the involuntary compliment, but her smile deepened. "Wait till later when the sky turns deep blue, like your cloak, and the stars come out—hundreds upon hundreds of them. As Fadir says, no hall could be so grand. You have never beheld such beauty."

"You are right. I never have."

Kaddi cleared his throat. He might have spoken, but, with all the cups filled, Tolljur Magnusson rose to his feet.

"My friends and neighbors, and our honored guests, it is long since we broke with the settlement at Husavik, where so many of us were born. Now Gunnar Fritisson comes telling us much there has changed, and it may be time for us to make new alliances. It is clear"—he paused for emphasis—"treachery is afoot. But for tonight we celebrate our strengths and pay homage to our visitors." He raised his cup. "Skål!"

The toast, repeated by every throat, echoed over the headland. Lodvar drank, surprised by the quality of the ale. A curious sort of speech, that could mean anything.

If Gunnar thought Tolljur a fool, he erred, and

badly.

Kaddi leaned forward to speak across Gyda. "We are fortunate in having this fine night. Storm is coming—by tomorrow morning at the latest."

Lodvar cast his gaze to the west. All clear. "I see— and feel—no approaching storm, Master."

Kaddi cackled. "My old bones tell me so. You mark my words, boy."

"Ja, so I will."

"What do you think of our hall?" As Tolljur had done, Kaddi lifted a hand. "Is it as fine as Gunnar's back in Husavik?"

"Finer," Lodvar acknowledged. He returned his gaze to Gyda's glowing face. "Your father never saw fit to build a hall here?"

"He did not see the point. Meetings of council are held at our house, and we seldom have visitors to entertain. Building supplies are hard to come by. The resources were better spent making sure all our people have what they need."

Very different from Husavik then, where the highest made certain they had what they needed, at cost to the lowest if need be.

In many ways, Lodvar had been fortunate growing up. Even though he'd been born to a slave and his existence might have been marginal at best, his father's honored status with the jarl had saved him from most deprivations. He'd grown up in the comfortable surroundings of the hall, which his father had managed, with always enough to eat.

What was the occasional thrashing for failing to lower his eyes swiftly—and respectfully—enough? What the showers of taunts and insults, compared to an empty belly?

Even so, his father's children from his legitimate marriage—already grown by the time Lodvar was born—had hated him and begrudged him the status he achieved as a holy man. Following their mother's death, they had not wanted Harald to wed his mother.

Yet Harald had, making of Lodvar—what? A half slave, at best.

Not worthy of the glorious woman seated beside him. Then why did he feel this deep connection to her?

Why had she called to him all his life?

Kaddi went on speaking about life at Husavik and here in Sorvagur. Down the table, Lodvar could hear Gunnar speaking also, to their hosts—boasting, from his tone of voice. No doubt bragging on himself as a preamble to requesting their daughter's hand.

He wondered why she'd never wed. She must be nearly an age with him—high time she'd taken a husband. Good, for his sake, she hadn't. Ill, if it meant Gunnar might get his hands on her.

Platters of food were brought around—fine baked fish and turnips and greens. Kaddi received his portion, which Gyda helped him sort.

She and Lodvar received one portion to share.

He watched her fingers, separating the flaky white fish from the bone, and could scarcely believe his good luck.

Nei, not luck. The gods had brought him to this. As clear as a Vision, he saw the two of them together, the berserker's daughter in his arms, their bodies and spirits fused into one.

"What is it, Master Lodvar?"

"Eh?"

"You seem distracted."

Should he tell her he was distracted by her beauty? By the warm scent of her, by every breath she drew, the movements of her hands? Her smile. What he saw in her eyes when she looked at him.

"I am merely listening to what Gunnar tells your parents."

"The lies he tells?" She whispered that in his ear, though he did not doubt Kaddi heard. "Ach, do not look so surprised. He does tell lies, nei?"

So she'd not been fooled by Gunnar's boasting. "I hope that your father takes all his guest says with…appropriate understanding."

"Of course. My father is no fool. My mother even less, and he always takes her counsel."

"As a wise man will," Kaddi put in. "It is not difficult to believe," the old man went on, "yon Gunnar's father, Friti, seeks vengeance against Tolljur Magnusson. Friti is a man made for vengeance. What is perhaps more difficult to believe is that yon Gunnar has any real concern for Tolljur's fate at his father's hands."

Lodvar leaned past Gyda. "He looks for an alliance that will be of benefit." No lie, that. Gunnar Fritisson looked always for the advantage.

Kaddi huffed. "The end is in the beginning, young man. You know this, as do I. It shall be interesting to see how this ends."

Chapter Thirteen

Just as Gyda had promised, the dark at length flowed in from the far horizon, and stars appeared there as if flung out by Odin's hand. They formed patterns and paths across the great indigo vault of the sky, trails the Fadir god might have followed on his fabled travels.

With the beauty of the night came a wildness born in Lodvar's heart. Always had he been forced to exercise discipline over his mien and bearing. "Stay humble," Modir often told him, "and they will overlook you." Even when he'd begun his rise to prominence, cupped in the hands of the gods, she had cautioned him. "Do not reach above yourself. They will punish you for it."

True, that.

Yet now he found himself sitting bathed in beauty, beside the woman for whom he'd longed most his life. How could he keep his heart from rising?

Speeches made, a few saga songs sung, Mistress Eadha arose.

"Ah," Gyda mused, "Modir is going to play."

"Eh?"

Mistress Eadha took up a harp. Lodvar had seen only a few such, back in Husavik, seized in raids launched on Alban lands. This instrument, clearly aged, had a battered aspect, well worn. She settled herself at the center of the open area, and everyone in attendance fell silent.

She struck a note, and magic ensued.

Not prepared for it, Lodvar experienced the music like physical sensation. So pure was it, so clear and sweet as it wound its way up through the indigo air toward the listening stars, he wanted to weep.

Alban music this must be, for he'd heard little like it in Husavik, where music tended to be wild and clamorous, with its own bright rhythm, except when his Modir had sung lullabies to him—old, old songs.

The beauty of this stabbed him through and made him understand suddenly why the hardened berserker, accustomed to endurance, had taken this woman to wife.

Moved entirely, he put out his hand. Gyda slipped her fingers into his, and they sat so, joined in flesh and by the magic of the music, until the final tune ended and Mistress Eadha arose.

Applause followed, warm and spontaneous. Under its cover, Gyda also rose, and tugged Lodvar's hand.

"Come."

"Eh?"

A new song had begun, played by two other members of the gathering, and people began to dance, women and women first, and then women and men together.

Did Mistress Gyda wish him to dance with her? But no, for she drew him away from the tables and torches, into the dark beyond.

They walked toward the cliffs, where still the gloaming held sway, with the light gathered over the ocean. Lodvar could hear the music, laughter, and teasing floating in pursuit of them. Folk enjoyed their world. Life here was fair, and good.

For how long, if Gunnar had his way?

He could not think about that now. Gyda's fingers held his, and awareness of her possessed him. He felt the sway of her gown around her calves when she moved, the slide of that glorious hair across her shoulders, the cool of the night air against her skin, as if it were his own.

"Look," she bade, pausing atop the cliff. "From here, you can see forever."

He gazed out over the water—a restless plane of dark blue, sparked with phosphorescent foam. The three long ships must still lie at anchor down in the bay, but he could not see them. Only, as Gyda said, eternity, with no seams.

Only the two of them existed as, from the first, it had been meant.

"Mistress Gyda—"

"Hush. Sometimes I must get away from all the voices and noise. When my heart is too full."

"And is your heart full?"

"Ach, ja."

She turned to face him. He turned likewise, and, gazing into the pale oval of her face, forgot anything else existed.

"Who are you, Lodvar Haraldsson?"

She had asked him that before, and he had given answer. But he understood why she asked again—she must sense the underlying connection between them, the same that drew him so relentlessly, must know something more than what he declared himself to be existed.

He whispered, "You know who I am."

"Ja, but whom—to me? What are you meant to be in my life?"

He drew a breath. "What makes you think I am meant to matter to you, Gyda?"

"You already do." She shook her head. "One thing I have learned in this life, Master Lodvar—one cannot deny the inevitable. And you feel inevitable to me. Can you not feel that also? It is as if, out of a world of darkness, a light has entered my life."

She stepped closer, into his arms. Any words Lodvar might possess fled him when she lifted her hands to cup his face, leaned in, and pressed her lips to his.

Madness ensued, a sweet kind of madness such as Lodvar had never imagined. Light burst in his head, warmth flooded his flesh. His spirit began to sing.

Surely, surely he'd been living all his life for this moment, surely he'd wanted it since the idea of her first occurred to him, back in Husavik. Since first he'd felt her calling him, deep in his heart. A world of longing, answered in the simple gesture of her lips meeting his.

What could he do but succumb to the sensation? Draw her closer, enfold her in his arms, and deepen the kiss. With a wordless sigh, she slid her hands up from his face and wound her arms around his neck. They melded together, tongues discovering one another, there on the edge of eternity.

Lodvar trembled on the verge of telling her he loved her, that he'd always loved her, even before they met. The urge rose up from the root of his being, a need to present her with his unswerving devotion, as he might a gift. Yet chains of duty lay heavy upon him. Better to forget the future and live entirely in this one particular moment.

If he could.

****

The man tasted of magic.

Gyda could not fairly say how magic should taste, but she knew its feel, its touch, its flavor, and Lodvar Haraldsson might as well be a font of it, from which she might sip if she chose.

She chose—she did. She must.

For he tasted as good as he smelled—like herbs and sweet resin, and warm male. He smelled the way Kaddi's hut did, when he read the runes, when the fire spewed holy smoke full of dizzying fragrance meant for the gods.

Dizziness possessed her now, along with desire strong enough to stun her good sense. The settlement at Sorvagur being a limited one, she'd known the available young men all her life. She could fairly say she liked and respected them. She certainly wished to wed with none of them. And she'd never wanted to lie down with any man she knew, either.

Until now.

It was madness. She'd just met this man, this stranger. Only she knew him to the depths of her being.

Still, one kiss should not be so powerful. One kiss should not change her world.

Closer. Hold me closer, she thought. His arms drew her in, impossibly near. He heard her—and it did not seem strange. Magical, and beguiling, but right, so right.

He had come over the ocean to her, for her. Now she need only persuade him to stay.

She had never been one to work wiles or play at

games. But now she persuaded as a woman does, with her lips fluttering against his, and her body pressing close. When the kiss ended, he did not release her but tucked her face into the crook of his neck and, aloud this time, spoke into her ear. "Gyda."

His voice sounded like the music Modir played on her harp. Gyda's whole body vibrated to it. She wanted his mouth on hers again. She wanted to touch him everywhere.

But he said, "We must go back."

Nei. She thought the word only, yet did he respond to it.

"You will be missed."

"Do you think I care?" She burrowed her fingers more deeply into his hair. "Something you should know about me. I do not always behave as I ought."

He laughed, with a catch in his breath. Gyda's desire sparked impossibly. So this was what it meant, for a woman to desire a man. Modir had tried to explain it, years ago. And Gyda had observed several of her friends go through it, becoming utterly foolish over certain young men. Several of them, besides Astrid, hankered so after Magnus, who sometimes played at the game of flirting with them.

Flirting had never appealed to Gyda. She had no time or patience for it. She had no patience now, when it came to this man. Every impulse bade her tell him she cared for him, that she wanted him.

"Let us slip away somewhere, Lodvar Haraldsson. Off into the dark—"

"Eh?" Wonder colored the word.

She built a picture in her mind—the two of them alone, she shedding her clothing for him and stripping him of his fine robe. He would come to her wearing only the sigils, the magic so much a part of him.

"Nei," he whispered again. "We cannot."

She breathed into his ear, "We can, if we wish."

"Gyda—"

"We will. It is destined."

"Perhaps so." He sounded troubled. "But we must be careful. Gunnar—"

"He does not matter, surely."

"I am afraid he does."

She lifted her face and looked into his eyes. The only radiance, now, came from the light of the gloaming, hanging out over the sea, and the distant torches. Still, his eyes gleamed with tawny light. Protesting, she told him, "I care only about this, *this*."

"Gunnar is dangerous. Not the man you should push to anger."

"Why should what lies between you and me anger him?"

"He has plans in his head, and they may include a marriage alliance."

"With me? Him?" Gyda's stomach clenched at the thought. "No, never."

"You may be sure he will speak of it to your father. Perhaps even tonight."

"And my father will leave the decision to me. There is no chance."

"Still"—his fingers tightened on hers—"we should return to the gathering, and act as if naught has passed between us."

Impossible. Yet, if acting so might protect Lodvar from Gunnar's ire, Gyda must manage it.

For his sake, she could do anything.

Chapter Fourteen

Rain pelted down across the island in sheets, chased by a sharp wind. Gyda, effectively trapped inside, bristled over the fact that the rest of her family had gone out, braving the weather for a number of reasons—Modir to a lying-in, Fadir to settle a dispute, and Magnus ostensibly to practice at arms, though she could not imagine it in such a downpour.

No doubt Magnus, rather, sat holed up somewhere with his friends, drinking the ale left over from last night's feast.

Why was she the one left here alone? She should go to see Kaddi, keep him company. His bones always ached in such weather, and she might provide some distraction from the discomfort.

And perhaps the young Husavik shaman might present himself there.

She needed to see him, the desire like a fever in her blood.

She'd just reached for her cloak when a voice called from the doorway. "Master Tolljur? Are you in?"

Gyda's heart fell. Gunnar Fritisson that was, come calling. Ach, how might she escape now?

Pasting a courteous smile on her face, she went and let him in.

Gunnar had dressed himself well for the visit, in the same fine clothing he'd worn to the feast. Or perhaps he'd never gone to bed. The ale had flowed freely last night. Who could tell?

Yet his eyes looked clear as they fastened upon her, and he gave her a brilliant smile when he said, "Ach, Mistress Gyda. I hoped for a word with your father."

"He has gone to settle a dispute."

Gunnar made a rueful face. "The fate of the jarl, eh? It seemed all my grandfather did, sometimes."

"I am not sure when Fadir will return. I will tell him you called."

"Would you turn me away so quickly, out into the vile weather? I confess, I would as soon speak with you as him."

Gyda hesitated. "I was just about to run an errand."

"Surely you can spare me a few moments? Ach— that fire feels good." Stretching out his hands to it, he came farther into the dwelling and seated himself comfortably beside the hearth, giving Gyda no further chance to chase him away.

"Master Gunnar, might I offer you some refreshment?"

"A warm drink would be most welcome. It is pleasant here out of the rain, with you."

Gyda sighed. Curse it all, the wrong man had come calling.

She brought him a mug of the hot draught Modir always brewed for Fadir in the morning. When Gunnar accepted it from her hand, he brushed her fingers with his, and his bright blue eyes held her gaze.

"I must say, Mistress Gyda, you make this poor morning beautiful."

A pretty compliment, and no mistake. Such a

young man as this, brimming with vitality, good looks and, she supposed, pure male appeal, might well beguile any lass. No doubt he'd beguiled more than a few. But never Gyda Tolljursdottir.

"It is lovely of you to say so."

He splayed one hand over his heart. "Me, I do not speak lies. If ever you hear words fall from my lips"—he fastened his gaze now to her mouth—"you may be sure they are true."

"Ah." Rarely the recipient of such nonsense, Gyda did not know how to respond. Folk here in Sorvagur seldom mentioned her appearance. Here, it mattered more what you did than how you looked. To be sure, Fadir sometimes called her his pretty girl, and once had told her she looked so much like his deceased sister, after whom she was named, he could scarce believe it.

But the young men of Sorvagur took her as found, having known her since she ran around the settlement with a snotty nose and scabby knees.

"Tell me, Mistress Gyda—tell me and quiet the greatest fear of my heart. Are you betrothed?"

Gyda shook her head, while disquiet burgeoned in her heart. For an instant, she was back in Lodvar's arms, beneath the glorious, star-strewn sky. *He has plans in his head, and they may include a marriage alliance.* She regarded Gunnar with caution.

"Ach. You reassure me." Gunnar gave her another of those blinding smiles. "Though I must admit I find it difficult to believe. A woman so matchless as you, why were you not claimed half a score years ago?"

Claimed. Was that how he defined marriage? Was the role of wife, to him, not much different from that of a slave, claimed as spoils of battle?

"Marriage is very different, here, from what you are used to, perhaps." Swiftly she turned away, so he would not see the expression in her eyes, and gathered up the last of the oatcakes to offer him as she would any guest, welcome or unwelcome. Since Modir could not make an oatcake to save her life, Gyda had produced these earlier, with her own hands.

She turned back, keeping her face carefully blank. "We have combined the traditions of our Norse forebears with some of our Alban ancestors. Women have a lot of say."

"I am beginning to see that. Women in Husavik speak their minds also, or at least, women of status do."

For an instant, in her mind's eye, Gyda saw it all—elevated women, such as his mother, perhaps, possessed a level of autonomy afforded by their husbands. Others, such as Modir had been, must struggle to retain the barest shreds of self-respect. Wed with such a man as this? She would rather go without a partner, lifelong.

But if she had her preferences—she wanted Lodvar, with his warm, brown hair and scents of magic. Ja, she could not let Gunnar see that. She could not let him so much as suspect. So even though she never played at love or courting, she supposed she must feed his opinion of himself now.

She placed the platter on the stone curb of the hearth and sat down. "And you, Master Gunnar? How is it that a warrior of your status and—and prowess—has no wife?" He might be wed, for all she knew. He might have a wife and ten female slaves, back in Husavik. He might play at some game, in speaking of a marriage alliance.

He made a deprecating gesture with his hands.

"That is just why. Not many young women in Husavik possess suitable status to be joined with our line. My grandfather insisted on an alliance that would benefit Husavik as a whole. I believe it is the duty of those such as we, who live in privilege, to fulfill such expectations. Do you not agree?"

Gyda did not, but saw no benefit in saying so. Widening her eyes, she gazed at him with what she hoped appeared to be admiration, rather than dismay.

"I am surprised," Gunnar drawled on, "your father has not arranged a marriage for you with someone in a neighboring settlement, or back in Norway. As daughter to a minor jarl, you have value."

And did she not have value as a person, with a warm and beating heart? She lifted her gaze to his face. "My father is not a *minor* jarl, or a minor anything."

"Forgive me. He is, ja, a man to admire. A living legend. Is that not what has brought me here, seeking a relationship with him? He is a great man. Yet if you could see Husavik, you would realize this place is but a rustic outpost. A man's worth may be measured by courage on the battlefield, ja, but it is demonstrated by the land he holds."

"Not by his honor?"

Gunnar flashed his beguiling smile. "That too, of course."

"If you consider my father's holdings so humble, we are scarcely worth your consideration."

"Ach—I have no intention of insulting your father and, through him, you. It is as I have said, I do not trust my father, who is now at the helm of the long ship called Husavik. My grandfather, with whom I was so very close, did not trust him. My father has vowed to

destroy yours, out of hate. He has also stolen from me
my inheritance. What better than to strike an alliance
that will both protect your father, and see me regain my
promised inheritance?"

"By destroying your father."

"Ja. He and I—" Gunnar waved a hand. "We were
never close. We saw things, always, far too differently.
It might have been better, back at the time of the trouble
that involved your parents, had Grandfather banished
him. But of course, I'd not been born yet, and had that
happened I might never have seen Husavik."

"You love the place." His voice had changed when
he spoke the name of his home, softened almost to
reverence.

"It is strong and beautiful. Ach, this place your
father holds is that also, in a different way. This is a
stark land, is it not? All cliffs and ocean. Husavik—
well, it is magnificent. You should see my grandfather's
hall. Big enough for a score of warriors, and also the
seneschal, to live there. Big enough for all the warriors
in Husavik to feast. Following a raid, there do we
gather. The hearth is large enough to roast an ox. All
the pillars are carved with runes and sigils—for strength
and luck, you understand. Each timber was earned, in
raiding."

"You are proud of your heritage."

"Proud? More than that. It made me what I am."

"Your grandfather, did he still go raiding up until
his death?"

"He sent us raiding, ja, though he no longer went
himself. Raiding, trading—is that not how we live?"

"Not here. Fadir does go to trade, ja."

"Of course he does. Else why would he have those

two fine ships? These islands, they are well placed for trading—and raiding also."

"We do not raid the southlands. Too many of us carry Alban blood. I do, myself."

He examined her closely. "It does not show. You look all Norse. Ach, I wish you could see a true Norse settlement—I wish I could show Husavik to you. Mayhap someday I will."

"I do not see that happening." Gyda had no intention of leaving Sorvagur.

He leaned toward her. "I believe it the work of Loki that you remain unwed, as do I. You could do much to help your father by agreeing to a marriage alliance—with me."

Gyda's stomach tightened. She said nothing, fearing to insult this man whose opinion of himself shone so bright.

"I intended to speak of it with your father. Indeed, I did mention it during the feast last night, but I do not think he took me seriously. I came here this morning to state my case with him. But it strikes me that an independent woman such as you will wish to make your own choice. I believe I was meant to find you here this morning, in your father's stead."

"You are suggesting a marriage alliance? Between us?" Gyda's voice sounded wooden to her own ears.

"Is it so surprising? You could do much to protect your father and this settlement. Even Friti Gunnarsson would think twice before murdering the father of his son's wife. Such a union could cement the alliance between us, make us family."

And would that truly turn a man like Friti away? Gyda knew little of the politics of such a place as

Husavik. In truth, she could think of little she would be unwilling to do for Fadir's sake. Except, perhaps, wed this man.

Gunnar tossed his head, and a steely glint entered his bright blue eyes. He did not like her failure to jump at the handsome offer he'd made—and the prize he considered himself. He imagined he flattered and honored her with his offer.

Yet…she sensed what went on beneath, as well as above, the surface of his demeanor. He played at being one sort of man. He might be someone entirely different.

She must refuse. But how to do so without insulting him? For that might well prove a fatal mistake.

She lifted empty hands. "I had planned never to wed."

"That is sheer foolishness and, if you permit me to say so, a terrible waste."

"I feel myself past the age of marrying now."

"Nonsense. You may yet bear many sons." He leaned toward her in what he no doubt considered an alluring manner. "My sons. Think on it. Consider of what great benefit you might be to your father. I will speak to him of this anon—but I will accept my answer only from you."

Chapter Fifteen

"I have her in the palm of my hand, Lodvar. Right where I want her. You should have seen her face when I proposed the marriage alliance. Sheer astonishment. She never imagined being worthy of an offer from a man such as me."

Lodvar, struck to silence, said nothing. Gunnar had returned to the long ship after his trek to Tolljur Magnusson's house and now stripped off clothes wetted by the rain. His movements revealed a body hardened by the rigors of a warrior's life and blessed by the strength he'd inherited from his father.

"She has but to agree."

"She may not," Lodvar croaked out.

Gunnar cocked an eye at him. "Have you seen this, in the stones?"

Lodvar shook his head.

"Then stop speaking such dire warnings. One would think you did not want me to succeed."

Somehow, Lodvar held Gunnar's glowing blue gaze. "An absurd assumption."

"Gyda will agree to the alliance. What woman could refuse all this?" Gunnar grinned like a wolf, and Lodvar relaxed marginally. "It will add to the revenge against the berserker, will it not? Just think—his beloved daughter in my hands and at my mercy, just as his søstir was once in my father's hands. You know the old story, do you not?"

"I do."

"Tolljur Magnusson accused Fadir of raping his precious søstir—also called Gyda—and causing her to kill herself. Foolish wench, she should have been flattered at having Fadir up inside her. Many another woman was. It is said he had most every woman in Husavik, back then. No one was safe from him."

And Gunnar admired that, did he? Lodvar wondered if the vile Friti had ever raped his mother, Catrin. No doubt, though she'd never spoken of it.

"It is a man's privilege to take where he wants. And in this case, I confess, I do want. It will be a pleasure, schooling the lovely Gyda. As my wife she will learn to be obedient, or feel my fist."

Lodvar's spirit rebelled at the thought. But he kept silent.

Gunnar paused, his naked chest glistening wet from the rain. "I wonder, can she be a virgin still, at her age? Or did she give herself to some childhood lover?"

"Lover?"

"There must have been someone, ja, a woman who looks like that. She would not say. I suppose I will find out for myself. It is unlikely she is still whole, though I must confess there is naught I like better than being first. But what matter? There are nights and nights ahead—and afternoons, if she learns her duty."

Lodvar fought to conceal his repugnance. He cared little whether Gyda had been with one man or ten. He needed to be with her both physically and in spirit. He had no doubt Gyda had been born for him. Even as a small child, he'd heard her voice in his heart, in his mind—one among those of the gods who also spoke to him.

Having held her, kissed her, he knew it for certain. Yet he must go carefully. He dared not let Gunnar guess he had feelings for the woman upon whom he'd set his sights.

Gunnar wiggled into a dry tunic and glanced at Lodvar. "Cast the stones on it. See how close I am to success."

Lodvar nodded. "And if the stones say she will not agree, this independent woman?"

"Then I will seek agreement from her father. He is no fool and does not wish to lose what he has built here to Fadir's sword. And she will obey him, I think. She adores the man."

Gunnar turned and looked full into Lodvar's eyes. "Perhaps I will share her with my father, after. How fitting would that be?"

****

"He suggested I marry him. He said it would strengthen the alliance between him and Fadir, and benefit us all."

Magnus turned his head and looked at Gyda, his hazel eyes full of astonishment, and paused in the act of polishing the blade in his hands. Gyda had found him in the armorer's shed, sorting through weapons. Why, she could not say, unless his sense of uneasiness matched her own.

She and her brother might not look alike, he taking after the Alban side and she the Norse, but they remained close in spirit. Though she had female friends in the settlement, she had gone looking first for him.

Fortunately they were alone, the rain still drumming on the roof of the shed in a wild tune.

"You did not accept the offer, did you?"

"To wed him? Nei!"

Magnus puffed out a breath. "Good."

"He behaved very much as if I should be flattered by his offer."

"I do not doubt many a young woman would be. The son and grandson of a jarl, and wealthy, if he's heir to all Husavik."

"How can he imagine I would want to leave here and live in that place?"

"Besides," Magnus went on as if she had not spoken, "I do not doubt women consider him handsome."

"He is that." Gyda shivered. "But I do not trust his pretty smiles. I do not trust him, withal."

"Nor do I."

"Even though he presents a fair and sunny face? He wants me to trust him."

Magnus grunted, which made him sound like Fadir. Despite looking like Modir, he harbored many of Fadir's qualities, including being slow to anger, or to speak. Of course, Modir's father, back in Alba, had also been a superior warrior, as well as a chief. Magnus, as Modir said, had inherited the best of both bloodlines.

And, so it seemed, he had not inherited what Fadir called his curse—to slip into the berserker's fit—as Fadir had feared before he was born. That tended to travel down the male line.

Gyda leaned into him. "You do not think the darkness I sensed, when first the long ship approached over the water, stems—from him?"

"I do not know. Can you not tell?"

Gyda shook her head. "It is as if the warning, or

most of it, has dissipated. I cannot feel it now. But he—he does make me uneasy."

"Could he be hiding his true nature, even from you?"

"Ja, Magnus, I fear so."

"Keep away from him. Keep clean away."

"And if he approaches Fadir about a marriage alliance?"

"Let Fadir handle it."

Easily said, that. Yet if Jarl Friti came with all his might to destroy Tolljur Magnusson—what wouldn't Gyda be willing to do in order to spare him?

****

The rain accompanied Gyda to the very heart of the settlement, tapping her with damp fingers on the hood and shoulders of her cloak.

Here lay Kaddi's hut, where she'd come so often as a child for amusement or solace. The old man had offered her the comfort she sought, along with, usually, a sweetmeat and laughter.

Now she came to him seeking wisdom, and the stillness that always lay here at the center of her world.

The hut lay dim and quiet, the old man drowsing and Aya at her spindle. The young woman rose with a quick smile when Gyda came in. "Good day, Gyda. Have you come to visit? I would be grateful for a chance to slip away and run a few errands."

"I am awake." The thin voice quavered from the blankets. "Besides, am I a child that needs constant tending?"

"To be sure, nei." Gyda shed her soaking cloak and went to sit beside his bed. "If it were so, would I come seeking your advice?"

Kaddi pushed himself up as Aya went out with a smile. A glint of interest appeared in his milky eye. As soon as Gyda settled beside him, he reached for her hand.

"I dreamed of you," he said abruptly. "You were in danger, out at sea. The sun—it wanted to scorch you, to burn you up."

Gyda froze in surprise. "A true dream was this?" she asked, thinking of her conversation with Magnus.

Kaddi shook his head, and a look of confusion possessed him.

"No matter," Gyda told him. "You may give me a blessing. And—" Should she tell him, speak of her feelings for Lodvar? After so long spent as a spinster, he might well think her rash, or mad.

"My child, you are always welcome to my blessing. But why do you come to me this day?"

"Change is in the air. With the arrival of the newcomers—well, a blessing from you seems an apt precaution."

Kaddi released her fingers and cupped her cheek. "Whatever blessing I may shed upon you, so I do. You are like a granddaughter to me."

Gyda smiled. "And you, in truth, like the grandfather I never knew."

"I knew him, your grandfather, even before we left Norway and settled in Husavik."

"Tell me about him." Kaddi had, in the past, given her brief glimpses of the man who had died long before she was born. She craved still more such knowledge.

"He was berserker, like his father before him—and like your father after him."

"Ja, it comes down the male line. Except it seems

101

to have skipped Magnus."

"Magnus has a goodly measure of Alban blood. Your grandfather took it hard when the fits came upon him. He suffered. But in battle he was invincible. He called it a curse, and one at odds with his nature—for he was a quiet man, for the most part. I could not help but respect and admire him."

"You were friends."

Kaddi shrugged. "I had that honor, ja. He confided in me. He came to me when he needed a refuge from the pain."

"As do I."

"Ja, girl. I was a young man then, also, learning the ways of the gods. I asked them for a means to ease Magnus's anguish. I learned to mix the potions that helped ease him into the fits and recover from them."

"So my grandfather was not a violent man, in ordinary life?"

"He was a very gentle man. I believe that is what your grandmother saw in him. You must understand, many a young woman followed after the berserker. They were impressed by his fame and his prowess. And some"—Kaddi's eye clouded—"some wished the honor of bearing the next berserker.

"Magnus, though, wanted something more. He wanted love. He confided in me how he feared he would never find that. What woman, he asked, could ever love a man who raged and bled and turned into a bear?"

"But my grandmother did."

"She did, ja—and only needed to convince him of it. A lovely young woman, was Solveig. But"—Kaddi searched for a word—"unstable. Seeing Magnus suffer proved difficult for her, and difficult for her children, in turn."

"You told me before that Fadir did not intend ever to marry."

"That is so. He had no wish to inflict his misery on any woman, or to beget a son cursed like himself."

"Then he met Modir."

Kaddi smiled. "She came into his life like a comet bursting across a dark sky."

Gyda drew a breath. "Kaddi, do you think it happens that way often?"

"Not often, but it does happen, girl. Are you trying to tell me something?"

She squeezed his fingers tight. "I'd never intended to marry either. I am, as you know, well past the age."

"Nonsense."

"I believed love had passed me by. But—but a comet has appeared, across my sky."

"Not Gunnar Fritisson."

"Nei, though he would form a marriage alliance with me if he could. I speak of the other." Gyda dropped her eyes. "His companion, the shaman."

"Ah."

"It is as you say—after all this time, it was the farthest thing from my mind. But I ask you, Master Kaddi, can one turn away from it, when it comes? Even if it may prove—unsuitable?"

"It is a good question. You believe the young shaman to be unsuitable?"

"Nei, I think he suits me—perfectly, in many ways. Yet despite his status he was born a slave. And now that Gunnar has expressed an interest, how could he hope to offer for me? Crossing Gunnar Fritisson could prove perilous for him."

"So it could. Tell me, girl, what are his feelings for you? Can you tell?"

Gyda remembered those moments in Lodvar's arms, and his lips on hers. "I believe I have captured his interest. I would not wish it to prove costly for him."

"I see."

"My question to you, Kaddi, is it wrong to turn away from such a love when it comes? Dare I turn away?"

"Wrong or right, I do not know that it is possible to turn away from what the gods send. Be it a vision, the berserker's fit, or love. But you are right. I would go carefully in crossing that one—Gunnar Fritisson. He may look pretty, and may seem to speak with a fair tongue. But I know from whence he came, just as I know from whence you came."

"Bless me, Grandfather. I fear I will need it in the days ahead. And speak to Fadir Odin on my behalf, if you will."

"My child, as always, I am here for you, to help in any way I might."

Chapter Sixteen

"Jarl Tolljur, there is no time to waste. When I sailed from Husavik to bring you warning, my father was already preparing his ships to come and attack. He will destroy you and seize your settlement. At any moment, his sails may darken the horizon."

The rain had finally moved off eastward, banks of dark cloud sailing over the sea. With the new day, bright sunlight burst across the land. It flooded in through the door of Fadir's dwelling, left open for that purpose.

The room seemed crowded with so many gathered. Fadir, his closest advisors, young Master Gunnar, and Lodvar Haraldsson were there. Even Kaddi had been brought down from his hut.

Gyda made sure to linger—both out of curiosity and because it afforded her a chance to see Lodvar, though she found it tortuous to be so near and unable to touch him. As she moved around the room, offering refreshment, she fought the desire to brush his arm with her hand or touch the brown mane that spilled over the shoulders of his cloak.

Modir, also present and listening avidly, left to Gyda the role of server. Gyda had prepared most of the food, Modir all too often turning out woefully inedible fare.

She turned her eyes on Fadir, measuring his

reaction to Gunnar's statement. Danger on the horizon haunted folk such as they, and always called for a swift response.

Yet Fadir appeared calm, his gray eyes, so like her own, revealing little emotion and certainly no panic. "If Friti Gunnarsson brings war to me, I will meet him shield to shield, as he comes."

Magnus grunted his agreement. He sat with his back to the door, and the sunlight made fire of his hair just as it did Modir's when she stood outside.

Gunnar glared at him. "You suppose that is what you want, do you—battle?"

"Only a fool welcomes war," Fadir replied. "And only a coward fails to rise to it."

Gyda did not want to see Fadir rise to battle. When she'd witnessed him entering the battle madness as a child, it had been terrifying. Modir's distress had made it even more so.

Yet he appeared so very confident, sitting beside his own hearth, speaking of life and death on a sunny morning.

Love for him convulsed her heart, this strong quiet man who loved so deeply and had protected her all her life.

Lodvar raised his eyes and met her gaze. No ordinary glance, this—for he gazed *into* her. Conveying a message, perhaps.

Gunnar leaned toward Fadir, all earnestness. "What benefits me, Jarl Tolljur, benefits you. You cannot stand against my father alone."

"Sure of that, are you?" Fadir spoke the words with a smile, not a nice one. Modir stopped abruptly in her fussing, and stared at him. His advisors exchanged looks before doing the same.

Gunnar tossed his head. "You know my father, ja?"

"Ja."

"You know what he is, when angry."

Fadir's eyes glinted silver. "You know what I am, when angry?"

"Tolljur," Modir began.

Gunnar stirred. "Now, I believe none of us wishes for it to come to that. Indeed, am I not here to prevent the sorts of unfortunate confrontations that occurred in the past?" His eyes glinted. "My father hates you. Even more than the conquest of what you have built here, he wants to see you repaid for ruining his relationship with his father, long ago."

"I did not do that—he did."

"What matters, Jarl Tolljur, is how my father sees it. For a score of years or more, he has mulled paying you back, has planned for it. Alone, it is not certain you can withstand his attack. Together, you and I double our forces. He comes with the full might of Husavik and two long ships. Likewise, I am not certain I can seize power in Husavik and right things, make it as my grandfather wished, without your assistance."

Gyda's gaze still rested on Lodvar, and she saw something flicker in his eyes. Agreement? Protest? Warning?

"Together, Jarl Tolljur, we have three long ships. We will stand him off here, and then follow him back to Husavik, where I will seize control. In future we shall stand united—and peace will endure between our peoples."

Gunnar glanced at Gyda. "To confirm the agreement between us, I do request your daughter's hand in marriage."

****

Fadir waited till Gunnar had gone before he exploded. Indeed, most of his advisors, save Kaddi, had also departed, each one looking hard into his impassive face before filing out.

Only the family, and Kaddi, remained when he took a stance beside the hearth and declared, "Never. Never shall that spawn of Friti Gunnarsson touch my daughter. I will lose all I own and die battling him first."

Gyda stared. So seldom did she see Fadir stirred to anger, she scarcely knew how to respond. Yet his eyes blazed. His scarred face paled before flushing red, and his hands fisted.

Looking at Modir, he said, "Should I allow him to do to my daughter what Friti did to my søstir?"

"Now…" Modir laid her fingers on his arm in an attempt to soothe him. "That young man is not his father. Far different, he claims to be." She glanced at Gyda. "And if our daughter chooses to agree—"

Everyone looked at Gyda then, Kaddi with his fogged eye, Modir wisely, Magnus in stubborn inquiry—Fadir with appeal. "Are you asking if I wish to wed with him?"

Modir whispered, "Surely it is up to you."

Ja, and how rare did that make her—a woman who could choose her own fate. It lay not in Gunnar Fritisson's hands nor even in Fadir's. Rather, it lay in the deep magic she'd seen in the eyes of the shaman.

Yet she needed to think carefully, and do what would best benefit both this place and this family she loved.

"Fadir, is it right, what he says? Is it the only way we can defeat Friti, by joining forces with Gunnar?"

"Nei." Fadir denied it soundly. "I can defend what is mine without the help of that—"

Gyda went to him and laid her hands on his forearms. "Fadir, are you certain? I would not wish it to cost your life."

Modir caught her breath, and anguish flooded her eyes. "Dottir, have you Seen—"

"Nei. But anything may happen, especially during battle."

Fadir smiled. "For a man such as me, death in battle is to be desired."

Modir cried out, "And what of me, Tolljur? How might I expect to go on living, without you?"

Tenderness flooded his eyes. He cupped Modir's cheek. "Never without me, lass."

Gyda bit her lip. "And what might happen to us, should you fall fighting Friti? Would the settlement not fall also? Should we not do all we might, to prevent it?"

"What are you saying, Dottir? That you are willing to accept Gunnar Fritisson?"

"Nei." She whispered it again. "Nei."

Kaddi spoke suddenly. "I sense a measure of deception from that young man. Given, he looks after his own interests, and that may account for it."

"I, too," Gyda agreed, "sense a certain—" Darkness was not the word. She shook her head in turn. "Why not treat him to deception in turn? If I pretend to agree with his proposal—well, that doesn't mean I will wed with him, after."

Magnus protested, "That is dishonorable."

"It is the same honor he offers us. And, brother, we

speak of survival. Honor comes second to that."

"Does it?" Magnus frowned. "I am not so sure. And I do not like it."

"Nor do I," Fadir agreed. "Dottir, it is my place to defend you, not the other way around."

"It is our place to protect one another in any way we may."

"Huh," Kaddi grunted, and closed his eye. "This is not a step to be taken lightly."

"No, indeed." Modir turned to Gyda. "Dottir—"

Modir, as Gyda knew, loved deeply—her husband, her children, and all those others around her made up her family. She'd loved those who, as slaves, had been taken to Husavik with her, and had even come to care for some of her captors.

Now anguish flooded her eyes. "I would not, ever, see you go to a man you do not love. It is a cruel fate."

"I know. But I need not go to him, Modir. We speak of a deception—one he may well deserve."

Fadir said, "His sire was a bad man to cross. He may be the same."

Kaddi spoke in a surprisingly strong voice. "Girl, do nothing yet. Let me consult with the gods." He waved a finger at Gyda. "And you do the same."

"Ja, Grandfather Kaddi." But would the gods respond?

****

Gunnar returned from the meeting at Jarl Tolljur's in a foul mood. Temper on a short lead, he went aboard the long ship and began snapping orders, calling the men lazy curs and worse.

"Why do you not practice at arms? There is no rain now to prevent it. Get out there and put on a show for our hosts. Let them see of what the warriors of Husavik are made."

The men moved reluctantly. Many of them had aching heads from ale they had taken the night before, shared by the men of the settlement. Gunnar kicked at two of them to make them rise, and cuffed a third on the head.

"Are you men or children?"

He turned to Lodvar as the men slogged ashore, anger and perhaps spite clear in his blue eyes. Lodvar had seen just such a look, many times, in the eyes of Gunnar's mother, Anaborg—beautiful eyes they were, that nevertheless could turn mad in an instant.

Did Gunnar also carry a touch of madness? Nei, he merely bristled over failing to get his way, back at the meeting. Someone—quite likely one of his men—would now pay for it.

Just so long as it wasn't him, Lodvar. Swiftly he said, "I will go up on the headland and consult with the spirits, see how the future lies. I may well be able to glean the signs."

"You do that, Lodvar. Cast your stones and read your runes. Tell me how to influence the berserker. He is made of stone."

His weakness lies in those he loves. But Lodvar would not say that aloud. "He is a man very much in control of his emotions." Until he wasn't.

"Does he think he can best me in combat? Me? That old man."

"You are a mighty warrior, Gunnar Fritisson." And had committed atrocities without restraint. Lodvar wished he could blot those from his mind. "Tolljur Magnusson is battle-hardened."

"And carries old injuries that may well hamper him. Every warrior his age does." A dark light appeared in Gunnar's eyes. "If we meet hand to hand in battle, I will destroy him. Then I will destroy his settlement, piece by piece."

Lodvar, struck silent by the spite he heard in Gunnar's voice, believed it. He believed it in full.

Gunnar sneered. "Now let me go beat my men into shape. They, too, have earned a thrashing."

Chapter Seventeen

The clash of weapons followed Lodvar to the headland. Sword upon shield and sword upon sword—Gunnar's angry voice, rising right up the vault of the blue sky.

How far did he need to walk before those sounds were lost behind him? He wanted only the rush of the wind in his ears, the pound of the surf on the cliffs below.

Ja, and he wanted Gyda's voice in his ears. Just as he ached for her in his life.

Ah, impossible.

Better to seek what peace he could find here, on his own.

He walked past the curve of the headland, past the rocky arm that formed one side of the bay where rode the three long ships, until the clamor died away. Here, the wind found him, lifting his hair from his shoulders and streaming it out like a banner.

Before his eyes stretched only ocean, vast and wide. A living thing it appeared from here, shifting eternally in its bed. Did it stir and breathe? Was it aware of him, poised above it like a speck on the cliff top?

Water carried magic for him. It always had. Once, when a small boy, he'd leaped into the bay at Husavik and taken off swimming. His mother had screamed and his father had leaped into the water after him.

When Harald hauled him ashore and asked why he'd done such a thing, Lodvar had answered, *I want to swim home.*

"Home?" Harald shouted at him, red-faced. "This is your home, foolish boy." And then Harald had thrashed him soundly.

Ja, Husavik was his home, born and raised. Yet he'd always felt he had another, elsewhere—perhaps the Alban island where Modir had been born and of which she spoke so often. Lewis.

Or perhaps she who spoke in his heart, and had from a young age, was destined to be his home. He had a name for her now.

Gyda.

The mere thought of her set him aflame. Now that he'd touched her, kissed her, the longing fairly possessed him. Her warmth filled the empty spaces in his spirit, her passion answered his own, dormant so long.

With a shrug—an attempt to quiet his desire—he hunkered down among the rocks and drew out his pouch of rune stones. This made a good place, screened from everything but the sky and his thoughts.

He'd fashioned these stones himself, as a young man, gathering them from the sea and painstakingly carving each symbol. A labor of love that had been, for he gave love only to his faith, his mother, and the woman in his heart.

Gyda.

He had wetted the stones, when finished, with his own blood—a bond between him and them. Since, they had served him faithfully, interpreting messages from the gods.

They'd forecast the voyage here, to Sorvagur. Urged him to accompany Gunnar, though Lodvar might otherwise not choose to associate with that young man. They'd warned of danger, and of a great, inconceivable reward.

He'd hardly dared believe that included meeting *her*. At last.

He centered himself now, holding hard against the emotions that tumbled through him, and slipped into prayer. He petitioned Odin and Freya to guide him, to protect those he loved.

He cast the stones, but before he could even begin his interpretation, a sharper message overrode all his senses.

She comes.

He rose and whirled to see Gyda climbing the headland, following the same path he'd taken.

As if she followed him.

Joy flooded his heart, magnificent and triumphant. Just as she'd summoned him across the ocean, his longing had brought her to him now.

She wore a plain gown and her gray-blue cloak that made smoke of her eyes. The garment belled out behind her, and it appeared she flew over the ground.

He might well believe she flew to him.

As soon as she reached him, she seized his hands. Heedless of who might be watching, and responding to the demand inside, he drew her into his arms.

Here she belonged—a missing piece falling into place, easing all want. For the first time ever, it occurred to him. *Perhaps when I leaped into the harbor back at Husavik, I did mean to swim here—to her.*

Wordless, they stood so, she with her cheek pressed into his shoulder, he with his arms wrapped tight around her. Time trickled away on the wind. The ground dissolved from beneath Lodvar's feet. He drank in the feeling of her presence, and the ensuing rightness of his world.

At length she stirred and lifted her face to his. Still wordless, she kissed him. His joy increased, rose to his head so he felt that he, too, might fly. Her kiss tasted of eternity. Soft as a dark night, magical as a trance, potent as storm. He melded to her—bonded on a level so deep it thrilled him. She claimed him, and he gave to her, gladly, all that he was.

He might have gone on so forever, with her lips on his, her tongue wooing him, sending green shoots of magic to twine about his heart. But she broke the kiss suddenly to gaze into his eyes. "Lodvar Haraldsson, I desire you."

Light sparked and flooded his brain before traveling through him in a powerful rush, forging ribbons of delight.

"Ja," he croaked, "and I you. But—"

"I have never before wanted to be with a man, not like this. But I think—I think with you, it will be easy. Easy, and right. Ja?"

Should he tell her he'd never lain with a woman, either? Ach, there had been kisses, and moments spent fumbling in the dark. But, despite those isolated incidents, he'd never wanted to join completely with anyone. Until now.

"Come." She caught his hand between both of hers.

"Gyda, are you certain? There is no going back from this—"

"You think I wish to go back?"

"I would not have you regret—"

I bid you come.

Did he hear those words with his ears, or in his heart?

He followed her, not back the way they'd come but farther off away from the settlement, twining between the rocks that studded the headland. The wind streamed her hair out behind her, a river of gold that brushed his cloak, and her eyes gleamed like silver when she looked back at him.

Some distance back from the cliffs stood a fortress of stone. Built by the hand of no man, it might have instead been raised by the gods, or by giants from out of Jotunheim. Lodvar sensed strong magic here.

He dragged Gyda to a halt. "What is this place?"

"We call it the giant's *hus*. Come inside." Her eyes shone. "Here we will make our bed."

"Gyda—" he began again.

"Lodvar. We know not what the future may bring, of good or ill."

They did not, and he had left his rune stones behind.

"Lodvar Haraldsson—whatever may come to us, I would have you first, ahead of it."

Pain flooded his heart. Did terrible things come? "Gyda, have you Seen—"

"Nei. But Gunnar Fritisson has brought trouble. Sacrifices will have to be made. Will you deny me my happiness?"

"Nei." *Nei.*

He stepped forward with her, among the stones, and paused again in wonder. The place lay steeped in magic so strong it vibrated along his skin. All his senses leaped to life, his eyes seeing colors in the filtered sunlight and his ears catching what sounded like music. Ach, and it was music—a tune played by the wind, feeling its way between the stones.

A holy place she had chosen for their joining. He wanted to fall to his knees, wanted to lose himself in reverence.

Or in her.

"What we do here today," she stepped once more into his arms, "must last us forever." She lifted her chin. "Lodvar Haraldsson, I do give myself to you."

Just as it should be, between two halves of one whole. Meeting her gaze, Lodvar drew a deep breath. He had lived his whole life for this moment. He would not hold back now. Casting all doubt to the wind, he claimed her lips and succumbed.

****

Always had Gyda believed in magic. From her earliest memory, when her mother taught her the sweet understanding of the gods from the south, the messages they might send. The soothing powers of music, the sustaining enchantment of love.

Never, though, had she expected she might find that on a personal level, might be willing to cast herself upon a holy fate with voluntary and unstinting passion.

But so she did now, within the shelter of Lodvar Haraldsson's arms.

He thought her beautiful—she could tell that by the look in his eyes. He desired her—she knew that also from the way his breath caught when she disrobed for him.

None of that mattered, though. Ja, she wanted him

also, as she'd never desired anything, and the physical demand felt strong. But it paled beside that other, the spiritual longing that opened inside her like a well, the need for him.

Ach, but the gods had been kind to her, though, as she saw when he stepped from his clothing. He was beautiful the way a young horse is, with strength and grace. His body, long and narrow, made her fingers tingle with anticipation.

They spread their cloaks on the ground, for a bed. When Lodvar came down upon Gyda, he whispered once again, "Gyda, are you certain—"

For answer, she kissed him. Bliss rose and overwhelmed her. Surely she had been born for this, for him. And nothing mattered but that they should become one.

Magic poured into her from the tips of his fingers, met the knowing inside her, and found its balance. Two perfect parts of the same being, their passions met. Equal parts giving and demand, they swiftly joined— bodies and spirits—and it felt as easy as breathing, as praying, as experiencing joy.

Gyda knew immediately the mistake she'd made. For she'd believed having him once would satisfy her heart. Having him once, though, would never be enough. She needed him for an eternity.

Eyes closed against the exquisite, beautiful pain of it, she struggled with that realization. She needed to anchor him to her, as the long ships anchored in the bay. She needed to hold him, as the runestones held magic.

How to express all that to him? She had always been a forthright person. Modir had given her the gift of owning her tongue and Fadir the gift of being heard without censure. Because of that, and driven by the certainty in her heart, she now found words she'd never expected to say.

"Lodvar Haraldsson, I do love you."

His eyes opened, long brown lashes lifting to reveal the tawny gold. What lay there, for her? Surprise? Acceptance?

Men, as her friend Kirstie told her, did not like speaking that word, nor did they do so readily. They considered it a trap, a harness like that put upon a pony for the first time. It had taken a year to persuade her betrothed husband, Snorri, to admit his feelings for her. Should this man be any different?

Yet the expression in his eyes revealed no doubt. Warm with tenderness, soft with admiration, it required no words.

He need say nothing. And yet, like music, the words flowed from his lips.

"Gyda, I have always loved you. Long before I met you, you were here—in my heart."

"How? How can that be?"

"You spoke to me, always. You called to me. I would have shifted the very world in order to answer that call."

Victorious joy flared in Gyda's heart. And yet—

She touched his face in adoration. "No one can know what has passed between us here this day."

"Nei?"

"Nei, my love." She pressed her lips to his in a lingering kiss. "For now, it must remain our secret."

A shadow flickered through his eyes.

Swiftly, she added, "I do not trust Gunnar

Fritisson."

"You are right not to trust him."

"If he should find out—"

A sound very like a sigh rumbled in Lodvar's throat.

"So this will remain between us, ja?" Though how she would behave when next they met, she could not say. "Just remember." She kissed him again, hot and hard. "Whatever may happen, it is to you I have given my heart."

Chapter Eighteen

"My father will be on his way even now." Earnestly, Gunnar leaned toward Tolljur where they sat once more outside the jarl's dwelling. "He was very angry when I left, and bent upon having his revenge. I say we meet him as soon as he arrives—surprise him, and see can we not stop him in his tracks."

Tolljur, gray eyes revealing no emotion, listened carefully. A cloudy day it was—the morning after Lodvar and Gyda had lain together in the giant's stronghold—and all the sunny weather flown. Rain would no doubt arrive before sunset, blowing in from the sea just like Jarl Friti's ships might.

The three of them—Tolljur, Gunnar, and Lodvar—sat alone in discussion, none of Tolljur's advisors present this time, and his wife elsewhere. Lodvar had hoped for a glimpse of Gyda, but she was apparently up at Kaddi's hut, tending the old man, who did not feel well.

Gunnar, like a hound upon the scent, beat at Tolljur for agreement. "My father does not know I am here. He thinks me off on another voyage. He will not expect us to meet him with a united front."

Tolljur remained impassive. Ja, difficult to read the man, or even guess what lay within his heart.

Lifting his eyes to Gunnar's face, Tolljur said, "Will Friti not tumble to the truth when he sails into the bay and sees your long ship?"

"I thought of that. I suggest we hide my ship—and perhaps one of yours—farther along the headland. Let him think you have less here than you do, and he will be taken unawares by our numbers."

"A clever plan." Tolljur spoke quietly. "And you believe he will arrive soon?"

"At any time. As I say, he prepared to depart Husavik even as I left. We should move the ships today, get our weapons ready. And, if I may speak freely—"

"By all means."

"You should give me your daughter's hand, that you and I might be pledged to one another in battle, the same as she and I in marriage."

An unidentifiable expression flashed in Tolljur's eyes. "My daughter's hand is not mine to give."

"Forgive me, Jarl Tolljur, but it most certainly is."

Tolljur shot one glance at Lodvar before he shook his head. "She will choose her own husband."

Gunnar bared his teeth in a smile. "That is lenient in you, Jarl Tolljur, and might be admirable during ordinary times. Which these are not. I can help defend your daughter. Would you rather see her in my father's hands—or worse yet, slain?"

"I would see her in the hands of no man who might abuse her."

"Nor would I—that brave and lovely woman—which is why I suggest this alliance. She, just like what you have built here, must be protected."

Lodvar shifted uncomfortably in his seat. Again Tolljur glanced at him, before his jaw grew tight. "Harm will befall my daughter only over my dead body."

"Forgive me saying, Jarl, but that too could happen."

"Ja, every man comes to death in his time." Tolljur looked Gunnar in the eye. "Every man. And it is best we speak plainly here."

"So I would hope."

"Speak to my daughter as you will. Her mind and heart are her own."

"I have spoken to her. I think a word from you would help her make up her mind. Women so often do not know what is best for them."

Tolljur shook his head again. "I will persuade her into nothing so important as a marriage."

Now disparagement gleamed in Gunnar's blue eyes, there and gone again so swiftly Tolljur likely did not notice. "Thank you, Jarl, for your permission to speak to her. I will do so again."

"Meanwhile, ja, I will ready my men and double the lookouts."

"And move the ships?"

"You may move yours. Mine will remain where they lie. Let Friti Gunnarsson see how matters stand, if and when he sails into my harbor."

****

"A stubborn man," Gunnar commented when he and Lodvar left the jarl's dwelling. "No wonder my father detests him."

Lodvar said nothing. When Gunnar took this mood, one did best to keep from offering a differing opinion.

"Any man who cannot keep his own women in line! That wife of his is a scold. And the daughter needs to learn her place."

Lodvar thought of Gyda, her smooth, strong body

flexing beneath his, meeting him on a wave of passion as strong as his own. Any man who would not delight in that had no belief in himself as a man.

By Odin's eye, he wanted her again, with a hunger that shocked him. Not usually prone to the seductions of the flesh, he tended rather to dwell upon spiritual matters and the life within—magic, signs, and portents. But Gyda called to something more in him, brought him to life in a way he'd never imagined. Having tasted that once, how could he possibly live in denial of it?

"What will you do when your father's ships sail into the harbor?"

Gunnar smiled. Not a nice smile, it turned his face into that of a wolf. "I will help Tolljur Magnusson set up his defenses, as promised, making sure one of our warriors stands at every third place. And when Tolljur gives my father battle—well, our warriors will make very certain the line of defense does not hold."

Lodvar turned sick inside. "There will be wholesale slaughter."

"There will. Tolljur Magnusson will be captured, and Fadir will have his revenge. It has been a long time coming, ja? Fadir may have a brutal hand, with many tortures planned, but I think the berserker will last a while."

By Odin's eye! Tolljur needed to be warned. But if he, Lodvar, went to Jarl Tolljur, he as good as condemned his mother, back home.

"After," Gunnar gloated, "this place, with its strategic position, will be ours. We will return home with Tolljur Magnusson's head on a spear, to decorate Fadir's hall. And—I think—with Gyda Tolljursdottir as an added amusement."

Lodvar drew a breath in an attempt to master his emotions. "You actually mean to wed with her?"

Gunnar turned those brilliant blue eyes on him. "Mayhap. I do not know, yet. It might serve me well. The berserker's blood travels down the line, does it not?"

"Possibly. Tolljur's son, Magnus, shows no signs."

"We have not yet seen him in battle, when he might well fall into the berserker's fit. I would not mind getting a son out of that bitch Gyda. It would bring a lot of status, having our berserker in Fadir's house. Either way, I will enjoy rutting with her for a number of days, till she cannot stand."

Gunnar gave Lodvar another smile, this one as cruel as any Lodvar had ever seen. "Even if I do not marry her," he drawled, "she may give me a berserker son. That would be a fine thing, even if he is born a slave. As you know—any slave born can be made as useful, or nearly, as a free man."

Chapter Nineteen

"Mistress Gyda, if you might spare a moment?" The polite query sounded at Gyda's elbow as she worked outside the armorer's shed, helping Magnus sort weapons. Spoken in an even, courteous tone, it should not make her body come to attention and her blood leap, yet it did, starting a gout of flame deep down in her belly.

Where its owner had already been.

She looked up, as did Magnus, in query.

There he stood, in his deep blue cloak, with the brown hair—that in which she'd buried her fingers—flowing over his shoulders, and something...something like magic flaring in his amber-colored eyes. He came as if in answer to the longing in her heart.

Denying what surged inside her, Gyda said, "Ah, Master Lodvar. As you can see, we are busy here."

"It is a matter of some importance."

Magnus shot Lodvar a close look. "Go, *Søstir*. Important, the man says."

Gyda rose out of her crouch. "Let us walk, then."

What could he want? To talk to her, truly? Or to touch her as he had before—run his hands down her body to that secret place between her thighs, trailing magic all the way?

She wanted him there. She'd awakened that morning aching for him. But ja, the man looked troubled, thoughts swirling deep in his eyes.

"This way." She directed him toward the cliffs. "We will not be overheard."

"Where is your father?"

"Out drilling the men. Why?" Gyda turned and gazed at him. "What has happened? Have the sails been sighted?"

An old term, that one. Her mother's people in the Alban islands had lived and died by such sightings. Was the reaction to that danger carried in her blood?

"Nei, not yet. But your father must be warned, all the same." Lodvar hesitated. "It will be easier for you to claim his ear, rather than me."

"All right." They'd nearly reached the headland. Gyda swept the broad expanse of the sea, reassuring herself no ships rode there, before facing him. "What must I tell him?"

Lodvar gazed at her a long moment, lips pressed together and eyes full of gravity. "That he dare not trust Gunnar Fritisson."

"I am sure he does not."

"All Gunnar has said to him since we arrived has been a lie—a deception from the very start. He never broke with his father, Friti. The two of them schemed together in this. Friti wants revenge, ja—and Gunnar is here to help him get it."

Gyda stared in horror. "But Gunnar would have us believe—"

"He would. He seems what he is not. An asp that lies in the sun seems harmless. It is still an asp. When Friti arrives, and Gunnar's men stand with those of your father, Gunnar will welcome Friti, rather than repel him, by turning on your men."

"A betrayal."

"Completely."

"Why—why did you not tell me this sooner? While we—" So intimate together, bonded so deeply. Why had he failed to tell her then?

He turned away toward the ocean. The late sun, emerging from a bank of clouds, lit his brown hair with strands of gold.

He swung back. "My mother—"

"Modir's friend, Catrin."

"Back in Husavik, she lies in Friti's hands. You do not understand what Friti is—"

"I can well guess." Gyda had gleaned enough from what her parents said. "And your mother is at his mercy."

"Ja, only he has no mercy, that one."

"Surely her master—Harald, is it? He will protect her."

"Husband. He has married her now. She is in fact a freed woman. But it will not benefit her. Harald may wish to protect her. And he had some hope, with the old jarl alive. Since Jarl Gunnar's death, everything has changed. No one stands against Friti. No one."

Gyda drew a breath. "I see. It sounds to me like this Friti desperately needs to die."

Lodvar blinked at her before appearing to consider it. "Ja, it would be a boon upon the world."

"Let him come here, then. My father will answer him. Or my brother will." Her chin jerked up. "If need be, I will."

"Gyda—" Lodvar caught both her hands. "Have you ever encountered evil? True evil? That is what I ask."

She shook her head. She'd sensed it—most lately in that darkness that rode out on the water before Gunnar arrived.

"In Friti Gunnarsson, you will meet it. His heart harbors darkness. He enjoys hurting others. More, he feels it is his right. You may not be able to defeat him."

"Or we might. In coming here, he may take a step too far."

Slowly, Lodvar shook his head.

"You are right," she told him. "My father must be warned—but not by you. Gunnar must not learn you have come to me." And not only for his mother's sake. What might Gunnar do to Lodvar, if he found out?

Lodvar might not care about protecting himself. She did.

"Let me go to Fadir—tell him of Gunnar's plans." A total betrayal.

"He will ask how you know."

She smiled. "I have ways, have I not, of Seeing the truth? No one knows we lay together. No one knows you've confided in me. Let it remain so."

Lodvar nodded. "What will your father do when he learns of this?"

"I am not sure."

"Will he confront Gunnar directly?"

"Mayhap. He chooses honesty when he can."

"Best warn him soon. Friti was not far on our stern when we left Husavik. He may well sail into that harbor at any time."

"Ja."

Lodvar gazed into Gyda's eyes. "Gunnar intends to cause you pain also, if he can. Provide what he calls discipline, because you stood up to him. It is why—"

He broke off.

"Why you have chosen to warn me, despite the danger to your mother."

Emotions sparked in Lodvar's eyes, bright and strong enough to consume Gyda. He nodded.

"Come." She tugged at his hand. "Where we cannot be seen."

This time she led him to a cleft in the rocks, a narrow fissure cloaked in green. Here, they slipped between the folds of the land, securely out of sight. She moved eagerly into his arms.

"Lodvar." She spoke his name in claiming, and demand. Lifting her hands, she cradled his face between her palms, and, without another word, pressed her mouth to his.

Euphoria flooded, her, nearly overwhelming. This had she needed. For this had she been living, without realizing it. Half dizzy with the rush of emotion, she pressed closer, and his arms wrapped hard around her, drawing her in.

Soon—all too soon—he broke the kiss. "We cannot be caught here. It is dangerous. You must go at once to your father."

"I will, you may be certain. But, Lodvar"—she searched his eyes—"I need you, first."

"Gyda."

"Need you. All of you."

"That is madness."

"It is like madness, for me, wanting you. Lodvar, it is a fever in my blood. Will you deny me?"

"I can deny you nothing."

"This—this may be the last time we can be together. If Friti Gunnarsson comes—"

"Do not say it."

Nei, she would not speak it lest it come true, yet the reflection lay banked in his eyes. He knew that if battle came, one or both of them could fall. And for the survivor, life might well change irreparably.

He unfastened the pin on her cloak, and it dropped away. She stood with her eyes half closed, absorbing the sheer pleasure of it as he unlaced her bodice. She shivered when her naked skin felt the air.

Exquisitely gentle, he palmed her breast and, with a groan, bent his head to taste her there. The strength of her passion for him rose, banishing all thoughts but one.

"Come to me, Lodvar. I beg you."

Please take me, she spoke to his mind.

My love, my love—his words and his emotions tumbled through her, even as they sank to the green moss beneath their feet.

****

"I must rise."

Not the first time Lodvar had expressed the conviction. Yet he did not stir from his place in Gyda's arms. Weightless he felt, almost lifeless or—better—as if he existed on another plane, high above this life.

He had come to her, as she'd begged, given her all of himself, body and spirit. She possessed, already, his heart. As he'd said, could he deny her aught else?

Curious, the way she made him feel—at once helpless *and* empowered. Humble, yet as if he owned the world.

Perhaps—for these few precious moments—he owned the most important thing in it.

He tried to stir. Her arms held him tight.

"Nei. Not yet."

"Gyda—"

"Say my name again. It sounds like music on your lips."

"Gyda."

"Talk to me. I cannot get enough of your voice."

He gave a gusty laugh. "What would you have me say? How much I love you?"

"Ja—that." She turned her head, and their lips met.

"And I feel like I have known you forever. Did I tell you—" He broke off.

"Tell me again."

"You spoke to me, back in Husavik. For years, you did. You called to my mind, my heart, an invisible companion."

"How can that be? I do not understand."

"Nor did I, until I got here." He smiled into her mist-gray eyes. "For a long time, I thought everyone had a voice in his or her head. When I found out I was different—well, then I thought I was mad. I must have been about ten when I took the matter to Modir. She said perhaps I was fey, had inherited the Sight from her people. It is, so I understand, a common enough trait there, in various forms, though rare in a male."

"Ja. I have it, and Modir—she can feel others' emotions. A curse, she calls it."

"So it would be." Fear, dread, anger, and lust— who would have all that thrust upon him?

"I decided, at length," he continued softly, "it was the gods I heard calling me. So I took up the holy studies." Reverently, he touched her cheek. "I have just realized, Gyda, it was you who led me upon the path that ultimately freed me."

Her gaze held his. "Perhaps it was the gods

speaking to you, all that time."

"Ach, ja, they did speak to me. But not in your voice. Once I'd learned enough to cast the runes and listen to the wind, I knew it was a woman who called me so persistently. I did not know who, not then. When Gunnar and Friti hatched their plans, and I knew that if I accompanied Gunnar I would have the chance to sail hence—by then, I knew what awaited me. My other half. That you are, and have always been."

"I called to you, without knowing I did?"

"So it seems."

"And, Lodvar, you trust in this magical tie between us?"

With absolute belief he answered, "As I must."

"Then I pray you continue to do so, and hold strong. Trust that my heart makes the second half of your own—whatever else may take place."

Alarm flooded him. "Gyda—"

"Nei, Lodvar. Trust." And she kissed him once more.

Chapter Twenty

"I should have known better than to consider trusting him. He is the son of Friti Gunnarsson and Anaborg Helmsdottir. Deceit is bred into his bones."

Fadir grimaced as he spoke, and paced the floor of their dwelling like a restless bear. Unlike him, to react so strongly to anything, and do more than listen impassively. Yet he'd risen half way through Gyda's account, with loathing in his eyes.

The three of them, Gyda, Fadir, and Modir, were alone, not even Magnus at hand. Gyda, catching them before they went to bed that night, thought it best to deliver her ill news at once.

Danger lay out upon the breast of the dark ocean. She could not afford to wait.

Fadir looked at Modir. "What do you sense in him, this Gunnar Fritisson?"

Carefully, she replied, "Much—layers and layers of feeling, and intent. Intelligence sharp as a blade. Cunning. But also a great desire to cooperate—"

"That," Gyda said crisply, "is a pretense. Ja, he is clever. And he deceives."

Still focused on Modir, Fadir asked, "And the other—the shaman? What do you feel from him?"

Modir glanced at Gyda. "Much. He is Catrin's son."

"And Harald's."

"I believe he speaks the truth."

"Ja, so do I. Dottir, why should he come to you, this Lodvar, and not to me?"

"It is dangerous for him. Should Gunnar suspect he has told us of this scheme hatched by Friti, the vengeance will stretch to him. And to his modir, back in Husavik. Right now, Gunnar does not know Lodvar has spoken to me. I suggest we try and keep it that way."

Fadir stopped pacing and looked at her. "Go on."

"Since Lodvar gave his warning through me, Gunnar will have no idea we know he means to betray us. I think it would be well to lull him in any way we can. When the defense begins, our men will be ready to turn upon Gunnar's, even before Friti's warriors come ashore. It is a great advantage."

Fadir looked worried. "Do we have enough men?"

"Men. And women," Gyda added.

"Aye." Modir took it up. "Gunnar's men will not expect that, either—for us to turn on them, even before they can turn on us."

"Nei." Fadir turned on her. "I will not have you, or the other women of the settlement, risking yourselves."

Modir's chin jerked up. "Why not?"

"Why not?" He went to her and caught her shoulders between his hands. "Because I love you and cannot imagine a future of trying to live without you."

Modir's gaze softened. "Yet you would have me watch you walk into battle and do naught but stay back and wait?"

"It is my place, Wife, and my right, to defend you and all those dear to me."

"Tolljur—once before, I stood upon a cold shore and watched others fight to defend me—to little avail. I watched my own da fall. I will not stand back idle again."

"I will be in that line of defense," Gyda declared. "Has Magnus not been drilling me at arms? But first," she lowered her voice, "I suggest we fight Gunnar Fritisson on his own terms."

Fadir listened to her suggestion, and his eyes turned cold as the slate stones of the shore. "Nei," he said at once. "It is far too risky. It gives this man power over you."

"Do you not see it also gives me power over him? He will think he has us where he wants us, and suspect nothing."

"It is a deceit."

"We deceive him even as he deceives us. I say I go to him in the morning and give him my agreement to the marriage alliance he seeks."

Fadir shook his head, very like the bear he sometimes became. "Dottir, I forbid it."

Both Gyda and Modir stared. Fadir never spoke those words.

He hurried on. "You know not what this man is. If he be one part like his father—"

"I make my own choices, Fadir. You declared as much. And this time, I must choose for the good of all."

****

Dawn flowed like pale water over the land, the light spilling from the eastern horizon. Gyda, who'd slept but little, rose early and readied herself for what would come. Only—who knew, in truth, what this day might bring? Friti Gunnarsson's ships in the harbor? A great battle? The deaths of those dear to her? Those thoughts had kept her from sleep.

She fussed over her appearance this morning as she seldom did other days. People sometimes described her as beautiful. She would rather be strong or useful. A shield to those she loved.

Outside, in the glorious wash of light, she drew a breath. In the bay, Fadir's two long boats rode at anchor on an ocean still as glass—Gunnar had moved his ship along the coast yesterday. The scene looked so peaceful, it felt impossible that the world should break open and violence ensue.

Sweeping the sea with her gaze, she caught sight of no telltale silhouette.

Not yet.

She closed her eyes for a moment, searching— searching. There! Far out, flying through the still water, and feeling like a shadow of what she'd sensed that first day, before Gunnar came—darkness, clinging in a blot, a threat upon the waves.

"Fadir Odin, help me." The rush of strength that came in response to her request, combined with her certainty of approaching danger, steadied her as she picked her way down to the harbor and around the headland. Only then did she catch sight of Gunnar's ship, tucked well in. If ever she'd acted to defend what she loved, it must be now.

Gunnar's men were already astir. Gyda could see several of them moving about on board, and one or two paced the shore. One of these, catching sight of Gyda as she came down the path to the cove, turned and gave a holler.

Gunnar promptly appeared. Even at a distance, Gyda knew him by the bright halo of his hair, catching the morning sun.

A darker, slimmer shape moved at his side. Lodvar. Thoughts stirred in Gyda's mind. *My love.*

Deliberately, she closed her mind to him. She dared not let him know what she intended to do. And she could not allow her love for him to distract her from that purpose.

Gunnar vaulted over the side of the boat with smooth grace and waded ashore. His eyes, fixed upon her, gleamed bluer than the distant sea.

Drawing another breath, Gyda stood on the rocks and waited. Let him come to her. Let it be convincing.

"Mistress Gyda, good morning."

"Good morn." She half bowed her head. He would want her humble—yet not so humble he failed to believe she'd made her own decision.

She glanced at him through her lashes. He must have arisen mere moments ago. His hair hung mussed, and a haze of golden beard traced his jaw. Neither had he taken the time to tie up his tunic, and she caught a glimpse of a broad chest, likewise marked in gold, and hard with rippling muscle.

An attractive asp, and no mistake.

"What a pleasure to find you here so early, Mistress Gyda. What might I do for you?" He frowned slightly. "Have Friti's sails been sighted?"

"Not just yet. But I hoped for a word, if you can spare me a few moments."

"For you?" He flashed his blinding smile. "Always."

"Let us walk. I can think better when I am walking. Besides, what I wish to say—it is private."

He took her arm and guided her away, along the shore. His fingers felt warm on her flesh, and not particularly unpleasant. As they moved off, she glanced over her shoulder at the long boat. Lodvar watched them from the gunwale, his form absolutely motionless.

The tide being out, they walked along the base of the cliffs, with the sea lapping beside them.

"I must say, Mistress Gyda, you have me curious. I would not wait any longer to hear what you have to say."

Gyda paused and turned to face him. Should she attempt to blush and simper? He might expect it, yet that was not her way, even in pretense.

Instead, she met and held his gaze. "The offer you made to my father and me—does it still stand?"

He half frowned. "Offer?"

"For a marriage alliance."

He looked surprised. She'd caught him off guard after all.

Good.

Recovering swiftly, he took light with what looked like victory. "Ja. Ja. This is why you have come to me?"

"It is. To be perfectly frank, my father and I disagree over the matter. Although he trusts you, and appreciates the prospect of an alliance with you, I think he does not wish for things to change. And he does not wish to see me sail away to Husavik with you, after."

"Ah." Gunnar caressed the flesh of her forearm, which he still held tight. "Husavik is not so far. And is that not in part a benefit of such an alliance? The Faroes are on our trading route. If you become my wife, he shall see you often. That is what you say, that you wish to become my wife?"

Gyda lifted her chin. "It is. As you may have

learned, I make my own decisions."

"And if you make this one, will your father accept it?" Earnest blue eyes held hers as he finished, "I would not wish you, close as you are, to fall out over it."

"Nei. What I do, I do to benefit my family. You will help in Sorvagur's defense. And we will help you reclaim your birthright. When you and I go to Husavik, you will take up the place of jarl in your grandfather's stead."

Gunnar's eyes gleamed. "And that will please you, will it?"

"What woman would not wish to wed a man of such influence?"

Satisfaction shone in his eyes before he swiftly banked it.

"Only one thing concerns me." Gyda pretended to muse.

"What is it?"

"In order for you to take up that place your grandfather meant for you—your father will have to die. Does that not trouble you?"

"My father is a madman. My ties to him are not strong."

"Ah—because I could not bear to see my father fall."

"You will not have to. Is what we do not all to his benefit?"

"Ja, I hope so."

Gallantly, he lifted her hand to his lips and bent his golden head over it. "Then let it be so. Mistress Gyda Tolljursdottir, I accept your binding word in this, our marriage agreement."

His lips pressed deep into her palm. Warm as they

were, they caused her to shiver, struck by sudden cold.

What had she done?

"May I have your kiss upon it, Mistress?"

"I—"

"Come, we are to be husband and wife." Without awaiting permission, he hauled her into his arms. The kiss came swift and hard, confident and consuming.

Gyda, finding she did not like having all choice taken from her, stiffened in protest. The strength of his arms gave her no chance to break away.

At last she turned her face to the side. "Master Gunnar—"

"Come." He whispered it in her ear. "Once we are wed, there will be more, much more. And ja, that is what I will be to you—master. You need one, I think. Left to run wild too long—you can use a bridle, ja?"

He bit her ear—a pinprick of pain, but enough to make her break out of his hold.

His blue eyes gleamed with laughter. "We may anticipate the wedding night, I think."

"I—I am a good lass. I have never—" She closed her mind to the thought of Lodvar plunging into her, in exquisite perfection.

"Of course you have not. But this is different. I am to be your husband. Prepare yourself, Gyda. Tonight— if we are not already in battle—you will have your first taste of me."

This time, the shiver started at Gyda's core and worked its way outward. Not—most definitely not— one of delight.

Chapter Twenty-One

"What have you done?"

Lodvar's voice, soft as it was, spun Gyda in place. She'd been expecting his arrival—all the morning long, she'd felt his thoughts beating at her mind. Now he'd caught her behind the armorer's shed, alone for the moment.

"You should not be here." After but a glance, she avoided his eyes, which burned with emotion. Not anger, nei, nor even betrayal. With those, she might have dealt.

They brimmed with hurt.

"Gunnar came back to the long ship boasting of his marriage agreement with you, saying how it gives him power over your father. Boasting also of the things he means to do," Lodvar added unsparingly, "in his marriage bed—if not sooner."

Gyda flinched. "Ach, surely no decent man would speak of such things."

"He is not a good or decent man. He laughs about the discipline he means to provide."

"I would like to see him try!"

"I would not. I have seen already what he does to his women, leaving them bruised and broken."

"It will not come to that. I but lay for him a trap—"

"Is that what you intend? And if this trap does not spring as you expect?"

"It will. It must. He suspects nothing."

"Gyda…" Lodvar lifted his graceful hands, hands that had touched her everywhere. "I fear you have made a terrible mistake."

"Nei. Lodvar, he comes—Friti Gunnarsson does." She jerked her head toward the sea. "I can feel him out there. It will be today, this great battle. And Gunnar will be vanquished."

Lodvar shook his head. "The portents are not good."

"What?"

"I have cast the stones—on his behalf, and on mine also." Grief flashed in Lodvar's eyes. "You have placed yourself right in his hands."

"All will be well." Gyda drew him to her, and trapped his face between her hands. "I ask you to trust me. Can you not do that?"

Doubt and trouble suffused his features, and a storm of tangled emotion filled his eyes.

Gyda, on edge, took it for an answer. "If you cannot trust me, or trust in our love—"

He seized her wrists in turn. "I have loved you as long as I can remember. I do not doubt that. But you have blundered here, most terribly."

Gyda tossed her head. "We shall see about that, when Friti Gunnarsson comes."

****

Sails were sighted early that afternoon by those of the watchers who had the sharpest eyes—moving on the horizon, they nearly blended into the gleam of sunlight on water. By then, Gyda could sense the attackers so strongly she'd been waiting only for the call. When it came, Fadir sent word to Gunnar, aboard his ship, to bring his men, that they might take up their designated places in defense of the settlement.

Then Fadir turned to Gyda. "Dottir, are you sure about this?" He intended to send most of the women, children, and elders inland to await the outcome of the battle. "Will you not go with the others, if only to guard them?"

"I have a place in the line of defense, and I mean to take it." Not far from where Gunnar would be stationed, in fact. She wanted to keep an eye on him.

She wondered if he would leave Lodvar aboard the long ship or bring him ashore to cast portents. Did she want Lodvar left aboard? Long ships could be fired, and being left back was no assurance of safety.

"You have trained well with your brother, ja, but you have no notion what this fight will be. Treachery and bloodshed we shall see, on a scale you cannot imagine. Tell your søstir, Magnus."

Magnus had walked up, his sword strapped on and his axe—a favored weapon—already in his hand. He looked steady, determined, and strong.

"Fadir is right, Gyda. Go with the women."

For answer, she jerked up her chin.

"Or if you will not," Magnus continued, "prepare to see those you love die—or die yourself. This is not play, and we will not all survive."

Gyda swallowed hard. But ja, it was the truth her brother gave her.

"I am prepared."

Magnus turned to his father and shrugged. "What can you do with her?"

Fadir clasped Magnus's shoulder. "Son, I am proud of you." He turned his gaze on Gyda. "Proud of both of you. But—your mother goes to wait with the other women. It would comfort her to have you there."

"I know." Gyda's lips quirked. "I heard you and her arguing about it last night, before you went to bed. She, too, wanted to stay." In truth, she'd heard Modir— as strong a woman as she knew—weeping over it.

What if I lose you?

Wife, you can never lose me. Has the past taught you nothing?

Gyda turned her eyes toward the headland, beyond which lay Gunnar's ship. What if she lost Lodvar, when she'd just found him?

Fadir, his lips pressed tight, turned her to face him. "Dottir, take your place in the line. But I want you to promise me something. If it goes badly—very badly— you will duck away and go join your mother." He glanced at Magnus. "I could not bear losing both my children this day."

****

When Gunnar arrived at the head of his men, he looked magnificent. Gyda could find no other word to describe him.

Golden hair gleaming as brightly as his armor beneath the sun, he fairly bristled with weapons, and no hint of his planned treachery shone in his clear blue eyes.

To be sure, none of Fadir's awareness of that treachery showed, either, as he greeted the younger man. They clasped arms as fellow warriors do. The instant they touched, a haze of red arose in Gyda's mind.

Blood backed by darkness. Death, ja, rode the water, but danger of a far sharper sort lay in Gunnar

Fritisson's eyes when he glanced at her.

"What is she doing here?" he barked at Fadir.

"She means to fight."

"Nei, and nei."

Gunnar marched to Gyda's side and yanked the sword from her hand. "Go join the women."

"I will not."

"You will."

"You have seen how well I can fight—"

His lips stretched into a grimace. "This is not the time for your foolishness. When it is over, I will come for you."

"You have no right to order me—"

"I have. You will soon be my wife."

"I am not that yet."

Gunnar, his glare turning ugly, raised his hand to her. Before he could level the blow, Magnus moved, placing his body between them. "Nei, you will not."

Into Magnus's face, Gunnar sneered, "You are all soft. This will be a short battle, I think."

"Come," Fadir called with—knowing him—deliberate irony. "Do we fight each other?"

With a grunt, Gunnar stepped away. Only then did Gyda see who trailed his warriors, taking the last place in line.

Lodvar had come after all.

Their eyes met—no more than that—and Gyda's heartbeat accelerated. She did not want him here, amidst the horror to come.

Better he'd stayed aboard ship. Surely, though, Friti would refrain from harming his son's shaman.

From the headland came a shout. Two long ships, now clearly visible, headed for the harbor. Fadir began calling orders and, swiftly, the lines atop the rise formed. Lodvar slipped away, no more than a blur of dark blue.

Would Gyda live to see him again?

The following moments did not go easy with her. She'd never been good at waiting—this felt like balancing on the edge of a blade.

For the long ships were fine, strong ones and far more heavily loaded with warriors than she had expected. When they anchored in the harbor, the men spilled over the sides like rushes from a tipped bucket and came ashore in a wave, all of them screaming.

She turned her eyes to Fadir. From whence did he get his calm? Ach, but he had entered scores of battles and was usually sent in first to soften the enemy, to daunt them with his ferocity and madness. Never before had she considered how terrifying that must have been.

This, though, was different. She and the men of Sorvagur stood interspersed with Gunnar's men. When the order came, they would need to fight not only the enemy warriors coming ashore but those stationed beside them. The treacherous enemies in their midst.

Gunnar expected this to be easy for him. It would not.

She must be prepared—prepared to take out Gunnar's man, standing next to her. Yet the enemy warriors, roaring as one, already reached the shingle beach.

The gods help them all.

Chapter Twenty-Two

In an agony that left him drenched with sweat, Lodvar stood behind the line of defenders—not far—and watched Friti's men come in. He'd been up before dawn, speaking prayers and looking for signs, casting the stones and searching for portents. The best he could tell, this could go either way.

And Gyda—his reason for living—stood there among the warriors on the shore, dressed in armor like any man. He wanted to rush in and seize her, argue with her. But there was no time. For as the attackers came ashore, the defenders rushed forward to meet them. Only to be attacked by the men at their sides.

Ah—but Tolljur's warriors were not taken unawares. Forewarned, they expected the treachery and even as Gunnar's men turned upon them, their swords and axes came up, at the ready. Tolljur took out one of the first—not Gunnar, as Lodvar had prayed, but one of his right-hand men, called Bjorgmar. The line, supposedly a defense, abruptly wavered as Gunnar's men absorbed the fact that they were undone. Lodvar saw Gunnar jerk about when he realized what had happened, that his scheme had been discovered, or betrayed.

When he did, he sent one scathing look toward the place where Lodvar stood, searching for him, before becoming wholly distracted by the fight.

Lodvar, with eyes for little besides Gyda, watched—he watched it all unfold, like a battle plan scratched in the dirt, ahead of the fight, only gone terribly wrong. In mingled horror and fascination, he saw the attackers, with Friti at their head, come charging up the slope. Tolljur and those of his men who had disposed of their traitorous allies rushed down and engaged the invaders. Others, including Gyda, stayed back to fight what remained of Gunnar's men.

A curse passed Lodvar's lips as he saw that Gunnar had survived the initial hand-to-hand fight and now rushed to meet his father and the newly landed warriors.

Lodvar had dared hope Gunnar might fall in the initial fray, thus freeing Gyda from the promise she'd made. And perhaps providing them with a future.

Gyda. Even as her name exploded in his mind, he saw her take a tremendous blow from one of Gunnar's warriors, sway, and go down. Her brother, Magnus, had been fighting near her but had taken off in his father's wake. And Gyda's opponent, with a brutal jerk of his arm, sent her flying, her sword tumbling from her hand.

Thanks be to Odin, the man did not take time to slit her throat but followed the battle down to the sea.

Lodvar dashed forward to the place where Gyda had fallen. She lay sprawled among others of the dead and dying, many of them Gunnar's men. Men he, Lodvar, knew and with whom he'd grown up.

He did not pause to do more than glance at them.

Did Gyda breathe? Odin save him, he could not tell. A livid cut traced her hairline and shed blood down her face. He could see no other wounds, and when he touched her cheek and called her name, her eyelids fluttered.

The roar of sound from the shore, below, told him the two waves of warriors had crashed together. A terrible storm it must be, from the sound of it.

But Gyda breathed. Nothing else, in that moment, mattered to him. She lived still. Ja, and she stirred beneath his hands.

"Lodvar?" She blinked at him, as if trying to clear her vision. "Help me up."

He wanted to protest, to push her down instead, longed to keep her where she lay, safe from what occurred below. For he could feel death rising, and smell the blood.

"Fadir," she gasped. "I must go to him. Help me up!"

She rose in a scramble, using Lodvar's shoulder to lever herself upright. He caught a glimpse of the expression in her eyes when she saw what was taking place down below. Indeed, they both had a sweeping view of a battle such as Lodvar had rarely seen.

The two lines of warriors—nearly equal in strength—had met just above the shoreline. This battle would have been an easy victory for Friti, had Gunnar's treacherous plan borne fruit. But with many of Gunnar's men struck down at the outset, Friti now had his hands full.

Lodvar picked out Jarl Friti, fighting near the center of the line, and saw also the man he faced, none other than Tolljur Magnusson. These two men must have fought side by side in the past, many a time, with Tolljur in his berserker's guise. Now they faced one another, roaring and hacking, Tolljur with a sword in one hand and his axe, rather than a shield, in the other. His ashen hair flew out behind him, like a banner. He did not appear above a score in age.

Friti—still fit and full of muscle also, and a brute in any battle—railed at Tolljur in return. He'd already lost his shield—it lay cleaved in two near his feet—and he had both hands on the hilt of his sword.

Men fought all around them, Magnus at his father's shoulder. The foam upon the shore already ran red.

As Lodvar and Gyda watched, Friti spun in a blur and struck. Tolljur backed off a step and the sword tumbled from his hand.

"Fadir!" Gyda screamed, her heart in her voice.

Unblinking, Lodvar watched what happened next. Friti pressed forward, seeking the advantage before Tolljur had time to recover. Tolljur's ashen head came up, and he gripped the axe handle in both hands. When he swung the weapon high, Friti struck, a slash to Tolljur's ribs.

Gyda shrieked, "Fadir! He is in trouble. Lodvar, Lodvar leave go of me!"

Lodvar had not realized till that moment how tightly he'd been gripping the woman he loved. Now he muttered, "Nei," and held on still more fiercely. "Wait."

"Wait? But—"

Even as Gyda spoke the words, it happened. Tolljur Magnusson tossed back his head and roared. Throwing off all restraint, and bellowing like the bear he would become, he slipped into his berserker's madness.

Lodvar, who had observed his share of battles and seen many a thing also in Visions, had never beheld such a transformation, or thought to. A man usually of ordinary size, Tolljur now seemed to gain in stature. His muscles bulged, and even above the clamor of the battle Lodvar could hear him bellow. Friti took an involuntary step backward.

What ensued stole Lodvar's breath. Tolljur Magnusson—transformed into a force before whom few could stand—charged forward. Swinging with devastating intent, he went for Friti's head with his axe. In defense, Friti's men, including Gunnar, mobbed Tolljur, striking at him with weapons and fists.

From where Lodvar and Gyda stood, it looked like insects overwhelming a behemoth.

"Fadir!" Gyda called again, in agony. Lodvar wrapped both arms around her and held on as she fought to escape him. Only that kept her from dashing down the slope and, quite likely, tossing away her life.

"Magnus is there," he told her over and over. "Magnus is with him—look!"

Indeed, Magnus, backed by many of Tolljur's men, rushed to his father's defense. Rarely had Lodvar seen anyone fight with such ferocity—in fact he wondered whether Magnus had not also fallen into some berserker's fit.

But Friti's men had now overwhelmed Tolljur. Arms rose and fell as they clubbed him down, and blood sprang bright red upon his brow.

"They have struck him down!" Gyda lamented. "Friti would know—of course Friti would know—it is the only way to defeat him. Let me go! Ach, Lodvar, let me go."

"Nei," he repeated, even while her horror at what had occurred flooded him, shared along the bonds that united them.

Below, Friti's men hauled Tolljur up. He appeared unconscious, and his head sagged between his shoulders. When Tolljur's men, still fronted by Magnus, rushed in, Friti hollered and put a blade to Tolljur's throat, his message clear.

Magnus backed off and lowered his axe, and the rest of Tolljur's men followed suit.

As swiftly as that, it seemed, the battle was done.

"Fadir," Gyda sobbed. "Why did you not let me go to him?"

"Gyda, if Magnus could not save him—"

"Is he dead? Is he dead?"

"Nei." Not yet, though Lodvar did not doubt Friti would finish him, once it suited his purposes. "Just taken down, amid his berserker's fit."

Gyda's expression turned wild. Tears marked the blood and dirt on her cheeks. "The fit? He will be in such pain. He is always in pain after—"

Ja, and no mercy shown him.

"I must go to him—"

Lodvar turned her to face him, and shook her slightly. "Nei, Gyda, you must flee. Go now, before Gunnar thinks to look for you."

"But Fadir, and my brother—"

"You can do them no good, staying here. Save yourself, and you can help free your Fadir, after. List to me!" He shook her again. "You do not want to fall into their hands."

"You expect me to run? When I am needed to fight?"

"Think of what your father would want. He would not want to see you in Friti's hands. Go find your mother. Set up a new resistance." That would appeal to her, surely? He would say anything, do anything, to see her safe away.

She could not tear her eyes from the scene below, where her father hung, appearing lifeless, between the hands of Friti's men.

"He is dead."

"He is not. For the love of Odin, Gyda, go."

She ignored him.

"Gyda, for the sake of all that lies between us."

At last she focused on him. Eyes wide with shock, she connected with his gaze and nodded. "Ja."

Still gripping her shoulders, he spun her about. Too late. From below came a strident call. "Shaman!"

Gunnar had caught sight of them there on the slope. He stood staring upward, and waved his sword. "Hold her!"

"Go," Lodvar breathed into Gyda's ear.

"But—what will he do to you, if he thinks you've let me get away?"

Lodvar shuddered to think. "It does not matter."

"You will feel his anger."

"It does not matter." He released her before giving her a shove. He would take any punishment Gunnar chose to deal out, before seeing Gyda at that bastard's mercy.

Too late again. With a bellow, sword still in his hand, Gunnar pounded up the slope, his hair flying. Even if Gyda ran now, Gunnar would chase her down, a hart after a hind.

He might even enjoy the pursuit.

Gyda stepped around Lodvar to face Gunnar. She stood with her fists clenched, distress bright in her eyes. When Gunnar reached them, she spat, "What have you done to my father?"

"Naught—yet." Gunnar smiled, revealing white

teeth spattered with blood. "He shall die a heinous death, at my father's pleasure. It will take him a long time to die."

"You betrayed us!"

"And it seems you knew we would." Gunnar's gaze flicked to Lodvar. "How, I do wonder?"

"You are naught but a snake!"

"And you are still my future wife."

That said, Gunnar reached out and dealt Gyda a tremendous blow across the face.

Gyda tumbled in a heap at Lodvar's feet, blood appearing at one corner of her mouth. It took every shred of Lodvar's will to keep him from kneeling down beside her and cradling her in his arms.

"Well," Gunnar told him, "do not just stand there looking foolish. Carry her out to Fadir's ship for me."

Chapter Twenty-Three

"A curious thing," Gunnar mused, "how Tolljur Magnusson and his men anticipated our plans to betray them."

"If betrayal it may be called," his father, Friti, rejoined. "A goodly plan, I call it. But, son, I think someone betrayed you, in turn."

They occupied Jarl Tolljur's house. Not, as Friti pointed out, that it was as grand as the hall back home in Husavik. But such occupation denoted their victory, and Friti never missed a chance to crow over anyone.

Had their victory not been complete? The berserker, Tolljur Magnusson—his old enemy—lay secure in their hands, bound hand and foot like a prize boar. Many of his men had also been captured, though his son, Magnus, had broken away, following his father's capture, and fled.

No matter. Magnus Tolljursson was badly injured and probably dying. And did they not have the daughter, Gyda, to use as a weapon, should Magnus try to attack them?

Now night had fallen—a beautiful night, as Lodvar saw when he glanced outside. All lay peaceful beneath a deep blue sky vaulted with stars. With Tolljur and Gyda held aboard Friti's vessels, the three of them sat beside the jarl's fire alone.

Gunnar raised a mug of ale to his lips. No mead, as

he'd complained, in this poor place. The ale would need to suffice.

"Betrayed—ja." He fixed his wide blue eyes on Lodvar. "But by whom?"

Friti laughed. Not a nice laugh, either. Even though for all the years of Lodvar's growing, Friti had been under the old jarl's thumb, Lodvar had always feared him. Feared the cruelty in his eyes and the air of entitlement he maintained despite his disenfranchised situation.

Now, with the old jarl dead, Friti was off his lead and, in company with his son, capable of most anything.

They knew very well who had warned Tolljur Magnusson of their plans. Ja, and they would make Lodvar pay. But first, being the men they were, they would toy with him, for their own enjoyment.

They both watched him now, with nearly identical expressions. Big men, comfortable with their power. Friti, perhaps a bit taller than his son and just a shade broader, had hair streaked with white and a face marked by deep lines denoting his bitterness.

His life had not been what he believed he deserved. He was a man to take out his dissatisfaction on others.

What could Lodvar do about it? He had no way to protect himself, nei. But Gyda? Her father? Could he find a way to protect them?

"I told you not to trust him." Friti nodded his gnarled head at Lodvar. "Is he not part Alban? In the end, you can never trust them."

Lodvar silently debated getting to his feet and making a break for the door. They'd brought him in here for a reason—to amuse themselves, ja, like two cats watching a trapped mouse. They wanted him to break.

They wanted to exercise their claws.

Both had been wounded in the battle. Friti, who had faced the berserker directly, bore a number of vicious wounds. He'd bound but one of them—the worst—in a filthy bandage. The others bled freely, disregarded.

Like his father, Gunnar bore his hurts as if they were badges of honor and beneath his notice.

"Alban, ja," Gunnar agreed, sweeping Lodvar with a bland look. "And he started out life no more than a slave. Yet look at the advantages we offered him. How would he dare betray us?"

"Indeed," Friti agreed, "he is Harald's son. Harald was ever loyal to my father, and to me. Always shared his women with me."

Lodvar flinched inwardly, though he fought to keep it from showing. His mother, in Friti Gunnarsson's hands?

Friti pulled a face of mock surprise. "You do not suppose, Gunnar, that the shaman is my son?"

"Nei, too craven. You breed better than that."

"True."

"This one," Gunnar gestured at Lodvar with his cup, "cannot possibly share our blood. Too much the traitor."

"Alban blood will out, it seems, in the end."

"Blood is blood," Gunnar concurred. "Yet how dare he open himself to our anger? What could the berserker possibly offer him, what valuable enough to make him turn?" For the first time, he addressed Lodvar directly. "Why did you betray us?"

Lodvar shook his head. Lying would avail him nothing. Would it help Gyda, or her father, if he held out from admitting the truth?

"He does not answer," Friti observed. "Perhaps his useless tongue needs to be cut from his head."

"Perhaps. Or," Gunnar suggested, "he might be made to talk."

"An interesting proposition. Anyone may be made to admit anything, under the right persuasion. I doubt he will endure as long as the berserker. But, still…"

Gunnar's eyes burned upon Lodvar. "Shaman, how long do you think you will endure questioning beneath my hands? Will your gods sustain you, do you suppose?"

Lodvar could only hope so.

"Begin by castrating him," Friti suggested. "That always gets them talking." He gave a laugh. "Or hollering, anyway."

Lodvar's balls tried to crawl up inside his belly.

Slowly, Gunnar got to his feet. The fire threw his shadow behind him, in a monstrous form.

"You," he told Lodvar, "cost us the lives of many men. The plan should have gone perfectly. Tolljur Magnusson would have been defeated before my father's men ever came ashore. It is the woman, is it not?"

"Woman?" Lodvar croaked.

"His daughter, Gyda Tolljursdottir. I saw the two of you together on the cliffs. Speaking. There is"— Gunnar wagged his head slowly—"something there."

"Perhaps he has been rutting on her," Friti suggested. "He may be a sodding shaman, but he's still a man—for now."

"Impossible. The girl's a virgin. She told me so."

"No doubt she lied." Friti gave another ghastly laugh. "Ask her. Like anyone else, she can be made to tell the truth."

"Nei." The word escaped Lodvar's lips before he could prevent it. *Do anything to me, before you harm her.* He wanted to scream it. He could not give them such a weapon against him.

"Did you rut on my future bride? Is that why you warned her?"

"Share and share alike," Friti grunted. "In my day, we passed women around like flasks of mead."

"This is not your day, Fadir. I mean to wed the girl, and beget sons on her. Do I want a slave's brat in her belly?"

"Especially his." Friti reflected. "But why marry her? Just take what you want. Not but she is beautiful. She looks very like her aunt did, long ago." For an instant, Friti's eyes darkened, and the bitter lines in his face bit deep. "She should have wed me, Gyda Magnussdottir. It would have prevented much of what came after."

"Why do we discuss the past? Fadir, you will have what you wished—revenge upon the berserker. And anyway"—Gunnar grinned—"had you not wed my madwoman of a mother, you would not have me."

The thought did not appear to lift Friti from his gloom. Eyes stabbing at Lodvar, he asked, "What will you do about him?"

"I have not yet made up my mind." Gunnar's smile broadened. "Let me think on it."

****

Pain, fear, and darkness. The victim of all three,

Gyda fought to steady herself and calm her frantic mind.

She had to think—make a decision about what to do next.

How to help Fadir.

Her stomach flipped over once more, bathing her in a cold sweat. Like her, Fadir was being held aboard one of Friti's longships, bound to the mast—conscious or unconscious, Gyda could not say. It was too dark now to tell.

Surrounded by guards, he had no chance of breaking free.

Gyda lay farther aft on the deck of the longship, with Friti's guards stalking past her at regular intervals. She might be aboard Friti's ship, but she had no doubt whose prisoner she was, in truth. Gunnar would be the one to deal with her—when the impulse moved him.

Both men had gone ashore, and Lodvar—Lodvar had not come from the place where he'd stood, when they dragged her away from him. She'd watched for him as best she could from her cramped position, straining to see.

Now a vast sky full of stars spread overhead, the eyes of the gods staring down. Would the gods aid her, if she asked them to? More importantly, would they help Lodvar? Fadir? She had no doubt Lodvar's fate also lay in Gunnar's hands.

How long would it take Gunnar to tumble to the fact that Lodvar had warned them of his intended treachery? Not long, she feared. What would he do to Lodvar then?

The whole side of her face ached where Gunnar had struck her down. Knocked her senseless he had, and she'd missed much of what happened after. From what she'd heard, though, she believed Magnus had got away.

Good. Good! There remained a chance he could rescue Fadir. He would move mountains to do so.

She tried to shift her position against the hard oaken planks. Her shoulders ached from the strain on her arms, with her wrists so tightly bound, and she could feel that the skin of her wrists had broken around the bonds. She wanted to scream. She wanted to weep.

Not for herself. For Fadir. And Lodvar…

What would Modir do when Magnus reached her and told her Fadir had been taken prisoner? That he'd slipped into his berserker's fit and been clubbed down—as terrible a thing as Gyda had ever witnessed.

She knew, for Modir had told her the stories, how Fadir suffered when emerging from his trance. Now he was bound, injured and alone, with none to soothe him.

Magnus would come. Her brave, strong brother would mount a rescue. She had faith in him.

But what could Magnus do against so many? Ja, some of their men had presumably fought their way free with him.

Would they have a strong enough force against both Friti's and Gunnar's surviving men? True, many of Gunnar's had fallen in that first clash.

Still…

A roar came from forward on the ship. At first Gyda thought it the bellow of an animal—a hart or bull. When she realized the truth, her blood ran cold.

Bound to the mast, her father called out his rage, his demand for release.

He called her mother's name.

Chapter Twenty-Four

Fadir Odin, hear me.

The night waned. Far to the east, above the shining breast of the ocean, a tinge of gold edged in upon the darkness and doused the stars one by one.

All lay in stillness. Well—almost all. From Friti's second ship, where Lodvar had been ordered, he could hear the roar that broke out at intervals from the throat of the berserker, who remained lashed to the mast of the other vessel.

Friti's men, and those of Gunnar's who had survived, patrolled the shore. Friti must expect an attack, perhaps led by Magnus Tolljursson, who'd made it away after Gyda was struck down.

Gyda.

But to Lodvar's disappointment, no such attack had yet come. He wanted Gyda freed before she fell victim to Gunnar's attentions. Even if such an attack cost his own life.

All night long, beneath the pattern of stars, he'd petitioned the gods for just that. He'd cast the stones over and over again, both in an effort to convince Gunnar he was still willing to work on his behalf and to find answers in this terrible tangle where he lay.

Gunnar no longer trusted him. The men aboard the long ship guarded him as much as the vessel. Perhaps in an effort to keep from angering the gods, Gunnar had not bound him. But Lodvar had no illusions. If he so much as lifted a finger wrong, he would be trussed up like the lowest slave.

Or killed. *Fadir Odin, please.*

Gyda lay aboard Friti's other vessel, separated from him by a short span of dark water, as did her father. He could almost feel her agony across the distance.

Ja, he could feel her.

Could she also feel him?

For the first time all night, he knew slight relief from the agonizing frustration that held him. All his life long, this woman had called to him. Could he not now call her in turn?

Closing his eyes, he focused upon her in earnest. Not fighting the rush of love and longing that came, he instead gave in to it, seeking to use its power as a means to reach out through the night and touch Gyda's heart, speak to her mind.

Gyda. My love.

No response. A wave of frustration crawled up from his belly and threatened to choke him. He fought to vanquish it the way a warrior fights against a foe. Now, if ever, he must make her hear him.

Gyda. Woman of my heart.

Something stirred in the darkness, like a glimmer of unseen light. In those first instants, he did not recognize it as Gyda, so brave and strong of heart. This spirit wept, it mourned. It ached with pain.

Yet she spoke his name. *Lodvar.*

Like a drowning man fastening his gaze on the shore, he focused all his will upon her. Clenching his fingers upon the rune stones scattered across his knees, he spoke to her as he might to his gods.

Gyda? Hear me, do.

Her spirit fluttered in surprise. Two beings held separately should not be able to communicate. He, too anxious to acknowledge his own wonder, pushed for a response.

My love, speak to me.

Fadir, he is bound, being held. He calls for Modir. I think he is dying. Can you help him?

Ja, that was his Gyda—asking nothing to alleviate her own plight, but only on behalf of one she loved. Like Lodvar, she'd been listening to Tolljur's agony all the night long, and desperation held her in its grip.

Gyda, are you bound?

Bound, ja—and under guard. I cannot reach him. Can you?

For an instant, Lodvar's despair overwhelmed him. Fearing the emotion would travel along the fragile bonds between them, he battled it down. He wanted to be this woman's hero, her warrior, the one who could salvage her world. All he had for a weapon was magic, and of that but what the gods agreed to lend him.

I am on the other ship. I do not see how I can reach your father. Gunnar no longer trusts me.

He felt the flutter of her alarm. *Does Gunnar know you warned us? Ach, Lodvar, what will he do?*

Lodvar hated to think. Gunnar's imagination, especially when it came to pain, had few restrictions. And, working in tandem with his father, he could provide both physical and mental agony.

I do not know. I believe he means to take revenge upon your father first. We must find a way to free him. But how?

166

My brother will come. But I do not know when.

Sooner rather than later, Lodvar hoped. Yet Magnus stood wounded, as did most his men. How much time would he need to recover?

List to me, he thought at her again. *Can you free your hands?*

I do not think so. I have tried. Tears colored her voice.

Do not weep, he begged. *I cannot bear it. You are strong. Are you not the berserker's lass?*

Ja, and the shaman's bride, she stated, on a rise of spirit.

Lodvar heard a shout from the shore. The bonds between him and Gyda quivered violently.

"Gunnar! Gunnar—" That was one of the guards. An attack? A rescue? Was it about to begin?

Even as he wondered, Gyda slipped like a shadow from his mind. The disconnect hurt as much as a physical wound. He clenched his fingers on the rune stones so hard, the skin of his fingertips bruised. He wanted her back. He needed her here with him, inside his heart and mind. This bond between them made far too frail a weapon—he must find a better one, if only for her sake.

****

His twelfth birthday had fallen some years before his mother's master, Harald, decided to wed with her, and so, on this day, Lodvar remained a slave.

He did not expect much. Even on his naming day, a slave did not receive gifts. His mother had hugged him when he rose, and showed him the new tunic she'd sewed for him.

No surprise, that. He knew she worked at it after he

was supposed to be asleep. But it had been a great effort for her to find the materials and get permission to use them. And the love sewn into the garment brought tears to his eyes.

Then—surprising indeed—his father Harald came to their sleeping place. Harald did not waste a lot of time on Lodvar, though he still came often to Modir's bed and grunted over her.

Harald had other sons, and daughters also, all grown. He rarely noticed Lodvar. Except this day, he came and hunkered down beside Lodvar where he sat at his breakfast.

"Well, boy—so you are twelve today."

"Ja, Master Harald." Lodvar did not call him Fadir.

"Twelve is a special birthday for a boy. It is when he starts, in earnest, training for a warrior."

Hurriedly, Modir said, "Lodvar will not be a warrior. He has other talents."

Harald looked at her. "I know. It is a special birthday, all the same. Lodvar, I have something for you." From his tunic he drew a small object wrapped in hide. This he handed to Lodvar. "Every boy—every man—needs one of these."

For an instant, Lodvar met his father's eyes—pale gray. He unwrapped the parcel and found—

A dirk. Right away he knew it for a fine one, with a good blade and a hilt wrapped in copper wire. It looked little like any other knives Lodvar had seen.

"For me?" he squawked.

"For you." Harald nodded at the weapon. "That came from Alba, it did. Taken from a Gaelic chief, so I am told. I had to bargain for it."

"Thank Master Harald, Lodvar, for his generous

gift," Modir whispered.

"Thank you, Master Harald." Curious, Lodvar ran his thumb along the blade. It left a narrow trail of blood.

Harald laughed. "You are to use that on others, boy. It is sharp."

So it was.

And so he would.

Slammed back into the present from that rare day so long ago, Lodvar drew a breath. He pulled his bag toward him, the one that held all his worldly belongings and into which he usually tucked his precious pouch of runes. Reaching inside—deep inside—he allowed his fingers to quest and search.

And he found it there, at the bottom. Neglected, as he had usually been in his own home.

As one of the few things Harald had ever given him, he'd carried it always. A token perhaps, if never used for its intended purpose. Shamans did not usually go armed, save with belief.

Was it still sharp?

By the mercy and intent of the gods, he meant to find out.

Chapter Twenty-Five

"Haul him up."

Despite the bonds that lashed him to the mast, Tolljur had sagged down over the course of the night, as he flitted in and out of consciousness, raving. Now, milky light flooded the deck of the ship and clouds drifted in, forecasting rain. Soon after dawn, Friti and Gunnar had gone to survey their prisoner and ordered him taken ashore in their company and under stout guard.

Gyda, watching from the ship, could not tell whether Fadir was aware of what happened to him. Blood from the wounds imposed when he'd been clubbed down streaked his face, and other marks, even more terrible, and all undressed, showed on his arms and torso. How could anyone survive such injuries?

Surely, surely she thought, Magnus would arrive now, before Friti had a chance to begin his tortures?

For such she had no doubt he intended.

Others of Friti's men, eager to see what would transpire, flocked to the side of the ship. Some went splashing overboard, to wade ashore. Her line of sight blocked, Gyda fought her way to her feet. Her wrists might be bound, but she'd not been tethered to the deck. No reason she could not press forward also—if she could bear to see.

For an instant, she swayed where she stood, and

her stomach heaved. Had she anything left in there, she no doubt would have lost it then. Ignoring her own sickness, she wriggled her way between Friti's men, who grunted in outrage and shot her scathing looks but let her reach the rail.

Fadir looked senseless. It took Gunnar and two of Friti's men to drag him ashore and prop him on his feet. She watched as his eyes rolled back in his head, and Friti's men were called, one on either side, to hold him.

They had loosened his bonds slightly. Enough? Why did he not surge to life, enter his berserker's trance, and kill them all?

Gyda.

The voice spoke in her head, and from close at hand. A voice she knew, and one with the ability to ignite her from within.

She turned. Lodvar, who must have swum across from the other ship, stood at her shoulder, hair messed and clothes damp from the water. All serenity had fled his eyes.

Nei, do not look at me.

She jerked her gaze away, back to the shore and Fadir, who now had his eyes open, regarding Friti.

"Where is the mighty Tolljur Magnusson now, eh?" Friti called out loudly enough for everyone to hear, and kicked at Fadir's feet. "It seems the bear has been hobbled."

Make them stop, Gyda shot at Lodvar, even though she knew he could not. *I cannot watch.*

Are you hurt? You are bleeding. Your hands—

I but tried to free myself. It is naught.

On the shore, Fadir roared. Awareness now possessed him in full. Almost better had he remained unconscious. What if he did enter his berserker's rage now, while bound? Might it kill him?

Tears ran down her face. She begged Lodvar, or perhaps the gods, *Do not let them torture him.*

She received no reply. Lodvar's expression had turned somber and tight, his eyes burned gold.

When Friti finishes with your father, then Gunnar will come for you. He intends to go through with the marriage.

I will not have him.

My love—my love, you will not have a choice.

But I am your bride. We swore we belonged to one another!

On the shore, Friti shouted, "We have an old score to settle, Tolljur Magnusson!"

Fadir glared into Friti's eyes. "Have we?"

"You ruined me in the eyes of my father, my jarl."

"You did that yourself, Friti Gunnarsson, through your treachery."

"I but attempted to clear my own path, that I might be first among our warriors, where I deserved to be. Now—well, at long last it shall be made right."

"I, and mine, are not in your way, Friti." Fadir's gaze found Gyda, there aboard the ship. With all her will, she strained toward him. Perhaps reluctant to draw attention to her, though, his eyes moved on.

"If you exist in the world, Tolljur, you are in my way. But not for much longer, eh? How do you wish to die? Shall I give you a choice?"

Fadir's lips stretched in a smile, and his eyes gleamed silver. "I wish to die in combat. Are you man enough to face me, Friti Gunnarsson? Or will you take the coward's way, as you did before?"

Gyda caught her breath. Badly wounded, no doubt weakened by the aftermath of his fit and being bound all night long, could Fadir win such a contest?

Would Friti take the bait? Challenged here before his men, did he have a choice?

"Ah," Fadir spat, "if you are too afraid—"

"I do not fear you, man-bear that you are. I have but planned other amusements."

"You can always torture me after you win the combat." Again, Fadir's gaze flicked to Gyda and away. Did he seek to create a diversion during which she might escape?

Friti grunted.

Fadir went on, almost as if he and Friti chatted over mugs of ale, "You know you always wanted the chance to defeat me. Here it is."

The onlookers waited, rapt, for Friti's answer. Warriors all, they lived for just such spectacles and, as Friti no doubt knew, would tell and retell the tale for many years to come.

High stakes, and much potential for boasting. But Friti would need to win.

He inspected Fadir's battered condition, perhaps weighing his chances. Then he spat disdainfully. "You think me a fool? When the gods touch you and you enter your trance, no single man—not even I—can defeat you."

Fadir looked disappointed. He turned to Gunnar. "How about you, boy? Are you more of a man than your father?"

Listening for Gunnar's answer, Gyda barely felt the touch at her wrists. But when her bonds tightened painfully on her torn skin, she sucked in a breath.

Nei, do not look at me. I have a blade. It sawed painstakingly through her bonds; her wrists came free.

Here, take it. The hilt of a knife pressed into her fingers. So numb were they, she almost dropped it. *So you can defend yourself when Gunnar comes to you.*

Ja, if Gunnar sought to force her, to rape her as he surely would either before or after a wedding, she could gut him.

Had anyone seen? Had any of the onlookers noticed Lodvar slip her the weapon? Nei, everyone focused on Gunnar, awaiting his answer to the berserker.

Swiftly, she secreted the knife in her dress, tucking it into a righthand pocket where her own blade—that Gunnar must have taken before tying her up—usually lay hidden.

Fadir tries to make a distraction. He hopes I may get away, she thought at Lodvar.

Can you?

Escape so many? I do not think so.

I may also try and create a diversion, at the right moment.

Do not endanger yourself. That thought escaped her before she could catch it back. Surely she should accept whatever aid Lodvar could provide. The safety of those she loved demanded it.

But if she also loved Lodvar—

Gunnar spoke, interrupting her harried thoughts. "I have always wanted to face off with a berserker."

Fadir returned swiftly, yet with deliberation, "This is your chance." And Gyda's also, maybe.

Before Gunnar could accept, though, Friti spoke. "Nei. If anyone faces the berserker, it will be me."

His men—all eager to witness combat between the berserker and most anyone—howled their approval. Friti's face flushed dark. "Untie him."

Did Gyda see a flash of victory, swiftly veiled, in Fadir's eyes?

"This contest, Friti Gunnarsson, is a long time coming—over twenty years. I suggest we fight it to the death."

Again, Friti examined Fadir, marking his wounds and the amount of blood he had shed, perhaps recalling how his men had clubbed him down. How could even a berserker, so battered, hope to defeat him? And ach, how he must want this victory!

"Ja. I will spill your blood here, on your own ground. Tolljur Magnusson, after all these years, it will end here."

"So be it." Fadir scanned the crowd, his gaze touching on Gyda for the briefest moment. In that moment, she saw—

Herself as a toddler, holding up her arms to him—the man with the deep, bear-claw scars on his cheeks and the softness in his eyes—and mewling for him to pick her up, "Fa, fa." Her, riding on his shoulder as they moved along the shore, searching out whelks and periwinkles so they might surprise Modir. The feeling of utter safety she'd always enjoyed in his arms, as if nothing in the wide world could ever harm her.

He would sacrifice his life for her now, if he had to. She knew that to the root of her soul, and she wanted to weep.

He and Lodvar offered her a chance—the two men who loved her did. She could not waste it.

Gunnar, though, also looked toward her. "You—

stay there." He glanced around for a man still aboard to guard her. Lodvar had already slipped away and, keeping her hands together behind her, Gyda pretended she remained bound. Leaning forward over the side of the long ship, she called, "This is unjust! My father is sore injured. It is not a fair combat."

"Hold your tongue," Gunnar shouted at her, "until I find a better use for it. No man who faces a berserker engages in a fair fight. Yet my father, a man of immense courage, will defeat him!"

His attention now turned firmly away from Gyda, Fadir smiled. "Then let us see this thing done. And someone bring me a sword!"

Chapter Twenty-Six

Lodvar, strung as tight as flesh and blood could endure, watched as the men faced off on the shore. The scene looked somehow unreal in the garish early morning light. He didn't doubt that Tolljur meant to sacrifice himself, giving Gyda a chance to escape. The man—berserker or not—was in no condition to attempt combat. Beaten and left to bleed all night, bound to the mast and raving, he should not be on his feet, let alone able to raise a sword.

And Lodvar had seen Friti fight. A strong warrior, perhaps even better than Gunnar, he tended to fight dirty, his abilities not much hampered by his age.

This could end only one way, in Lodvar's estimation. He had to make sure, whatever it took, that Gyda got away and Tolljur's sacrifice was not in vain.

Most the men aboard Friti's ships now abandoned them to go ashore. These men comprehended what it took to fight while injured, but few of them had seen a berserker, before yesterday.

The men Gunnar had chosen to stay with Gyda looked unhappy about it. All their attention focused on the scene setting up on the rocks, where Tolljur and Friti faced each other.

Lodvar glanced at Gyda, who stood drooping slightly, hands clenched behind her as if still bound.

Go over the other side of the boat, once it begins.

She nodded, the smallest of movements.

Lodvar looked to the sky. The morning light, flung from the east, now met a bank of cloud moving ashore from the western sea. Was there enough radiance for him to gather and use? He closed his eyes and sent forth his will, gathering the elemental energy. He needed to be ready, when the moment came.

Fadir Odin, aid me. Not for my sake. For hers, all for hers.

On the rocks of the shore, the combat began. It started with a wild cry from Tolljur Magnusson's throat and a leap that took him straight at Friti.

Gyda's guards moved forward to hang from the side of the long boat, straining to see. Even Gyda took a step toward the rail.

Go, he told her.

Not yet.

Did she measure her moment with a warrior's eye? Or did she merely want to see what happened to her father? Lodvar also glanced ashore, and for an instant forgot everything else.

Beneath that garish light, everything appeared too bright. The two combatants no longer looked aged, for they moved like young men.

Friti had more bulk, and a bit more height, than the berserker—his shoulders wider, his reach longer. But, despite his injuries, Tolljur moved with greater agility. Trained, Lodvar supposed, to disregard his pain and discomfort, he now leaped repeatedly at Friti, causing him to step back and back on the damp stones beside the water.

What if Tolljur won? Would Gunnar let it end fairly? Or would he then take the berserker on himself?

Go now, he told Gyda, and looked around for her.

She had gone. Disappeared from the deck of the ship as if she'd never been there.

Ashore, Tolljur bellowed again and leaped. A stripe of bright red appeared across Friti's chest.

If Tolljur killed Friti, could it all end here and now?

For an instant, Lodvar had hope. Then he caught sight of Gyda, moving with powerful strokes around the prow of the long ship, on an angle away from the other moored boats.

He must act now.

Closing his eyes once more, he called upon the light—not that of the dawning, already fast losing its battle against the incoming storm clouds, but the lightning that lurked within those clouds. *Come to me. Serve me.*

He felt Gyda pause, as if she'd heard him. His eyes flew open, and he told her with haste, *Go. Swiftly. Fast as you can.*

On the shore, Friti now went on the attack, fueled no doubt by his anger and old hatred. As Lodvar knew, Friti and his son excelled at harboring hatred. Only their self-love served them better.

No one on the shore, or left aboard the ships, had eyes for anything except the combat. Tolljur now fell back, and back again, catching Friti's blows on his borrowed shield, and otherwise defenseless.

Lodvar threw himself into the summoning.

The rain came first, washing over the scene from west to east in a heavy curtain. Everyone and everything became instantly wet, including the head of the lass who stroked her way steadily toward the far side of the harbor.

Though Lodvar knew she was there, he could no longer see her. Hard spears of silver rain danced upon the water, struck the shore, and blocked his sight.

The combatants, presumably, kept fighting. Above the bright rattle of the rain, Lodvar could hear their blows crashing, but he could no longer see who looked to overwhelm whom.

Unnoticed by the supposed guards, who also struggled now to see the combat, he slid over the side of the ship in Gyda's wake.

Not to follow her, nei. He needed to be on shore to see how went the combat, and how best he could help. Thunder rumbled overhead, and the first bolt of lightning struck even as he stepped ashore.

If Friti proved victorious in this battle, if the berserker died, he, Lodvar, would likely die also in the most painful way Gunnar could devise.

That did not matter, so long as the berserker's lass survived.

On the shore, he could once more follow the combat. Both men, now dripping water, remained on their feet. Bright red wounds marked them, and a wash of blood mixed with rain colored Tolljur Magnusson's face. Even as Lodvar watched, he bared his teeth in a snarl.

Friti held one arm—badly slashed—close to his body. But the other wielded his sword with confidence.

Tolljur, Lodvar decided, needed help that he could perhaps provide.

Where was Gyda, though? Safely ashore on the far rocks?

He sent out a thought. *Where are you?*

No reply. His heart leaped from his chest to the back of his throat and, despite the driving rain, his mouth went dry. Had she been caught? Ach, by Odin's eye—

Gyda.

The faintest reply drifted to him. She secreted herself. She must have reached the shore.

Guard her for me, Fadir Odin. Brodir Thor, I summon you!

Throwing himself into the summoning, he lifted his face. Above his head, the clouds boiled and lowered. Lightning flashed between them, as if the very clouds contested in combat, just like Tolljur and Friti.

He squeezed his eyes closed, fisted his hands, and called.

****

On the shore, soaked to the skin and huddling behind a line of rocks, Gyda saw the lightning flash overhead. Bright as a sword—as her father's sword—it slashed down toward the combatants and observers on the shore.

The men there cried out. So hard did the rain now pelt down, Gyda could barely see them. Their voices sounded like the cries of distant gulls.

Should she run? Dared she? Would the falling rain hide her? Shifting on her heels, she forced her fingers into her pocket and gripped Lodvar's blade.

Lodvar. What would happen to him? Would Gunnar suspect he'd helped her escape?

And Fadir?

She got to her feet and narrowed her eyes, trying to see through the rain. The two men still fought, circling, circling—even as the clouds churned above them like foam in a cauldron.

And there, near the prow of the ship—was that Lodvar standing facing them, straight and tall, power in his every line?

She ached to return to him but knew she could not. The cost would be far too high. She sent him a thought, winging like a bird through the intervening murk. *Save my father, if you can.*

Lightning struck again, ripping a seam in the heavens through which poured silver light. Light, even in the heart of darkness.

It forked down, striking one of the combatants. For the rain, for her tears, Gyda could not tell which one.

She turned and, with all her might, ran.

Chapter Twenty-Seven

"Jarl Friti, Jarl Friti! Is he dead?"

Lodvar heard the question repeated over and over again. He knew he should use this opportunity to slip away, while the combatants and everyone else remained distracted. He needed to dash along the shore in search of Gyda.

But if he did, the storm he held above the island would dissipate and die. And if that happened, it might make a tremendous difference for Tolljur, as well as open both Gyda and himself to exposure.

How long could he control the crashing elements by will alone? How much of himself would he exchange—for Gyda's sake?

He splashed through the water, the hem of his cloak trailing behind him. When he drew near enough, he saw that one of the combatants had fallen, though he could not see whom. The men on the shore, including Tolljur's guards, had backed off in a half circle, partially blocking his sight. It felt as if everyone there collectively held his breath.

Then the shout came again. "Fadir! Fadir! Stop!"

Lodvar recognized Gunnar's voice. A man in front of Lodvar shifted, and he saw—

The cluster of men, all soaked by the rain. Their eyes glittered, when flashed the lightning, as bright as the weapon in the hands of the single combatant who remained on his feet.

All the breath left Lodvar's body in a rush. The berserker stood, the sword raised high, his gaze fixed on the man who had fallen at his feet. Jarl Friti—he lay weaponless, both his hands held up as if he sought to keep death at bay. For an instant, Tolljur appeared to consider him, before he disobeyed Gunnar's command, and brought his broad weapon down in a sweeping arc, straight for Friti's head.

Everyone there bellowed. Gunnar leaped forward, and the scene broke up into chaos. Gunnar threw himself at the berserker, who turned entirely sane eyes on him. This was no berserker's fit that had allowed him to defeat Friti, but sheer determination and brawn. Now he would need to fight for his life against the many.

Alone but for him, Lodvar.

Exhaustion tugged at him. He held the storm as a strong hound on a leash, and it drained him. No one even knew he had a part in this battle, yet if he did not battle on, Tolljur would die.

Without hesitation he ran toward and not away from the confrontation, his wet robes swirling out behind him, spreading like the wings of a bird. Accustomed to his presence at all such gatherings back in Husavik, the circle expanded to admit him. Looking at the scene, he blinked the rain out of his eyes, and looked again.

Jarl Friti lay, beheaded, on the ground. His sword had fallen ready to his hand, but those fingers would never again grasp a sword, or a woman. The rocks of the shore ran with red, blood chased by the rain and diluting into the sea.

Lodvar lifted his gaze to Gunnar's face. This young man he had known all his life, alternately fearing and detesting him. Never had he seen such a look on Gunnar's face. Disbelief filled his wide blue eyes, and his mouth hung ajar.

Lodvar looked next at Tolljur Magnusson. Nei, Tolljur had not relied upon the berserker's trance in this. He looked beaten, bloodied, and exhausted, but he still stood on his feet. For how long?

Lodvar's gaze met Tolljur's for an instant. He heard Gyda's voice again, in his mind. *Save my father, if you can.* Could he? Magic demanded almost as harsh a price as combat. His strength was nearly gone.

Yet what did he matter, compared with Gyda's happiness? With the berserker's courage? He might as well burn himself up to ash, here on the shore, and count his life well spent.

Time hung suspended for one fragile moment while Gunnar remained clasped by the shock of seeing the man he never believed could be vanquished lying on the shore. As soon as he recovered, every weapon there would be turned on Tolljur Magnusson.

With a sigh, Lodvar released the storm, which at once abated and hurried away eastward. Tolljur shifted and set himself. He prepared to fight to the death, if he must. He would not stand alone.

Gaze still holding Tolljur's, Lodvar gave a nod. Surprise and recognition flashed in Tolljur's eyes. He glanced at the sky, watching the clouds stream away.

"Tolljur Magnusson!" Gunnar bellowed. "Face me!"

Gunnar had recovered from his shock, if not his grief. His relationship with his father, as Lodvar knew, had always been a strange one, more like that of two competitive brothers than father and son. Gunnar had, in truth, lived beneath the sunshine of his grandfather and the favor of the old jarl. Yet when the moment came for him to choose between siding with Friti or following the old jarl's wishes, he had not hesitated to fall into this scheme with his father.

Blood would tell.

If that were so, he, Lodvar, should be back in Husavik tending the jarl's hall and keeping his stores. Yet other blood besides that of Harald ran in his veins. He knew little enough, in truth, of the Albans or their gods. Someone—someone had blessed him with the ability to weave magic. He needed to call upon that now, in full.

Once more he threw back his head. He felt the weariness drag at him, like bonds on a slave's wrists. He could not heed it. He must have enough strength left.

In the time it took Tolljur to turn and face Gunnar, he made up his mind. From the air and the sea, he drew in great gouts of power, even as he watched a wry smile twist Tolljur's lips.

"You want to fight me, boy?" he asked Gunnar.

"I will avenge my father."

Did Tolljur stagger slightly as he braced himself on the stones? "Do as you believe you must."

Clenching his fists, Lodvar once more raised his face to the sky. The wind, still strong, blew his cloak out behind him like the wings of a bird. *Birds, come.*

He made of it an invitation, then a call—then a demand. As the wind streams, so did he stream his will to the creatures of the air, the demand of it causing him to waver where he stood.

Young and strong he was, willing to give all of himself for Gyda's sake. Surely he had strength enough.

In the time it took for Gunnar to raise his sword, the first of them came. Ravens were common to all battlefields and places where men fought and died— always looking for the chance, they were. These, though, were not ravens, but gulls. Out of the diminishing rain they flew, wings gleaming as silver as the lightning. They wheeled, screaming, above the heads of the men on the shore, many of whom raised their arms and covered their heads.

Lodvar might not be a warrior, but a childhood filled with persecution had taught him when to run. He tucked down his head, the cries of the birds echoing in his ears, and dashed into the circle, nearly stepping on Friti's headless corpse.

"Come," he told the berserker.

For an instant, he did not think Tolljur would heed him. The berserker had been taught to stand and fight rather than to flee. But his eyes, bright as two polished shields, met Lodvar's, and for an instant frozen in time, Lodvar caught a glimpse of what lay in the man's mind. Death hovered there, and bright, silver madness. Had Tolljur Magnusson slipped into his berserker's trance after all?

Not allowing himself to hesitate, Lodvar seized his arm and pulled. "Away now, for Odin's—for Gyda's sake."

Tolljur's hands, torn and bloodied, came up and clutched at Lodvar in turn. "Shaman."

"Me, ja. Come."

Surrounded and yet untouched by the attacking

birds, they broke through the circle and ran. Up the shore and toward the rise, with voices hollering behind them, they went, Lodvar following the berserker. Even over the din caused by the shrieking gulls and by the men trying to swat them away, he could hear Tolljur's strained breathing. Lodvar could have run much faster, but he had no clue in which direction safety might lie. As it was, they made it to the heights—no easy path— and the cover of the rocks there.

Cries of agony sounded behind them, and what Lodvar believed was Gunnar's wail of frustration.

"He escapes! The berserker—and the shaman!"

Odin, aid us.

Had he already burned up all his favors from Fadir Odin? The aged god could be capricious, sometimes abandoning men to seize success or fail on their own.

When they reached the height of the headland, Tolljur paused. The man blew like a winded pony, and his wounds ran freely with blood. But a certain calm possessed him as he looked down at the scene below.

The birds now circled, still screaming, above the men on the shore, but they no longer attacked. Gunnar had broken away from them and stood trying to rally his men to follow Tolljur and Lodvar. Even as Lodvar watched, they began to organize.

Tolljur still held his sword. Lodvar went unarmed. How long would it take Gunnar's men to make it up the slope? How long did he have to live?

"Come," he told Tolljur again, urgently.

The berserker ignored him. Laying aside his sword at last, he picked up one of the rocks from the stony ground. Without hesitation, he hurled it at their pursuers.

With a gusty breath, Lodvar followed suit. When the rocks came down upon them, some of the men fell back. Gunnar, and most of the others, came on.

Lodvar tugged at Tolljur's arm. "Come," he beseeched again.

Tolljur looked at him, gray eyes full of resignation. "I go no farther, Shaman. I am spent. You go on."

"Nei. I will not go without you. What would I tell Gyda? She will never forgive me."

"Tell my daughter I love her."

"You must tell her yourself."

Light appeared in Tolljur's eyes. He snatched up his sword, and they ran. Up over the headland, through the rocks, and on a tack Tolljur indicated, though he labored behind. Now the breath came hard in Lodvar's lungs. His legs burned beneath him. He could not pause nor allow Tolljur to flag. Back on the stones, Friti Gunnarsson lay dead. And that meant Gunnar would never stop pursuing them.

He could not allow himself to think about that. Nor about whether Gyda had made it to shore alive. There was just one more step, and one more breath, each following the last.

Chapter Twenty-Eight

They climbed steadily before veering inland, leaving the headland behind. As they went, Lodvar sought Gyda in his mind, groped for her, but caught only a faint thread of awareness.

Sheer will kept him moving ahead of Gunnar's and Friti's men, who still pursued them. Lodvar knew the pursuers came on, even though their cries had died away like those of the birds on the shore. He and Tolljur spoke little, unwilling to spare the breath.

At last, well inland from the cliffs, Tolljur paused among a scattering of rocks and bent over, struggling to breathe.

"Ribs," he tossed at Lodvar, when he caught his look of concern. "I think some are broken."

"The beating, yesterday?"

"Ja." Tolljur stepped around the nearest rock. Lodvar heard him vomit violently.

How had the man bested Friti in combat? How hiked so far after? There must be magic in it.

This time it was Tolljur who told Lodvar, "Come. We are almost there."

"Do you think Gyda made it away?"

"I hope so." Tolljur gave him a crosswise glance. "You have strong feelings for my daughter."

How would the berserker react if Lodvar admitted he did? A man who could take out Friti Gunnarsson might deal harshly with an unwelcome suitor.

"I have a powerful attraction to Gyda. Never have I known its like."

Tolljur merely nodded. Then he raised an arm and hailed someone up ahead, in the distance. Several figures there ran toward them—not men, but women standing guard over a gathering of rocks like a fortress.

"What is this place?" Lodvar asked.

Tolljur did not answer. His wife, Eadha, numbered one among the women. She flew at Tolljur and embraced him, nearly taking him over backward. They clutched at one another.

Eadha sobbed, "Och, I did not think I would see you ever again. How did you get away?"

"This young man helped. Called down a storm, so I do believe, and a flock of gulls. Is Gyda here?"

"Ja."

"Safe?"

In answer, Eadha, still clinging to him, gestured behind her where Gyda came, with Magnus at her side.

Her gaze met Lodvar's, and a rush of rightness engulfed him. He drew a deep breath, and his unbearable tension eased.

"Our men," Tolljur called to his son. "How many are left?"

"Enough, Fadir. Enough to escort those bastards to Hel."

"Good thing it rained so hard," Eadha said. "Else Friti would be able to fire our dwellings—and your ships."

"Friti Gunnarsson is dead."

"What?" Eadha stared, as did the others who'd gathered around them in a flock.

Tolljur gave her a smile, terrible to behold in his scarred and bloodied face. "Ja, Wife. He lost his head."

She blinked at him. "Come. Let me tend you, my hero, as you deserve."

Arm in arm, they moved off toward the stone fortress, most of the others following them. Lodvar turned and found Gyda at his side. His heart leaped painfully as bright emotions stirred inside him, tumbling to rightness.

"Am I welcome here?" he asked.

For answer, she held out her hand to him. Their fingers intertwined effortlessly, just like their spirits. "Most welcome, here in my heart."

"They will be coming, not far behind us." Lodvar glanced over his shoulder. "This thing is not done." With Gunnar alive, he had escaped nothing.

"As Modir says, we will worry about that anon."

The encampment, hidden deep in a fold of the land, felt secure. It encompassed a small, level area and a number of caves, all easily defendable from the rocks above. A large number of women and children and a surprising number of men had gathered there. All of them hurried forward to greet Tolljur, including the ancient shaman, Kaddi.

How had they got the old man here? He looked weary but still impressive, wearing his raven-feather cloak.

Kaddi grinned as he joined Gyda and Lodvar. "I am happy to see you, boy. Do you bring trouble with you?"

"Perhaps."

"He also brought Fadir home, Kaddi," Gyda put in, her fingers squeezing Lodvar's tight.

The old man snorted. "Ja? The work of a hero, that is. So." His milky eye focused on Lodvar. "You called down a storm, did you? And helped Tolljur escape?"

"How did you know that?"

Kaddi clasped his arm. "I felt the power, and the draw upon the magic. The birds…" He jerked his head shoreward. "Did you call those too?"

"Ja."

"Come, we will sit together. You can tell me."

Lodvar longed to be alone with Gyda—ached for it. He wanted to hold her, kiss her for a day. Or two.

Yet he followed the shaman to a place beside one of the several fires that burned, down in the depression among the rocks. Folk gave them curious looks as they passed, and Magnus a hard stare.

Would he have trouble with Gyda's brother?

Once she'd seated them beside the fire, Gyda hurried off to fetch Lodvar a draught of ale. Kaddi clutched his arm with a claw-like hand. He searched Lodvar's face with his milky eye.

"So tell me—upon whom did you call for your magic?"

"Fadir Odin."

The old man looked pleased. "Him do I also serve. Eadha, she follows the Alban god—Lugh. Since your mother was once also Alban, I did wonder about you."

Before Lodvar could answer, Kaddi went on, "And what magic did you work against Friti Gunnarsson?"

"Fire and water—lightning and storm. But Master Kaddi, this is not done. I suspect I will be required to pay a price for it. I believe I will be asked to pay dear."

****

Rain moved back in, not long after nightfall,

creating misery for those on guard. The men who had followed Tolljur and Lodvar up from the shore, however, had not yet attacked, and hung just out of sight. Perhaps, it was suggested, they had insufficient men to try and take the natural fortress.

Some time after midnight, Gyda sought out her brother, on patrol, at Modir's request. "All quiet?" she asked as she joined him on the rocks above the caves.

"So far, ja. But I would not be surprised if they burn our houses, and Fadir's boats."

Gyda started, and looked at him. Though nearly a year her junior, he stood much taller than she did—taller than Fadir, for that matter. Modir said he took after her father, who had been a strong, strapping warrior. He had a touch of Modir's Sight also, just like Gyda, and sometimes made such pronouncements, though he did not See so much as sense changes to come.

"Nei," she breathed. "What makes you say so?"

He shook his head. "It is what I would do, if I found myself in possession of my enemy's holdings. Would you not?" He shifted the axe in his hand. He often favored an axe above the sword, and could throw one with startling accuracy.

In that, he was all Norse.

"How is Fadir?"

"I cannot say. I just came from the caves—Modir sent me here to you. She will not budge from his side. It has been so long since he fell into the berserker's fit. And he is badly wounded."

"The fit—it takes much from him."

"Ja."

Magnus drew a breath. "He is not going to die is

he, Gyda?" For an instant, Magnus sounded like the boy he had been, deeply attached to his family and capable of much affection.

"Modir says he will survive. And it is something, that he came here on his own feet." Modir had also wept over Tolljur while he slept, and called upon her gods with raw desperation, but Gyda would not tell Magnus so.

"Good. Because I am not ready, Gyda."

"Ready?"

"To lose him. Or to take over in his stead. I do not think it my place."

"Of course it is your place. You are the grandson of an Alban chief."

"And a berserker."

"Ja, and the son of one also. But you have never shown any tendency to take a fit—" Gyda paused. "Have you?"

"I have felt the impulse, Gyda. I felt it, back there. And—it is not the first time."

Gyda stared, aghast. "Nei! You never said—"

"I did not want to alarm Modir. Or Fadir. You know what dread he has of seeing me follow after him in that way. It is his greatest fear. Since I am so much like Modir's fadir, I let them think…but now that this danger comes to our door, I feel it hovering, like a great bear, extending its claws for me."

Was that part of what Gyda had felt approaching, before all this began? This threat not only to their lives but to Magnus's wellbeing?

"I will do as I must to defend what I love," he said heavily. "Even if it means I must give in to the call of the bear."

"But"—Gyda touched his shoulder—"you are unprepared. It takes much training, much...much endurance to withstand the trance, when it comes." In the old days, Kaddi had eased Fadir's path into the madness, and that of his father before him, with potions, in part.

Indeed, Kaddi had come to Modir now, asking to brew a mixture that would restore Fadir's strength, only to have Modir turn him away again.

Magnus nodded. Gyda looked at him anxiously. "What does it feel like, when the madness threatens to overtake you?"

He hesitated. "It is not easy to describe. Something like a storm coming, only stronger. Hot as fever, with prickles all over my skin. Giving in to it—but I cannot imagine."

She put her arms around him, and held tight. "Do not give in, Magnus. No matter what."

"Easily said, Søstir. Not so easily done."

****

Half way through that night, Gyda went looking for Lodvar. She'd spent the last stretch of time helping Modir tend Fadir, who had at last fallen asleep in the alcove where they'd made their bed. Eventually, she found Lodvar in one of the caves, sitting beside Kaddi. Kaddi slept with his one good eye closed, and the other open, disconcertingly, over its empty socket.

When Lodvar saw her, he lifted a hand and got to his feet.

"I have been searching everywhere for you." Gyda ached with longing for him, a sensation not helped by the fact that she could feel his presence, hanging in her consciousness, but could not tell from exactly where it stemmed. After what they had endured apart, she needed time with him—alone, preferably.

He clasped her hands. "I have been here. I wanted to keep the fire going for Kaddi while he slept. The damp is hard on his old bones."

"Ja. Where is his minder?"

"Somewhere about. I think her brother was injured in the battle, and she tends him."

Far too many of their men—and women—were injured. Gyda cast a glance at the old man. "He is well, now, and the fire will hold for a time. Come you with me. I will find you some breakfast."

I want you, instead.

His thoughts sounded clearly in her mind. Their eyes met in a long exchange.

Ja, but where? Gyda thought furiously, and tightened her grip on his hands, before releasing them. *It has stopped raining. I think I know a place.*

Careful not to touch each other, they threaded their way through the sleeping folk of the settlement—injured warriors, young mothers with babes in their arms. Outside, a brisk wind swept the night clear, chasing the rain to the east. All around the caves, people stood at guard. The nearest, who was Astrid, turned her head and looked at them.

"No sign of anyone?" Gyda asked her.

"Nei. And no smoke from back home. Magnus is convinced that Gunnar will torch the settlement, and your father's boats."

Lodvar gave his opinion. "Gunnar is much too shrewd to torch the boats. He would rather take such fine vessels for himself." He glanced at Gyda. "How is your father? He was sore hurt when we got here."

She gave a tight smile. "He was, and is. Modir is in an agony over him. But I think he will recover. His endurance is legendary, is it not? He is berserker, with the strength of a bear."

Lodvar appeared to consider it. "The strength of a bear when in the grips of the trance, ja. But when he comes out of it—"

She shot him an assessing glance. "Most folk do not comprehend that. I am grateful you do." Addressing her friend, she said, "Astrid, we are going to slip away for a time. Master Lodvar has prayers to say, and rune stones to cast."

"Is it safe?" The girl looked concerned. "Magnus will not like it."

"We will not be long."

Several of the guards watched as Gyda led Lodvar up and over the top of the fortress. How quiet it seemed, and how peaceful beneath the flying clouds. Hard to imagine that, just a short distance away, death waited.

"Magnus will not like it," Lodvar agreed with Astrid's opinion. "I do not believe he likes the prospect of you and me together."

"You saved Fadir. Fadir said so."

"Still."

"I love my brother dearly, but he does not make my choices. Come."

She linked her fingers with his. They wove their way between the stones and through the broken scree on the slope beyond. Ja, and perhaps it was foolish, leading the shaman away by the hand, for all to see. Yet desire rode her, and not just of the physical kind. Her heart needed him, and her spirit. She'd never imagined such feelings, or such longing.

Beyond the hollow where lay the caves, the land continued to rise. Great slabs of gray rock thrust through the green turf, and the wind scoured them.

Hair streaming out behind her, fingers still linked with Lodvar's, Gyda paused. "I like it up here, I always have. This place looks like a sleeping giant, does it not? There—you can see his head tucked down. The rocks are his bones. And there—you see the waterfall?"

"Ja."

"The giant's tears."

"Gyda—" Lodvar turned her to face him. His hair streamed out, just like hers, and light filled his eyes. Meeting that gaze, Gyda felt her connection with him vibrate, much like one of the deep notes on Modir's harp, and quiver through her, like her passion.

"I want you here," she told him. "In this most meaningful of places."

For answer, he drew her into his arms and kissed her. The wind twined their hair and clothing together, and wrapped it around them. They swayed and melded into one, and the peace Gyda had sought all night—or perhaps all her life—flooded her.

Two, stronger than one. It sounded like something old Kaddi would say. But Gyda did not want to think of Kaddi now.

Because Lodvar tasted of honey. He tasted of belonging. He tasted of eternity. The intensity of the feelings swayed her where she stood. She broke the kiss and, with the exquisite flavor of him on her lips, invited, "Come."

"Where?" She felt his desire, as strong as her own, and also his bewilderment. "Where, that we will not be seen?"

"There—behind the waterfall."

He balked slightly.

Trust me, she told him mind to mind.

She picked her way down through the rocks onto the narrow ledge of stone, never releasing his hand. The sound of crashing water surrounded them, its wild song matching the fever in her blood. She'd been here before, as a child, and caught her parents' displeasure for it.

Nothing here now but pleasure.

Behind the waterfall existed a shallow cave, little more than a nook, bedded with dry sand. A perfect mix of two holy elements—earth and water—and she and Lodvar would add their breath and the fire of their passion.

He glanced about. "There is magic here. I can feel it."

"You are right. Here, we are disappeared from the world and everything in it."

He looked at her, and she had no need to wonder what he felt. She sensed it all, from the beat of his heart to the leap in his blood.

"Here"—she stepped up to him—"there exists nothing but you and me. No yesterday. No tomorrow. I was born for you, I think."

He raised his hand to her cheek. "I know it."

"I need to touch you. Taste you. Become one with you as"—she tried to explain what lay in her heart—"the two parts of a sword are made one in the fire of the forge."

"That, Gyda Tolljursdottir, is all I have ever wanted."

****

Shedding her clothing, which Gyda did eagerly, was not enough. Nor was stripping Lodvar's garb from him, laying his grand cloak aside carefully on the sand. Pressing her naked body to his did not completely satisfy, but only intensified the fire that burned deep inside. Kissing him, twining her tongue with his even as she wound her arms around his neck and twisted her fingers in his hair, felt better.

She wanted him inside her. She wanted to be inside him, her spirit mingling with his in answer to her wild yearning.

Never before had she wanted to lose herself this way. Her strength and independence mattered. They did still. Yet combined with his magic, she became more than she was, all she'd been born to be.

With the sound of the waterfall in her ears, she could hear nothing beyond his thoughts, sounding in her mind. She could feel nothing except the warmth of him and his hands sliding over her skin in a dance that turned her molten—palm to breast, fingers wooing her to open for him. She could taste only the sweetness of his mouth, the faintly salty tang of his skin beneath her tongue.

They fell to the sand as one, and strength rose up inside her, reaching—reaching for him. She spoke to his mind, even as she stretched beneath him. *Take me. Now.* When he entered her, the perfection of it almost hurt. Her body drew him deeper and deeper before convulsing in ripples of pleasure, and her spirit clung to his even after the sharp ecstasy of it began to fade.

The tiny cave still enfolded them. The stream of silver water still crashed down. Nothing—nothing else remained the same.

Fighting for breath, fighting for sanity, she tried to remember the rest of the world. The danger that lay beyond this sacred place. The peril contained in promises given.

I want to stay here forever, she told him, deep in his mind. *Nei, do not move. Not yet.*

He drew away, just far enough so he could look into her eyes. Unlike her, he spoke aloud. "You are so beautiful. I did not expect that—for you to be beautiful, as well."

"As well as what?"

"The other half of me. All the answers, in one. The end to all my searching. I have felt you calling, forever calling me." Tenderly he touched her face. "I am grateful to the gods who let me find you."

Gyda sobered. "Even here?"

"Eh?"

"Here, where there is war and strife and—and perhaps terrible consequences." She laid hold of him in turn. "Lodvar, list to me. This fight is not done."

"That I do know."

"I want you to understand something. From this moment, whatever might come, I am your bride. You, and nobody else, ever, hold my heart. You are forged to my spirit. If Gunnar comes—"

"When." The expression in Lodvar's eyes changed. "I know him. He will come."

And when he did, would he try and enforce the promise she had given him, that of a marriage alliance? Ach, she could not bear it! She belonged to this man—this and none other—till she died.

She snagged the back of his neck and drew his

mouth closer to hers. "I am your bride," she whispered. "None other. And we are together now. I cannot get enough of the taste or feel of you. I doubt I ever will."

He kissed her deeply, and the exquisite fire rose once more to fill them.

"Lodvar," she broke the kiss to ask, "can you trust me? Whatever may come?"

He gazed once more into her face. Golden fire burned in his eyes, a bottomless sea of devotion. "Trust is not easy for me. Gyda, I trust only where I love. And if ever I could trust anyone, it would be you."

Chapter Twenty-Nine

"First we must discover when Gunnar Fritisson will attack." Tolljur spoke with a wheeze that caused Lodvar a qualm of disquiet. Mistress Eadha had confirmed he had at least one broken rib. Lodvar, recalling the man's labored breaths when they'd made their climb of escape, believed it.

Tolljur waved off his wife's concerns with a careless, "Eadha, you know how swiftly I heal."

No sooner had Lodvar and Gyda returned from their time away from the world, at the waterfall, than folk came running, saying Tolljur was awake and asking to see them.

Did he suspect what they'd been up to, together? Lodvar couldn't say. He expected the berserker to upbraid him, but Tolljur had immediately expressed his concerns about Gunnar, instead.

With a scowl, he said, "I do not question if he will attack—I have slain his father. But when? Can either of you tell?" He fixed his smoke-gray eyes on Lodvar. "Can you, through your magic?"

Lodvar shook his head regretfully. "I can cast the stones, but if they indicate danger, I will not be able to tell when it will come."

Tolljur switched his gaze to Gyda. "Dottir?"

"Nothing has come to me, Fadir." She did not add that the blistering connection she had shared with him,

Lodvar, had blasted away nearly every other perception, but he suspected it was so. "There is danger, ja, that I can sense. But as Lodvar says, I do not know when, or whether he may arrive by stealth or direct attack."

Tolljur moved restlessly on his pallet. "We must prepare. Since we have little enough with which to fight, we must use our resources to best effect. I have asked Kaddi." His gaze once more fixed on Lodvar. "He suggested I turn to you. He seems to feel you are well-suited to fill his place."

"Jarl Tolljur." Lodvar squeezed Gyda's fingers. "Might I speak with you alone?"

Eadha immediately bristled. "I will not leave my husband, not with him in this condition."

"Ja, Wife, you will." Tolljur gave her a rare smile, one that softened him perceptibly. "Just for a moment or two."

"Very well." She leaned in and kissed him. "Only because you will tell me everything that is said anyway, later."

"To be sure, I will."

The women left the enclosed area where Tolljur lay, deep within the cave. Tolljur's gaze, full of tenderness, followed his wife away before switching back to Lodvar.

"Now, young man, we may speak plainly and honestly, as I like. Make no mistake, I saw what you did back there on the shore—saved my life, and gave me the chance to get away. I owe you much. My wife— she would not have fared well, had I fallen there."

"Nei," Lodvar murmured, wondering how best to proceed with this conversation. The man asked for honesty. He lifted his gaze to Tolljur's face. "Master Tolljur, I am in love with your daughter."

"Ach." Tolljur grimaced, which Lodvar did not find encouraging. His gaze moved over Lodvar slowly, as if measuring him. "And how does she feel for you? Do you know?"

"Ja. She has admitted she returns my feelings." Arms and legs twined with his, tongues and spirits tangling.

"I will admit, you are not what I ever thought she would choose—a shaman, of all things. She has taken her time in selecting a husband. No man ever suited her. But if she did fall, I expected it to be for a warrior. She has a warrior's spirit."

"I cannot explain it either. I am naught but the son of a slave—"

"You are far more than that."

"Despised by my masters, even as they sought to use me. It is the way of the Norse, perhaps, to use, and use without thought. I recognize that, in your eyes, Jarl Tolljur, I can never be worthy of Gyda—"

"Is that what you think? Young man, Kaddi has been like a father to me, all my life. He walks in the steps of Fadir Odin, which demands respect. Should I honor you any less?"

"I am not Kaddi. And we speak of your daughter."

Tolljur have a short laugh. "At least you are humble. Not like Gunnar, eh?"

"Then you have no objection to—?"

"List to me, son. Eadha was a slave when I first saw her, in the process of being distributed along with the other goods seized in our latest raid. She was also the daughter of an Alban chief. Who am I to say where worth may lie? And who am I to object to my daughter's choice?"

"I am glad to hear you say so. Gyda and I...we are like halves of the same whole. I wish I could explain it better—"

"No need. I understand. Sometimes the gods—and different gods at that—send this to us. It is both wonderful and terrible."

"Terrible, Jarl Tolljur?"

"Ja, for it is a perilous way to live. I tell you that in all honesty. Deep need is accompanied with the risk of deep loss."

"I begin to see that, ja. And I see that you, as a warrior and foremost among your people, would rather protect Gyda from that kind of loss."

"Ha." The laugh sounded painful. "There is no protecting Gyda from anything, much as I might wish to do so. You want to wed with her?"

"I do."

"Then I will not object. However, there are other complications, the foremost being that Gyda has betrothed herself to Gunnar Fritisson."

"Ja." There was that.

"You know Gunnar far better than I do. Is he the sort of man to surrender his claim?"

"Nei." Definitely not.

"Not even to you?"

"Especially not to me."

"Why?" The gray eyes pinned him.

Lodvar shook his head. "We grew up together, yet the relationship between us has ever been strained. In Husavik, it is not approved for slaves to move beyond their station."

"So I recall."

"Gunnar, the favorite of his grandfather, the old jarl, and named early to succeed him, did not much like the recognition that came my way."

One corner of Tolljur's mouth quirked. "But as you say, he did not hesitate to use your talents to his own advantage. I had hoped he would prove nothing like his father. I see that hope was in vain."

"My mother always preached to me that I must be of use to our masters, else I would never gain their respect." Lodvar thought about it and admitted, "I am not at all certain, though, I ever attained anything approaching respect. Gunnar would as soon gut me as look at me."

Tolljur grunted. "Especially now that you have provided assistance to me. You cannot go back to him. You see that?"

"Ja." Lodvar's whole life had just changed, all he'd ever known of belonging and identity flown away with a single decision. Gunnar was not the man to cross. And what of Modir, whom he'd sought always to protect? "If he brings us battle, and defeats us, I will suffer the same fate as the rest of you."

"Or worse." Tolljur frowned. "Gunnar, being a traitor, detests a betrayer most of all. Ironic, nei?"

Lodvar met the smoky-gray gaze of the man on the pallet. "There is no question, then. We simply must defeat him."

"Ja, young shaman, we must."

"We cannot let Gunnar return to Husavik." If he did, it would be without him, and how could he speak, then, on Modir's behalf? Harald might well try to speak for her, but Harald was not now, nor had he ever been, a match for Gunnar.

Ach, he had been selfish, for once in his life—choosing Gyda, choosing even a few brief moments of happiness. And it would rebound upon him.

"Not if we can prevent it." Tolljur leaned forward slightly. "The question is, do we let him bring the fight to us, or take it to him?"

Lodvar eyed the berserker. Battered and visibly weakened, he did not look able to lead an attack, one most likely centered on his own settlement, no less.

Gravely, Lodvar said, "I believe Gunnar will bring the fight to us."

"Do you?" Tolljur cocked a brow.

"He is not a patient man. But he is clever. Always looking for the best chance. What my mother would call an asp."

"Ja, the blood breeds true. Young Shaman, we need to be certain the gods are with us in this fight. Cast your stones and render your foretelling as best you can. If we must fight them here—well, this place may make a fine trap, as well as a shelter."

Lodvar nodded. Once more he raised his eyes to Tolljur's face. "You killed his father. He will be angry. And he is one whose anger must be feared."

"Feared?" Tolljur did not scoff, not quite. "Cast your stones, son. Let us hear from our gods on the matter. And while you are doing that, I will see if I can get up from this bed."

****

With his energies depleted by yesterday's battle, and his senses still blasted by those moments in Gyda's arms, Lodvar found it difficult to still himself within. Even though he sat with his eyes closed, seeking to shut everything else away, far too much intruded upon him. He could feel the berserker's emotions, a mighty current beneath the stalwart surface he presented. Tolljur feared for those he loved—far, far more than for himself.

Beyond the leather sheet that screened the space, people called to one another, further distracting him. Fear and uncertainty filled the very air. And, as Lodvar had learned long ago, one did not approach the gods in uncertainty or fear.

Fadir Odin, heed me.

Somewhere out in the cave, a young child began to cry. Lodvar was taken back to a time long ago when Harald had struck him for getting in the way when some of the old jarl's men occupied the great hall, which was their home. Just so had he cried and run to his mother. She had caught him up in her arms and swiftly hushed him.

Comfort, he had thought it then. But had she just wished to silence him, so he would not receive another blow?

He had learned to be quiet, and to keep his thoughts—and his grievances—to himself. He had learned that Modir, alone, cared enough to comfort him, and put his safety ahead of her own. And now, what had he done? Placed her at risk, and left her prey to Gunnar's revenge, if and when Gunnar returned to Husavik.

All for the love of Gyda, which, given the way they were bonded, was self-love, after all.

Nei, he told himself. I must concentrate. *Fadir Odin, I sue thee for answers. I submit to your judgment. I request a share of your wisdom.*

Before his inner eye appeared a traveler. Wrapped in a long leather cloak and hood, he carried a tall, crooked staff and came walking out of a mist. Nowhere and everywhere had he been. Bound for unknowable places, he nevertheless paused and turned to face Lodvar.

Deeply lined was his countenance, within the cowl of his hood. He had but one eye, and that gray as the mist on a damp morning, but so full of intelligence it fired Lodvar's spirit.

Ach, ja—this felt akin to connecting with Gyda, a strong and sacred thing—the same yet so different. Powerful. Consuming.

My son, what would you ask of me?

Lodvar, eyes still closed, fumbled with his bag of rune stones. He could no longer hear the voices or other noises surrounding him. Instead, a rushing like the music of the waterfall filled his ears.

Guide me, Fadir, as I cast the runes.

Cast them, my son.

Lodvar did so. Still, he did not open his eyes.

Odin smiled the smile of a raven. *They are cast. What more would you ask of me?*

Dared he ask too much, and take advantage of what was offered? He must choose carefully among the many things he wished to know.

His heart bade him ask for protection for his mother, and for Gyda. His head wanted weapons he might use against Gunnar. Could one accomplish the other?

Tell me, will we defeat Gunnar Fritisson?

What is defeat? It comes in many forms. The blade that saves one man kills another.

Can I succeed in protecting those I love from him?

If you can summon enough light. If you and those who stand with you have the courage to be what you are.

Riddles.

Odin laughed. *You ask me for answers, when the stones are cast but not yet read.*

The future is not yet decided.

It is not.

Will one of us die—Gunnar Fritisson, or me?

The god waved his hand, a motion Lodvar felt rather than saw. A scene opened before Lodvar's inner eye.

Jarl Tolljur's dwelling, back at the settlement. A fire burned, casting the only light—enough to let him see Friti stretched on a litter, his head placed back on his shoulders where it belonged. Eyes closed, he looked very much younger, and almost handsome, with the cruelty wiped from his face.

Above the litter stood another form, stock still. Like a shadow he appeared, yet Lodvar knew him for Gunnar. He spoke in a voice like gravel, roughened by grief.

"I will avenge you, Fadir. Only death will halt me."

Lodvar emerged from the Vision to find the god departed, gone upon his eternal journeying about the world. The berserker watched him quietly, with steady gray eyes. The rune stones had been flung wide, across the floor at Lodvar's knees.

Hands fisted, he narrowed his eyes at them.

Chapter Thirty

"They come." Although Gyda, standing at Magnus's side, whispered the words, they sounded like a shout.

The two of them kept watch together upon the rise above the caves, gazing back toward the settlement. The land, brilliant green and studded by rocks, unfolded before them, and beyond that the sea stretched like a flared cloak, impossibly blue.

Gyda, her senses heightened by her time with Lodvar, felt she could see almost too much. The threads of their connection tensed and vibrated, quivered as she did when he was inside her and they became one. Even apart, he belonged to her now.

He'd lent her part of his magic, and it heightened her own poor store. Always had her Visions been visited upon her—rarely had she successfully sought foreknowledge. But she felt Gunnar coming, the darkness and power of it, very like what she'd sensed out upon the water that very first day.

Magnus looked at her, his hazel eyes overbright in the clear light. "Are you sure, Søstir?"

"Ja." Part of her wished it were not so. Another part wanted to end this—to see Gunnar answered as he deserved. If only she could be sure the price would not be too high.

Magnus turned and gave a bellow, raising the axe

in his hand.

"To arms! Everyone, prepare! Gunnar Fritisson and his warriors are on their way."

Folk scrambled. The majority of them were women, but the women of Sorvagur were not loathe to lift a weapon. Gyda herself already gripped her sword. She also still had the knife Lodvar had given her, tucked well into her clothing. From it, she felt a tingle.

Magic.

Others, men and women alike, pounded up the slope toward her and Magnus, all armed. Fadir still lingered inside the cave—probably being fussed over by Modir, if Gyda did not miss her guess.

She, or Magnus, would have to lead this defense.

"How near are they?" gasped Brita, her face tense. Brita had once been a slave in Husavik, like Modir.

Magnus shot a look at Gyda. "How close, Søstir?"

Gyda closed her eyes and sent out her consciousness, as she did when she wanted to contact Lodvar. "Just out of sight, beyond that swell in the land. They hold back."

"Do you think they will wait and attack in the dark?"

"Perhaps. Or they may wait out of sight until morning. Who can tell?"

Brita licked her lips. "No matter. I will fight to the death before I return to Husavik." She grinned. "I am just disappointed Friti is already dead. I have been waiting a score of years to plunge a blade into his guts."

For an instant Magnus looked shocked. Then he returned Brita's grin.

Modir bustled up, her skirts caught high in her hands. In the morning light, the birthmark on her cheek stood out like a brand.

"They come?"

"Ja. Gyda says so. Not certain how soon."

Brita linked her arm with Modir's. "We will fight them off together, eh, Eadha?"

"To the last breath. Magnus, I hereby place you in command. Your father insists he will fight, but I fear he is not fit, and I would not have him at the head of our warriors."

"Not fit to fight, you say?" Magnus gazed past her toward the front of the cave. "I would not be too certain."

The rest of them also turned. Tolljur came puffing up the side of the cut, his ashen hair—now well-streaked with silver—flowing out loose behind him. He had one hand pressed to his chest, and he moved as if he hurt. In his other hand, however, he clutched his sword.

"I am here," he called to his son.

Magnus's face brightened. "Fine, that. The two of us always fight better together than apart."

Modir called to Fadir, "You cannot possibly fight, not so soon."

Brita laughed.

Tolljur said, "Do not tell me that, Wife. It will only make me more determined." He glanced around. "I might have chosen a better place to make a stand."

"It is defensible," Magnus insisted.

"Ja, to a point. If they drive us off this high ground into the hollow, we are done." He looked at Brita. "Brita, organize the women with children. Send them on to the waterfall, where they may be safer. Tell them—tell them if we all fall, they should make their way to the settlement at Vagar. Send some of our strongest women as guards. Perhaps you would go."

"I will not. I mean to stay here and gut Gunnar Fritisson, in his father's stead."

"You may not get the chance." Fadir smiled. "Not if I reach him first."

"Curse it! I want that pleasure for myself."

A tickle on the back of Gyda's neck caused her to turn. Lodvar stood there, gaze resting on her. Her spirit leaped in response.

"How soon?" she called to him.

He shrugged. "He is waiting—I can feel it. But for what, I cannot say."

"What say the rune stones?" Brita demanded. "Will we be victorious?"

Lodvar gave her his rare smile. "Fadir Odin refused to say. With his best wishes, he has left the matter in our hands."

****

All the day long, they awaited movement from the direction of the settlement. Gyda, strung tight enough to break, remembered Gunnar's arrival, and how long he had lingered out upon the ocean before sailing into the harbor. Did he play games with them? Did he hope uncertainty would cause them to break? Or did he merely give those of his men that remained time to recover from the last fight?

She had no answers but could sense him and his men there upon the land, just out of sight. By dark—which fell late, indeed, at this time of year—tempers were short and the defenders felt anxious. Fadir alone remained calm and seemed to make use of the respite to regain his strength.

"He will wait for full dark," declared Kaddi, who'd insisted on being carried out from his refuge in the cave.

"Fadir, let us attack him," requested Magnus, who had turned downright irascible with waiting.

"Nei," Tolljur returned calmly. "That is what he wants. He will have sent a scout ahead, and seen we are dug in fast here, among these rocks." He shot a look at his son. "Do not let him lure you out. You must learn to wait."

Magnus swore under his breath and said nothing more.

Modir fretted, "What if they circle around in the dark and attack us from farther up?"

Gyda moved to her father's side and laid a hand on his arm. "Perhaps we should send a scout to see exactly where they are."

He gave her a look in which acknowledgement warred with refusal and the desire to protect. "Ja, Dottir? And who should I send?"

"Me. I can move swiftly in the dark, and I know the path well. Also, I have the advantage of being able to sense where the bulk of Gunnar's forces lie. I am the right person to send."

Kaddi chuckled. "There speaks Eadha's daughter. Tolljur. Can you tell her nei?"

"I can." Fadir scowled.

Eagerly, Gyda rushed on, "Fadir, Gunnar does not know the path, has no way to tell he must circle up and around from the headland to avoid the ravine. He may try to take the shortcut of the bridge."

"The bridge"—a structure built from little more than decaying tree trunks—"is not sound."

"He will not know that."

"They will be following our trail up from the settlement. They will see we did not come across the bridge."

"He will be impatient and may take the chance."

Fadir looked at Magnus. "Son, you take the best of our men. If they attempt the bridge, give them a reception."

Modir gasped. "Magnus—"

Ignoring her, Magnus shifted the axe in his hand, and grinned. "Ja."

"Fadir," Gyda protested immediately, "that is not fair—"

"It is fair, Dottir. I need you here, where you can relay to me what you feel coming."

"But—"

"Tell me, Gyda, what kind of leader fails to make the best use of the warriors available to him?"

He had called her a warrior. She supposed she must be satisfied with that.

As she turned away, Lodvar touched her hand. Their fingers meshed together, and she heard his voice in her mind. *I am glad to have you here.*

She turned her head. Their gazes met and clung. In his eyes she saw a hundred things—his love for her, backed by helpless desire. The longing to protect her. A deep well of strength and—ja, fear.

He voiced none of it. Tearing her gaze from his, Gyda turned back to her father. "If you need me here, you will need Lodvar also."

"So I will. Both of you, keep near to me when the fighting begins. We will need every weapon available to our hands before this is done."

****

Kaddi came stomping up not long after, leaning heavily on his tall stick and looking disquietingly frail. Another argument arose when both Fadir and Modir tried to persuade the old man to shelter with the women and children in the caves.

"Nei, Tolljur Magnusson," Kaddi declared. "There is to be a great battle. I have cast the stones." He glanced at Lodvar who, with Gyda, stood by. "As, I am certain, has my counterpart here."

Fadir fixed Kaddi with a fierce eye. "Will we be victorious?"

"The stones did not tell me that. Only that it will be a dire battle and the cost will be high."

Modir seized Fadir's arm. "I do not like the sound of that."

"No one likes the sound of it, girl," Kaddi replied. "You speak to your gods, and I will speak to mine."

Modir looked nonplussed.

Lodvar said suddenly, "The true danger is that Gunnar Fritisson does not come for the sake of conquest. These islands, ja, would prove of benefit to him, a good location and post for trade. But he comes for revenge and will not be satisfied until the ground runs red with blood." He looked at Kaddi. "Perhaps, Master, it would be wise for you to go stay with the others, in the safety of the caves."

"With the mothers and the babes, you mean? With the old men? Ha!" Even though Kaddi lacked his cloak of feathers, he looked ruffled. "I am still a man, and a shaman, the same as you. I never was a warrior, true, but I have served Tolljur long, and his father before him."

He lifted his chin. "If I am to die, should it not be here, engaged in the sort of battle only you and I can fight?"

Lodvar narrowed his eyes. "Magic, you mean."

The old man smiled. His face broke into a wealth of wrinkles. "Magic. Each must act by his or her own nature, boy." He pointed at Eadha. "Her. And him." He indicated Tolljur, and lastly Gyda. "Even her."

Gyda wondered, later, if the old man spoke in prophecy. She never had the chance to ask him.

Chapter Thirty-One

Not long after, they heard it traveling to them through the stillness of the black night—the sound of a clash not far away, the clatter of weapons and raised voices. Everyone tensed and stole anxious looks at one another. Errant children were chased back into the caves, and their mothers with them. Eadha clutched her husband's hand and leaned into him.

Lodvar edged up to Gyda, who insisted on remaining at watch, a borrowed sword in her hand. "Tell me of this bridge," he requested. "I caught but a glimpse of it when your father and I came here, and he edged his way well around."

"It is not actually a bridge," she answered, keeping her voice hushed as if still listening to the sounds from beyond. Trouble hovered in her eyes. Her brother had gone forward into this fight—and much hinged upon it. "Long ago, when my parents first came here from Husavik, they made their home here, in this dell, whilst the settlement was being built. I was born here, as a matter of fact. The way across the ravine was constructed then, out of wood brought from Iceland. It saved much time for folk going back and forth, but it was never safe. There were accidents, and when it became unsound, Fadir eventually forbade us to use it."

"He never built another?"

"Nei, we had not the supplies to waste, plus he

considered it too dangerous. Some lads, pushing and shoving as lads will do, fell and were killed. All the parents told their children not to cross there. It was not such a hardship, since we were all living in the settlement by then."

"Ach, I see. But"—Lodvar thought hard upon it—"Gunnar will not know that."

Gyda shot him a fierce glance. "You know him better than I, and you declare him impatient. Do you think he will take a chance and try to cross there?"

Lodvar shook his head. "He might."

"Then," she said it flatly, "the island may do our work for us. We can hope—"

Cries from the distance arose, and Lodvar narrowed his eyes. Might those be the cries of men fighting, or those plunging to their deaths? Cursed if he could tell. Amazing, how the sounds carried through the still air. For there was no wind, and Lodvar's ear caught even the distant stir of the sea.

"Faith," he told Gyda. "If we stop believing we can win, all is lost." Yet standing there so and feeling the woman he loved vibrate with agony on behalf of her brother and his company was hard to do. "Trust Magnus."

"I do trust him. It is just—"

Lodvar closed his fingers on hers. "I know."

She squeezed his hand hard, and spoke into his mind. *You have cast the stones. How bad will this be?*

Bad. He would not disguise that from her. He respected her too much.

Will my brother die? My father?

We will lose many.

Grief rose within her and spilled over to him. *If I*

am to number one among them, I am glad I knew you first. I am glad I touched you, kissed you, lay with you. At least I have had that. Remember, I am and will always be your bride.

Do not weep. He turned her to face him. Tears brimmed in her eyes.

If I do not weep for this, then for what?

I wish you need never weep, Gyda, my beautiful love.

Then tell me all whom I love will survive.

The gods make no such promises.

A crash resounded through the still air, spinning them both around. All along the ridge, the guards shifted, and others came running up from behind.

"What was that?"

"Can you see?"

A wild chorus of cries arose from the direction of the ravine. Cries of loss, or of victory? And from whom, defenders or attackers? Lodvar could not tell.

Eadha and Tolljur pushed in beside them. "The bridge," Eadha whispered. "It has fallen—tumbled into the fissure."

"Ja," Tolljur agreed.

"How many of our men went with it? Magnus—"

"He is strong, this son of ours, Eadha." Tolljur shot Gyda a look. "Both of our children are strong. We shall see now, eh, of what Magnus is made."

Eadha did not appear reassured.

Gyda wiggled her fingers against Lodvar's palm. He felt her strength and pride in her brother. She was right, he decided. Whatever happened during this night to come, at least he'd found her first—the one who'd called to him for so long, his mate, his destiny. If he were fated to die in this fight, he would hold for eternity to those moments of perfect happiness in her arms.

And ach, no matter what happened—no matter what he had to sacrifice—*please, Fadir Odin, let her survive.*

****

"I detest waiting," Modir complained. "It is worse than anything else." She added, after a moment's thought, "Almost anything else."

Gyda could do nothing but agree. Standing hand in hand with Lodvar, the sword Magnus had lent her clutched in the opposite fingers, she felt ready to defend this fortress and everyone in it—nerves and senses all stretched tight. But when her eyes caught movement at last, out from the lip of the ridge, she lost all her breath in a rush. Someone approached. But who would it be? Magnus and his men, ahead of the attackers?

Or was this Gunnar, and did Magnus lie at the bottom of the ravine?

A thousand thoughts and memories flooded her mind. Magnus, barely a year her junior and a near-constant companion when they were small—laughing, always laughing. Hazel eyes full of light, chasing and teasing her, always there to take her part.

What if she never saw her brother again? How could she go on with such a gaping hole in her life?

"Here they come." Fadir spoke with his eyes closed. Sure enough, shadowy forms now came into sight, struggling as they approached.

"Who is it?" Ragged desperation tore Modir's voice.

It was Kaddi who answered. "Ours. Ours!"

Gyda's relief caused her to stagger. But ja, she

could now see who they were—Fadir's old comrade, Mica, who came supporting a wounded woman. Two others followed after, visibly struggling—a litter improvised from shields carried between them, its burden unrecognizable.

Alive? Or dead?

Others of their warriors came after the injured, barely visible in the poor light.

"Magnus?" Modir called, and Gyda strained to see. Was he there?

Ja. Ja! He came last, his axe still raised. Had he stayed back to fight, making sure the others got away? When he drew near enough, Gyda got a good look at him. Spattered with gore, his face streamed blood from a cut along his hairline. He'd lost his sword, but the cherished axe, its blade wetted, had obviously served him well.

Disregarding everyone else, he sought Fadir's eyes. "We battled them—we battled them at the bridge until the spars fell in. Some of them went with the bridge. But the rest—they're going up and around. They will be here soon."

"How many?"

"Most. Gunnar survived."

Ill news, that—for Gyda, in particular. Would Gunnar come looking to make good on their marriage agreement? Surely not.

Fadir stepped up to Magnus and clasped his shoulder. "Son—are you hurt?"

Surprisingly, Magnus grinned through the blood on his face. "I can still fight, if that is what you ask."

"Go to the caves. Get your wounds tended."

"Fadir, they are not far behind. Who will—"

Fadir's eyes glinted. "I will wait to greet our…guests." He raised his sword.

Magnus did not argue. He moved off, helping others of the wounded.

Fadir looked at Kaddi. "I do not suppose I can ask you to reconsider, and fall back?"

"Nei," Kaddi returned.

Fadir gauged Lodvar with his gaze, but said nothing. Instead he turned to Modir. "Eadha—"

"I will not leave you. Do not ask it of me."

"My love—"

"You waste your breath." She gazed away down the slope. "And I am thinking you will need it."

Following Modir's gaze, Gyda gasped. Was she ready for this?

Ja, Magnus had trained her, but that had been sparring, done among friends. Not true combat—brutal and intense. Life and death.

Many would die this night. Perhaps she would.

Gyda. Lodvar's voice sounded in her head even as he caught her hands and drew her aside to face him. They had only moments—the last they might ever spend together.

Many things might be said. She could feel his emotions, a strong current that matched her own. Instead of speaking aloud, he leaned in and kissed her, the warmth of it flowing through her like life's blood, lending strength.

You do I love, now and forever.

You do I love. Against all likelihood, Gyda's heart rose. *I will see you on the other side of the battle. Wherever that might be.*

****

As a shaman, Lodvar usually stood outside the battle—monitoring the enemy perhaps, or eyeing the forecasts for victory. When Gunnar's men appeared and swarmed up the rise, little more than fierce shadows in the dark, he found himself instead in the thick of it. Unarmed.

Save for his magic.

The fact that he'd once served Gunnar as shaman would not keep the jarl's son from taking his head. Gunnar sought revenge on his father's behalf, but he came also wanting revenge for Lodvar's betrayal.

No one, no one betrayed Gunnar Fritisson and got away with it.

So he spoke the prayer now, into the chaos and the darkness.

Protect her, so do I ask. Or give me the power to protect her. I care far less what happens to me—

He got no farther, even in thought. The shadows that were Gunnar and his followers—mostly Friti's men, or what remained of them—came up and over the rocks. Madness ensued.

He wished immediately, and to his own surprise, that he had a blade. Seldom in the past had he entertained the impulse to use one, but now he felt naked, as the crashing wall of screaming, hollering men broke upon the defenders. Tolljur's people met them, stepping forward with stout courage, Tolljur at the fore.

Even injured and supposedly past his prime, the berserker made an impressive sight, weapons raised, shoulders bulging with muscle, hair flying. Yet Lodvar had seen those wounds he carried. How long could he endure?

Two women flanked him—neither one his wife—

and another warrior near his own age held one side. And Gyda—

In the weird half dusk that surrounded them, only partly lit by torches, he could feel her better than he could see her. He felt the thoughts rushing through her mind, a sensation so disquieting it made it hard for him to breathe. He felt her fear, coupled with determination, and the strength of their connection, proving her love for him.

Beside him, Kaddi began speaking aloud, a chant, an imprecation. The old man stood with his single eye squeezed shut and, in the gloom, power shimmered around him.

Lodvar should do the same—summon what power he could and fashion from it a weapon. Yet how to focus in the face of the crashing, the screaming, the peril? How to protect the men and women falling—for ja, they did fall amid the bellowing and the blood.

Fadir Odin, aid me.

How many of Friti's men had Gunnar brought? He had lost most his own when Tolljur's folk turned upon them. For that, he would blame Lodvar.

Upon that thought, the line of defense broke directly in front of him and he saw Gunnar, golden hair reflecting the torchlight, teeth bared in a grimace, and eyes full of fire. Their gazes met, and Gunnar roared. Bringing up his sword, he slashed at the woman he faced, the blow knocking her down. With a howl of pure fury, he leaped forward.

Straight for Lodvar's head.

Chapter Thirty-Two

"Back. Get back!"

Someone crashed into Lodvar and, by association, Kaddi, nearly knocking the old man off his feet. Suddenly, Gyda was there, imposing herself between them and Gunnar, weapons raised.

Blood already marked her, running down her left arm and trickling from one cheek, a sight that nearly convulsed Lodvar's heart. Never, never had he wanted to protect anyone so strongly. His will rose wildly, in defense of this woman he loved, like a shield—like a wall of flame.

And then there was a wall of flame, springing up between the defenders and the attackers. At least, it looked like flame. It must be real, for the combatants— attackers and defenders alike—leaped back from it and several, who did not move swiftly enough, cried out as if seared.

Gunnar roared in frustration and swept his blade through the flames. His action caused them to leap higher and turn deep blue in color, shot through with silver.

A moment's respite, they offered—only that. Like Lodvar's spike of alarm, they would subside all too soon.

Tolljur, fighting beside his daughter, staggered. Eadha ran to him just as Gyda turned to Lodvar.

"Get back, for the love of Odin," he beseeched her.

She shook her head. Eyes luminous in the garish blue light, she pushed at him with violent hands. "Nei. You fall back behind the rise. Take Kaddi, and use your magic."

Already the blue flames were less. The defenders, with Tolljur at their head, reorganized. The severely wounded were hauled away toward the caves. Others, mostly women, stepped up to take their places.

On the other side of the dying flames, Gunnar continued to roar like a madman. He waved his sword and called to Lodvar.

"Shaman! Shaman, I am coming for you!"

"Lodvar, for my sake," Gyda gusted desperately, "Go. Take Kaddi to safer ground."

That, he might be willing to do. Supporting and half carrying the old man, he started away, only to swing back again and beseech her, "Come with us."

"I will." For a blinding instant, their eyes met. "I will be with you always."

Lodvar's heart protested. A thousand things he wanted to say to her, but he spoke only three words into her mind. *For my sake.*

The fight broke out again behind them as they went. Glancing over his shoulder, Lodvar saw the combatants meet over the remnants of the flames— those born of his love for Gyda.

"Here. No farther," Kaddi demanded when they reached the rocks on the lip above the caves. "I need to see!"

"Ja," Lodvar agreed.

From here, the entire scene lay spread before them like a drawing scratched in sand. Gunnar's attackers did not number so many, but they fought in a determined knot, with the discipline characteristic of Friti's men. Experienced and battle-hardened, they now faced defenders who, other than Tolljur himself and Magnus, consisted mostly of women. Fierce women they were, though. Tolljur's force ranged across the top of the rise, using the stones there for cover.

Yet from Lodvar's point of view, it seemed unlikely they could stand against Gunnar's forces, despite their courage.

Though—maybe they would.

For Tolljur Magnusson, battered and wounded as he might be, stood to the fore of them, sword in hand, an unstoppable force even though he'd not entered his berserker's trance.

The man fought for what he loved. That, Lodvar understood.

His gaze found Gyda, fighting just behind Tolljur and slightly to the rear of her brother. Any attackers who got by Tolljur would face those two.

She fought well and, having felt her body beneath his, Lodvar knew her strength. Not battle-hardened, however. How long might she endure?

A cry went up from the defenders. Tolljur had taken a tremendous blow to the upper chest. Even as Lodvar watched, he wavered and nearly went down.

"Wind!" Kaddi howled beside him. "Boy, call your fire. I will fan the flames."

Almost too distracted to concentrate, Lodvar tore his gaze from Tolljur and closed his eyes, wondering how much punishment human flesh could withstand. And Gyda—now in danger with the shield of her father damaged. Lodvar hated to take his eyes from her, lest she go down.

Yet—he too had to fight. He could feel Kaddi's will, seeking and calling up his own, and then summoning something else again.

The wind began to rise. Unlike the rain Lodvar had brought out of the west, this came from all four corners at once—East, South, West, and North—and met above the place they stood. Little more than eddies at first, they swept this way and that.

The old man grunted in effort, and Lodvar threw his will into the calling. The wind strengthened, collided much like the warriors below, and formed a mighty maelstrom.

In response to the power of it, Lodvar's flames, now all but dead, revived. He felt them leap up and opened his eyes to see a scene transformed.

Something out of a nightmare, it might be. The blue flames turned the faces of everyone below lurid and garish. He saw Gunnar, still at the forefront of his men, vault through the flames and aim another blow at Tolljur, even as many of Friti's men fell back, arms raised to defend their heads against the wind.

Outlined in blue light, Tolljur went down—a mighty tree falling.

Gyda immediately rushed forward into the breech he left, but Gunnar did not meet her with his sword. Instead he knocked her weapon out of the way before grappling with her, catching her body against his and clasping her tight.

Lodvar cried out, losing focus. The flames died and the wind subsided to a hush.

Kaddi hollered at him, "Nei! More!"

Gyda called out also, in Lodvar's mind. *Lodvar,*

Lodvar! He has me. Nei—

A great wave of possessiveness arose within Lodvar. Rampant, it lent him power such as he'd never known. Eyes fixed on the pair struggling at the edge of the blue flames, he directed the wind. It rose once more and, like a spear, darted at Gunnar Fritisson. Struck hard, and with Gyda still in his clutches, Gunnar swayed and trembled.

And spun away.

Nei, nei, nei!

Friti's men closed in behind the departing pair, covering their escape. Tolljur lay still on the ground. Dead? Lodvar could not tell.

Kaddi's hand, a tense claw, clutched at Lodvar's arm.

"More!" demanded. "More."

Their wills joined, Lodvar's with a wall of anger behind it. Once more they raised the wind. It screamed around the stones where they stood, almost knocking the old man down. It scoured the ground where Friti's men fought, giving Tolljur's warriors a chance to drag him back from the fray.

It did not halt Gunnar, who moved steadily away into the darkness with his captive.

Suddenly a new figure emerged from the fray and rushed like a madman to take a stance in front of the fallen Tolljur. For an instant, Lodvar did not recognize him as, lit by the blue flames, his face twisted into a mask of fury.

Indeed, he knew the man by his armor before aught else, and the reddish-brown hair, so like his mother's, that flew out behind him.

Magnus, as might be expected, had stepped out in

defense of his father and sister. But this was a man transformed.

By a berserker's rage.

But—

Gyda had told him her brother did not suffer from his father's affliction, had never fallen into a berserker's fit.

Not until now.

Blood flew from the blade of Magnus's axe as he hacked and swung, making contact with flesh at every blow. Friti's men fell back and back, in Gunnar's wake. Fearless, Magnus charged after them, over the lip and down into the darkness beyond.

Nei, Kaddi hollered in Lodvar's mind. *They will club him down.*

Wind, Lodvar answered.

Wills once more combined, they summoned power from the four directions, reaching their limits and endurance, sending the might of it chasing down the slope to attack Friti's men.

And to halt Gunnar, who made away with Lodvar's heart.

Abruptly, Kaddi's power drained away. Lodvar felt it lessen and nearly stop flowing into him, though the shaman's fingers still clutched his arm. He increased his own effort to the point of anguish, only letting up when the old man's knees buckled, and he went down behind the stones.

The blue flames died, and Lodvar could no longer see what happened below. He heard the fight, led by Magnus, move down the slope.

He sank to his knees at Kaddi's side. Already the wind had subsided, making his ears ring. Deserted by their power, the two shamans were alone.

Lodvar touched Kaddi's face tentatively. The old man's single eye stretched wide, as if he strove to see through the gloom but could perceive nothing. Lodvar, laying tentative fingers beneath the old man's ear, felt no pulse.

Kaddi had given all, and more, in defense of those he loved—like any warrior. He had poured his power into and through Lodvar.

Lodvar bent his head. Above him the sky, swept clean by the powerful winds, revealed a vast field of stars. When he looked up, fighting his emotions, Lodvar saw one shoot across the firmament, brightness burning into infinity.

Kaddi, gone. Tolljur—possibly slain, and Magnus disappeared into the dark.

Gyda gone also—in Gunnar's hands. A fatal blow to Lodvar's heart.

He screamed into the darkness of his mind. *Fadir Odin, help us!*

Chapter Thirty-Three

Blood ran freely down Gyda's cheek; the wound there burned and stung. A second wound at her shoulder seeped blood persistently, but she knew enough about wounds to figure it would not kill her. The rest of her felt battered and bruised, scraped and torn, her knuckles grazed raw.

She had struggled against Gunnar as he dragged her away ahead of that terrible wind, but to little avail. His punishing grip on her arm nearly paralyzed, and he struck her repeatedly, making her head swim. Down the steep slope, with her ears ringing, and out through the water. Hauling her aboard his father's ship, he threw her down onto the oaken deck like so much meal in a sack.

Angry and still raging, he shouted to the men who'd been left aboard. Gyda, scrambling back against the mast, sought desperately to take stock of herself. Gunnar had wrested her sword away from her back at the fortress, but he did not know about the knife secreted deep within her clothing, the one Lodvar had given her.

Lodvar.

She could barely think of him, for the ache of it, could not calm her mind enough to reach for him.

Had he survived that terrible battle? The ravening wind... Fadir, going down—dead? And Magnus, ach,

Magnus…her brother, in a berserker's rage.

Nothing like that had ever occurred before, not to him. As a family, they'd believed Magnus safe from the gift—or curse, as Fadir termed it—of the berserker's fit. Ja, Magnus had told her he sometimes felt the impulse pull at him. She had not truly believed it. Magnus so rarely fell into anger for any reason.

Like Modir's father, so Modir always said. A strong yet measured man.

Yet a berserker's fit did not truly qualify as anger, did it? Even though some folk called it a rage, it was actually battle-madness.

And Fadir's blood did run through Magnus's veins.

From where she huddled on the deck of Friti's ship, she strained to look across the short stretch of water. Impossible to tell what happened so far off, though she fancied she caught the flicker of blue flames from the heights.

Lodvar had fought with that flame—and the wind also. She'd felt the power build in him, and felt it unleash.

Men fought for what they loved. Fadir—her heart skipped a beat. Magnus. Lodvar.

Finished with bawling at his guards, Gunnar stood at the side of the ship, also gazing over the side to the land. Did he wait for the rest of his father's men to arrive? What would he do when they did? Cast anchor and sail away into the darkness of the wide ocean?

Take her away from everything she loved? Would she ever see this place again?

Once more, she fought to calm herself, and reached for Lodvar with her mind. *My love?*

No reply. She caught just a faint echo from him,

weighted by grief, before Gunnar swung about and marched back to her.

"So—your brother is berserker, just like your father. You hid that secret well."

Gyda gathered her limbs and her will, preparing to move if he tried to strike her again. He looked very much like he wanted to. "I did not know."

"You expect me to believe that?" he spat. "I do not. But it is interesting." He inspected her slowly, his gaze lingering in one or two places. "If it runs so strongly in the blood, I might well breed a berserker from you."

Several of his men, who had followed him down from the battle and splashed aboard, turned their heads, listening. Gyda tried to disguise her horror. Did he mean to take her—rape her—here and now, in front of everyone?

The hard and vengeful gleam in his eye said he might.

"A berserker," he pursued, "makes a fine weapon—as we have just seen. Even if you have to wait for him to grow up."

"Would you use your own child so? As a weapon?" Gyda hated that her voice cracked, as if broken. Not fear, she told herself. That was grief.

Several more of Friti's men climbed aboard, shedding blood and water.

One of them gasped, "The berserker—Tolljur Magnusson—still lives."

Gunnar turned to regard him. "And the other berserker? His son?"

"Alive also, with that axe of his still in his hand. By Odin's eye, he did some damage."

Gyda's heart leaped, even as Gunnar agreed, "So

he did. But we have a weapon of our own now." He aimed a vicious kick at Gyda's legs. Hastily, she drew them in tight, out of his reach.

A terrible smile spread across his face. "My lovely bride to be."

"Nei." Gyda reacted instantly to deny it.

He hunkered down beside her. His golden hair had come loose during the attack and hung down, wet with blood. More blood marked his face—spatters, and not his own. Gyda could only wonder whose. A jagged wound, to which he gave no heed, traced the length of his left arm, and blood seeped at his shoulder.

Softly, almost conversationally, he said, "You gave me your word, Gyda Tolljursdottir. You pledged to wed with me. Do you mean to go back on that promise?"

Gyda gazed into his eyes—handsome eyes, wide and blue, they should have been filled with light. Instead, spite glinted there, like the spark off a honed blade.

"It seems you and the members of your family need to learn a lesson, eh? About keeping your word, and about loyalty to those you are sworn to serve. Ach, I have heard the stories. Have you? My father and yours were once the foremost among my grandfather's warriors. As his future jarl, Tolljur owed my father his allegiance. His respect. Instead, he—and that bitch of a mother of yours—destroyed Fadir in Grandfather's eyes. Nothing—nothing was ever the same."

"Ja, I have heard the stories. Your father tried to kill mine."

"There is a brotherhood among warriors. At least, there should be. Tolljur switched his loyalty to an Alban slave."

"He loved her." Gyda lifted her chin. "Will you sneer even at love?"

He laughed. "Love is a weapon, like any other, and meant for the weak. But I admit—I might fall in love with you. Would you like that?"

Gyda, desperate to disguise her reaction, said nothing.

Reaching out with a blood-spattered hand, he touched her cheek. "A pity you have torn your face. But you are still beautiful, one of the loveliest women I have ever seen. Tell me you will keep your vow and become my bride. Do so, and I will sail away from here and leave your father's holding be. For now."

He leaned in, so close his breath skittered across Gyda's face. She could smell the blood and sweat on him, and feel his banked emotion.

He meant to kiss her. She dared not let him see her flinch. Carefully, she asked, "You vow to sail away, if I agree to come with you?"

"Ja, back to Husavik. There we shall start a new dynasty, and lead like a king and queen—we will reign over everything. You need only keep your word."

She need only keep her word. Leave her home here. Doom herself and agree to endure life with this monster for always.

To save all she loved, she need only sacrifice all she loved, including Lodvar.

Lodvar.

Again, she called to him with her mind, with her will, with her heart.

Had he fallen, back there at the fortress? If he had, then ja—she might as well make this hideous bargain and sail away with Gunnar. She could perhaps spare her family more hurt, and anyway, her heart would be dead.

Suddenly, clear as the cry of a tern across the distances, she heard his voice in her mind. *My love*. Sweat broke out all over her body and, had she not already been on the deck, relief would have knocked her down.

Again she strove to hide her reaction from the man who crouched so close to her.

"Like a king and queen, you say?" She pretended to muse. "I have never seen Husavik, but I have heard much, and that it is very grand."

"My grandfather's hall would make your father's dwelling seem a sty. It will all be mine—ours. With Fadir out of the way, there is naught to stop me. I"—he struck his chest—"will be jarl."

Gyda squeezed her eyes shut, unable to face the avarice that consumed him. What should she say? She wished she knew what was happening back on the heights. If Fadir and Magnus had survived, as Friti's men insisted, would they mount a rescue? With her here aboard Friti's ship, was a rescue possible?

Again she sought Lodvar with her mind. But now she encountered only a wave of grief.

Leaning still closer, Gunnar whispered, "Whether you agree or nei, you are going back to Husavik with me. And one way or another, I will beget the next berserker on you. The world, Gyda Tolljursdottir, lies in the palm of my hand."

Chapter Thirty-Four

"Gunnar Fritisson has my søstir. We must go after her. I will not leave Gyda in that bastard's hands."

Magnus did not speak loudly, but he captured the attention of all around him. In the wake of the battle, it had gone quiet, with the wind and the flames died away and dark gathering above the caves. Above, in the vault of the sky, stars looked down, like bright eyes.

The quiet also allowed Lodvar to hear the sound of sobbing. Tolljur's wife, Eadha, wept over Kaddi's lifeless body, stretched out between the stones where he'd fallen after lending Lodvar all his power for that final spell. Lodvar had felt it drain from him, along with his life, flowing swiftly through his own body and transforming into burning, searing light.

No doubt it was the way Kaddi—or any true shaman—would choose to die, a warrior at his apex. But now he lay broken as a scattering of brittle bones bound by frail flesh. And grief ran rampant.

Tolljur, who certainly should not be on his feet, moved forward and laid his hand on Magnus's shoulder. The berserker's skin ran with blood. Covered in wounds, he made a gory sight.

"Son, I understand how you feel." Wonder flared in Tolljur's eyes. "The battle madness is not easy to endure and leaves a man—shattered. Scarred and changed. Give yourself a moment—"

"My søstir has been taken." Magnus's eyes looked too wide, his voice that of a drunken man. He still clutched the stained axe in his hand, as if unable to put it down.

Ach, what he had done with that axe—Lodvar did not want to recall it, did not expect to forget.

Gently, Tolljur turned his son to face him. "We will rescue your søstir. Do not doubt that. But first, tell me, did you know the fury lurked within you?"

Magnus blinked at him. He shook his head slightly, and droplets of blood flew from him. "Nei. And ja. There was something inside—something that asked me to give in. But a man learns to handle his anger. You taught me that."

"Ja."

"They cut you down, Fadir. They attacked everything I love. And Gyda—"

"Ja, son, I know." Tolljur's face twisted with emotion. "Kaddi lies dead—he who was like a father to me."

"And to me." Eadha's voice drifted to them, choked with weeping. She lifted her face from the old man's hand, clasped in hers.

Magnus said, "We can do nothing for Kaddi. My søstir needs us. I will not leave her in the hands of Gunnar Fritisson."

"Nor I." Lodvar stepped forward to Magnus's side. "If you go after your søstir, I will go with you."

Magnus, still possessed by the remnants of his berserker's rage, covered with blood and wounds, eyed him up and down. "You?"

"Me." Lodvar lifted his chin. "She is mine to defend, as much as yours."

"How is that, Shaman? She is my søstir."

"She possesses my heart, and I hers."

Magnus stared. Lodvar felt him emerge from his fit—his first ever—and picked up clearly on the remnants of the glory, the exhilaration, the confusion. "What can you do?" he challenged.

"Who do you think called up those flames?"

"Kaddi."

"Him, and me."

Magnus gusted a breath. He gazed away down the slope toward the bay where lay Friti's ships, as if measuring his chances. When his gaze returned to Lodvar, it held acceptance. "Ja, I will go get my søstir. You come with me. I want Gyda to know she is not forsaken."

"That you may safely leave to me."

****

Lodvar sat, with his legs crossed and his eyes tight closed, on the cliff high above the shore. The night swiftly faded, and below lay Friti's two moored ships, where Gunnar, with Gyda and all his father's remaining men, had withdrawn. Around Lodvar stood the men and women of Tolljur's settlement, well-armed and determined.

He clenched his fingers together on his knee. Never before had he found it so difficult to concentrate and reach beyond himself—to contact Gyda, just below.

Well, there had been that time after his father beat him soundly for failing to lower his eyes when his betters spoke to him.

Betters—ha!

"You are a slave," Harald had told him, landing the first blow across Lodvar's face. "Do not get big ideas.

You will do yourself no favors."

What were big ideas? What was above his place? The gods spoke to him, sent him messages and power beyond measure. They had made of him something more than a by-blow and a slave. They had given him the ability to speak with the woman who owned his heart, mind to mind. Only now—now he could not.

He ached from head to foot. The gods, nei, did not give without taking. The same whiplash of exhaustion that had cost Kaddi's life had scoured him also. Ja, well, he'd hurt after his father beat him, too. And still he'd fallen into a vision of Odin, walked with the father god, and spoken with him.

What do you want from life, boy?

Her. I want her, only. Even then, Gyda had haunted his mind. He merely had not known who or where she was.

The old god laughed. Pacing beside Lodvar, he looked like an ordinary traveler, his hood shadowing his face. *A woman? You would pin all your hopes on that?* He sounded almost teasing.

Not just a woman. She is the other part of me.

Ja, I know. You, my son, walk only lightly in this world.

You mean, in Husavik?

With a laugh, Odin told him, *I mean Midgardr. You keep one foot in Asgardr, in the highest of Yggdrasill's branches. Not an easy way to live. But I think you are up to the challenge, eh?*

When will I find her? When will she be with me?

When you find and claim your strength, and understand how to wield it.

Sitting on the cliff with the light of a new day

hanging on the horizon, Lodvar unfolded his hands. He would not reach Gyda by straining or by forcing a connection.

He would reach her by believing—as he had always believed.

My love. He sent the call out through the murky morning light with confidence. *Gyda!*

Lodvar. The reply came almost at once. And then he reached her, able to speak to her mind and heart.

Are you hurt? Has he harmed you?

Nei. Just these minor wounds—

Are you with him? Aboard Friti's ship? Which one?

Closest to my father's boats. I am trying to convince Gunnar—

You can convince him of nothing. Trust him in nothing. Can you get away?

Nei. He guards me.

Your brother and I are coming for you.

Lodvar, my heart, I beg you, nei. Do not risk yourself—

Do not ask me to leave you in his hands. How many men are on board?

Perhaps a score. Enough.

Gunnar—how badly injured is he?

I cannot tell. He carries wounds but disregards them. My father—

Injured, but on his feet.

And Magnus—I saw him fall into the berserker's fit. We did not know—

He will come for you, as will I. Believe.

I do believe in you, my love, and in him. But listen—I can deal with Gunnar, convince him to bargain with me. If I tell him I will honor our betrothal, I may be able to save you all.

Nei, Gyda.

But—

Nei. You are my bride. Sworn to me.

Now and always. No matter what happens.

Always, Lodvar repeated, and arose from the clifftop.

****

Tolljur found them there on the rise overlooking the bay, with daylight washing in all around them. Limping, and favoring his right arm, he approached Lodvar and thrust a long, twisted staff into his hands.

"Take this. It belonged to Kaddi."

Lodvar recoiled. The old man's body, barely cold, had been lovingly shrouded and moved into the caves before they left, Tolljur taking part despite his horrific wounds. Now grief filled his eyes, and heavy certainty. "Nei, I cannot. It is part of him."

"Ja," Tolljur agreed. "I cannot remember him without it. But I think it still holds the last of his power. That makes it a weapon, and one you may need if you are to rescue my dottir."

With a nod, Lodvar accepted the staff. It tingled between his fingers, and tickled the palm of his hand. "Power—ja."

Tolljur said, "It grieves me more than I can say, losing Kaddi. But you will bring Gyda home." He smiled unexpectedly, amid his scars and blood. "It will be good, having another shaman in the family."

Not until Tolljur walked away did Lodvar realize what had just happened. The berserker had given him his blessing.

Chapter Thirty-Five

"Did you expect that to happen? To fall into the berserker's fit, I mean."

Lodvar asked the question of Magnus as they hunkered down side by side at the edge of the cliffs, eyes on the ships below. Most of Friti's surviving men, with Gunnar and Gyda, had retreated to the boat on the right, closest to Tolljur's vessels. Only a few guards and a shrouded form that might have been Friti's corpse, well-wrapped, remained on the other ship.

Gunnar had set guards at the edge of the water. They looked nervous and continually scanned the clifftops, keeping Magnus and his company low to the ground. They should be nervous, Lodvar thought, even as he probed the deck of the ship for any sight of Gyda. He could not see her but knew she was there.

Magnus shot him a look. It did not appear entirely friendly. For all his efforts, Lodvar could not quite decide what Magnus thought of him. But Tolljur had left it in their hands—his and Magnus's—as to when and how to attack the long boats. Tolljur numbered one of the company, ja—nothing, including Eadha's arguments, could hold him back. Yet he left leadership to his son.

Magnus, as anyone including Tolljur could tell, had set himself the mission of rescuing his sister and would let nothing get in his way. Determination fairly shone from him, and he'd barely taken time to wash the blood of the last battle from his face and hands. The handle of his axe still bore a tracing of blood.

He gestured with the weapon before he replied. The axe seemed part of him, as if it shared his intent. "Is this a time for idle talk?"

"Far from idle. I need to know whether I can expect it to happen again."

Magnus closed his eyes briefly. "By all the gods, I hope not."

If Magnus had been Lodvar's friend, as well as Gyda's brother, Lodvar might ask him what it felt like, falling into the fit. The toll it had taken showed clearly in Magnus's eyes, and the wounds that marked him.

Maybe Lodvar did not need to ask.

Magnus gestured with the axe again. "But I will suffer ten fits if it will win my søstir back to us." He stole another look at Lodvar. "Just so long as you know—I will take apart any man who ever hurts her, bone by bone."

"That is reassuring. Just so you know, I will never hurt her. I have loved her most of my life."

"How is that, when you have just met her?"

"It has to do with the realm of spirit and magic."

Magnus grunted. "Just what we need, another accursed shaman. I loved Kaddi, do not mistake me. But such men are forever giving advice they cannot back up with the sword."

"Shamans and berserkers—you must admit, it is a daunting combination."

"They have walked together a long time. I never thought I'd live to see my søstir choose a shaman for a mate. To be sure, I never expected to become berserker, either." Magnus nodded at the bay. "Before we go down there, what help are you able to give me?"

Lodvar bent his gaze on the water. Deep blue near the horizon, it took on a shade of green closer in where the ships rode. What could he do? His efforts in tandem with Kaddi had left him depleted. If he tried to whip up another storm, how successful might he be?

He would need to work with the power that already lay beneath the surface of that ocean, call upon it to serve him.

"Waves. I can give you waves."

"Waves?" Magnus repeated doubtfully.

"Mighty ones."

"Enough to overset the boats?"

"Perhaps."

"We need to persuade Gunnar to release Gyda, first of all. None of this will be any use if he decides to slit her throat."

Lodvar's life would be no use, if that happened. Ja, his body might march on into a future dark with hopelessness. His spirit would wither and die.

He nodded, suddenly grim. "I can persuade them off the boats and onto the shore."

"Where I and the others will slaughter them." To Lodvar's surprise, Magnus extended his hand. Lodvar clasped it, and could feel his strength.

"So we work together. For Gyda."

"For Gyda."

Trial by fire, and no mistake. Or should that be trial by water? Lodvar balanced on the balls of his feet, and regarded the bay. A glance behind told him Tolljur and the others from the settlement who had come to fight regarded him with cautious curiosity. Turning back to the sea, he carefully narrowed his focus, striving hard to shut out the feelings of fear and desperation. Those emotions would not serve him now. Even making contact with Gyda would not serve him.

Closing his eyes, he sought for the currents running deep beneath the green water, and even deeper beneath the blue. Untapped power lay there—a swirling wealth of it—and his heart leaped in hope.

Kaddi's gnarled staff, now laid across his knees, jerked and quivered in his hands.

Raising it, he spoke aloud. "Waters that feed Yggdrasill, blood that nourishes root, leaf, and stem, might of the maelstrom, power of the deep, and favor of all the gods, flow to me."

The staff jumped violently in his hand. Power flowed in from the direction of the sea, through the ground, up through stone and the twisted wooden column.

Ash wood, just like Yggdrasill itself. Behind him, he heard those who waited to fight with Magnus exclaim. He opened his eyes.

Far out in the deep blue of the ocean, the water stirred. Where it had been still as glass, a swell rose, slow as the back of a breeching whale, and a hundred times more powerful. Narrowing his eyes against his wonder, and the power that now filled him, Lodvar watched it come. In from the horizon it rolled, growing ever higher as it neared. Behind it, a second wave, this one topped with a crest of white foam, and beyond that still another.

Magnus swore. "Come," he called to Tolljur and the rest of his attackers. "We will be ready, ja, when they tumble over into the brine."

He glanced at Lodvar. "I will bring her back."

"Bring her to me." *And*, Lodvar beseeched the gods, *keep her safe.*

****

Gyda, look out!

The cry sounded clear in Gyda's mind. She knew the voice—her heart did—for it had become anchored in her very spirit.

An instant later, she felt the swell lift the boat. She'd spent time enough aboard her father's vessels, from a young age, to become attuned to the temperaments of the sea. Now, what had once been calm turned angry and wild.

Lodvar, Lodvar, is this your doing?

Hold on fast!

No other reply, yet she could already feel the well-built deck of oaken planks beneath her feet begin to tilt. The men on board cried out, and Gunnar, who had been sitting forward and watching his guards on the shore, leaped to his feet.

Gyda seized hold of the nearest line, one of those that ran down from the mast. Gunnar had tethered her there so he might not need to set a guard on her, but he'd bound her hands in front of her, and she wound her fingers into the rope.

All around them, men began to exclaim and swear. Several called Gunnar's name. Others gazed away over the side, toward the mouth of the bay.

Turning her head, Gyda followed their gazes. There, far out to sea, and racing at incredible speed, came a series of waves, one behind the other, bearing down upon the row of anchored ships.

The breath caught in Gyda's throat, and her eyes

stretched wide. The sea seemed to rise above their heads, first blue, then deep green, threatening to crash down upon them. If the boat overturned, tethered as she was, she could drown.

Fadir Odin, she whispered swiftly, *save me*.

The men began to scramble across the deck, nearly crashing into her as they sought for some handhold or toehold. Leaving go of her grip on the line, Gyda thrust her bound hands into her skirt, fingers searching, searching. She found the hilt of Lodvar's knife and extracted it hastily. She had precious little time to free herself before the first of those waves hit. Awkward as it might be to wield the knife with bound hands, her life depended on it.

The first wave hit. Had it taken them broadside, they surely would have been swamped. But Fadir always anchored his boats prow facing to the land, and when Friti arrived, he had anchored alongside them. Gunnar's boat, she knew, was still hidden farther along the coast.

Now, nearly in unison, the four dragons tilted, their tails rising high above their carved heads, their oak beams flexing almost as true living beings might.

Men bellowed. Gyda, still bound to the mast, slid along the oak planks as if weightless, only to be brought up by her bonds. In the mad rush, one or two of Friti's remaining men went over the prow.

Built to weather the open seas, the boat settled back down, falling into the trough between the first wave and the next.

The next.

Salt spray blinded Gyda so she could not see. But she felt the swell rise up beneath the rear of the boat.

Madly, she clung to Lodvar's knife, now clutched in numbed fingers. Thanks be to Freya she had not dropped it.

She heard shouts from the shore, a wild bellowing that sounded like challenge, and clawed her way up. Blinking hair and water from her eyes, she saw her brother on the shingle, engaged in battle with Gunnar's guards. Others stood with him, ready to dispatch any of Friti's men who abandoned the boats.

Her eyes found another figure there. His dark blue robe billowed out behind him on the breath from the water. He held a tall staff in one hand. The other he had raised high, as if in command, and he stared straight out toward the boats.

No, to her.

He it was who summoned the waves.

Ach, if she could only free herself and get over the side before the next wave struck, she might reach him. Then Magnus and the others would finish the fight, there on their own holy shore.

If she had time.

Frantic, she plied the knife again. It slipped, and the blade sliced the skin of her forearm. Stout leather thongs Gunnar had used to secure her. Yet Lodvar's blade proved equal to the task. She cut through one of the ties before Lodvar's voice sounded in her head.

Watch out!

Instinctively, she looked over her shoulder. The wave loomed behind the tail of the ship like a blue mountain. With an agonized gasp, Gyda threw her arms around the mast and hung on.

Whatever else happened, she must keep hold of the knife.

This time, the dragon groaned as its back end rose high over its head. Still half-tethered to the mast, Gyda wondered what would happen if it twisted and shattered and came to pieces around her.

Eyes clenched fiercely shut, she screamed. The tremendous wave passed under the boat, which leaped beneath her.

Please, Fadir Odin, let me survive so I might be with him.

It is up to you, girl, whether you survive.

Odin sounded an awful lot like Kaddi. Gyda's eyes flew open in time to see men flying from the boat like fleas from a wetted hound.

With another groan, the boat once more settled. Someone crashed into Gyda—hard—and clutched at her with hands strong as iron. Trying to save himself? Ach, but it hurt, that impact.

Had it jarred the knife from her fingers?

The man raised a sopping, tangled head and looked at her. His face, contorted by an evil grimace, might have been unrecognizable. But she knew him by those sky-blue eyes.

Her betrothed, Gunnar Fritisson.

Chapter Thirty-Six

"Let go of me." Gyda spoke in a low voice, as if they shared an intimate conversation. "Your fight is done. You have no chance against him."

"Him?" Dangerous light flickered in Gunnar's eyes. "Your brother?"

"Nei. I speak of Lodvar Haraldsson."

"Traitor." Gunnar spat the word. "Before this is over, I will carve out his heart and feast on it."

"Do you not feel how powerful he is?" Gyda should hold the words that tumbled from her, she should for Lodvar's sake, but they came far too fast. "Who do you think it is who calls up the power of the seas? He has the favor of the gods, and that is—"

"And I have you. My passage away from here, so I think."

Before Gyda could reply, the next wave hit. She gasped, thinking to be torn from Gunnar's grip, but he'd locked his arms around both her and the mast.

Trapped, with no hope of escape, she hollered in her mind, *Lodvar, I cannot get away.*

No reply. Above the groans of the tortured planks, she could hear the battle on the shore. It sounded like a slaughter. Lodvar was there, and Magnus. She need only get away—

To Lodvar.

Yet he might as well be separated from her by an

ocean.

She blinked the water from her lashes and glared into Gunnar's bloodshot blue eyes.

"Let me go, and he may spare your life."

"Magnus?" Gunnar asked again. "You think I fear—"

"Lodvar, and you should fear him." Gyda felt the power streaming from the man on the shore, the man she loved. It filled her as it filled the sea, called her as it called up the waves.

What wouldn't she do to be with him? Her other half, her place of spiritual belonging, her one true home.

"Gunnar, Gunnar!" One of Friti's men came by and slammed into the two of them, crushing Gyda against the mast. "What to do? They are slaughtering our men in the tide. They are wading in after us."

Gunnar glanced into Gyda's face before he replied. "Kill the shaman. Without him, they cannot succeed."

"It cannot be done." The man's eyes stared out of his head, his face streaked with seawater and blood. "No one can get near him. And our other ship—it is all but destroyed."

Gyda's gaze flew to Gunnar's. Friti's corpse had been aboard that ship, destined for an honorable funeral.

"Leave it. Cast off the anchor. Do we have enough men to sail?"

"I do not know!"

"See to it."

Suddenly, a painful tug came at Gyda's wrist. Gunnar had broken the second of her bonds.

With brutal strength, he dragged her to the prow of

the boat, hard up against the carved dragon.

Bobbing wildly in the wake of the last great wave, he drew her up so they balanced perilously.

"Shaman!" Gunnar called out. "Shaman, do you want to see her die?"

Gyda? Out of the madness and the wild waves, Lodvar's concern came rushing. *Gyda!*

"Call off the attack. Call it off and still those waters—or she dies."

Everyone on the shore froze. For an instant they looked like mere carvings of men with white foam roiling around them—Magnus, his axe still raised, his body spattered with blood. Others of his warriors, men and women Gyda knew from childhood. The dead lying about their feet in heaps. Lodvar.

Lodvar.

Not a large man, he nevertheless exuded power—the same Kaddi always seemed to command—that elevated him. In response to Gunnar's call, he waded out through the water, as if he wanted to face Gunnar at the prow of the boat. He stopped when the waves broke at his chest.

"Gunnar, let her go. Let her go, and I will let you live."

Gunnar laughed. "You think to defeat me? You, a slave?"

The aftermath of the last wave hit Lodvar, floating his blue cloak out around him like dark wings. Spray wetted his hair. His face held an unearthly calm.

Yet Gyda could feel what lay beneath that composed surface, shared the wild protest that beat in his heart, his fear and desperate love for her.

"Call me what you will, Gunnar Fritisson. The

gods are against you. You cannot prevail."

"I can, so long as I have this prize. Wife or hostage—it makes little difference now. She will bear the next berserker, and he will be my son."

Lodvar met Gyda's gaze. *I will not let him take you from me.*

No one can ever take me from you. Yet Gunnar could drag her off, sail with her far across the sea. He could rape her, force his seed upon her, keep her forever from the one she loved. What torment would it be to hold Lodvar forever in her heart, speak to him in her mind, long for him, but never, never be free?

The thought made her dizzy. It started a low buzzing in her blood, a wave of rising anger strong as the waves Lodvar commanded. Her heart began to hammer overtime. Her skin flushed and her limbs trembled.

She twisted in Gunnar's grip. "Leave go of me."

"Ach, nei." Gunnar sneered. "I have told you, you are my passage out of here."

He called to Lodvar. "Calm the waters, and she lives. Call up another wave, and I will snap her neck where she stands."

His fingers curled around Gyda's throat. Curiously, the strong grip—tight enough to constrict her breathing—caused her no fear. Courage—or was it something else?—streamed through her, an elemental force.

Gunnar called to his men, "Cast off! Those of you who can, row. Row!"

"Master Gunnar," one of Friti's men protested, "your father's ship—"

"We will return and settle this score," Gunnar

replied before shouting to Magnus, who rushed up through the water to stand at Lodvar's side, "We shall avenge my father and slaughter all those who stood against us. And I will dine on the shaman's black heart."

Nei. The fury inside Gyda exploded in a maelstrom of protective love. For an instant in time, she stopped breathing. Her emotions consumed her, and the world turned white.

White it was when she glared into Gunnar's face— as if bleached out by a blinding sun. The heat came from her rage, all-commanding, and no sun ever burned so bright. She could no longer hear anything except the rushing in her ears. No voices, no waves—not even Lodvar's voice in her mind.

The beat of her heart, in time with her pulsating rage, was all.

Gunnar's gaze, first startled and then horrified, connected with hers. His eyes widened, and his lips moved, but she could not hear what he said.

His fingers tightened around her throat. She could not breathe. She did not need to.

The rage was all.

With casual strength, she broke Gunnar's grip on her and shoved him off. Not far—he still clung to her, the two of them trapped there beside the carved prow of the boat.

She wanted to strike that dragon down and use a piece of it to spear Gunnar's heart. Instead, she bared her teeth at him and flexed this new, scorching strength.

Within the folds of her skirt, her fingers again found what she wanted.

"Die," she told Gunnar through the wild humming

in her head. *Die.*

Lodvar's knife, so firm in her fingers, entered Gunnar's body just below the heart, and surged upward.

Warm blood ran over Gyda's hands. Gunnar stared into her eyes, shocked. He opened his mouth again to speak, and blood dribbled out.

The fury filling Gyda would not relent. She drove Lodvar's blade deeper, still hauling it upward, the handle clutched in both her hands, until it encountered bone. The white-hot mist rose and consumed her vision.

Gyda.

Like the pealing of a bell, Lodvar's voice cut through the pulsing mist, calling, calling for her attention.

Gyda! My love.

Love.

She repeated the word. Slowly, slowly the mist began to abate, and then to clear. She turned her face from Gunnar who, wedged between her and the prow, remained upright. Struggling to see through the remnants of her rage, she looked shoreward.

There—she saw her brother, Magnus, an expression such as she'd never beheld on his face. And there, with the sea foaming all around him, the other half of her world, of her being. Her home. Her love.

She tumbled from the front of the ship and into the sea.

Chapter Thirty-Seven

Without a thought for his own safety, Lodvar splashed forward through the sea. The turmoil inside him—the berserker's rage that he'd experienced right along with Gyda, by extension—fell away, consumed by his fear for her. For now he could feel nothing from her. *Nothing.*

A berserker's rage, and she a woman. Had it killed her? Was she dead?

He reached her in four bounds. Magnus came after him, barely a step behind, and when Friti's men poured over the side of the ship, Magnus set about with that great axe of his, affording Lodvar a chance to pluck Gyda from the sea.

She floated face down, her hair making an ashen cloud.

He turned her over, letting the swells bear her up, and looked into her face—stark white. Her eyes stared, open and sightless. He could catch no trace of her thoughts, no hint of her spirit.

Desperate and frantic, he called with both his mind and heart. *Gyda. Love. Come awake to me. Come awake.* She did not stir.

All around them, Magnus and his attackers battled the last of Friti's men. No time to waste. Dead or living, Lodvar wanted Gyda out of the battle.

He gathered her up in his arms, the way he might a

child, and with Kaddi's staff tucked beneath his arm, bore her landward.

Behind him, the storm of his emotions raised a like storm from the sea. An eddy formed, gathering power as it swirled. It turned Friti's boat—no longer anchored—side landward.

Magnus hollered. Everyone—Magnus's warriors and Friti's alike—abandoned the sea, now a roiling cauldron.

Ignoring what occurred behind him, and the slaughter that littered the shore, Lodvar stretched Gyda on the rocks.

Hair and clothing clung to her. She could not look more lifeless. Skin like alabaster. Eyes, like gray mist, that did not see him.

A shadow hovered over him. Magnus. "Does she breathe?"

"I do not know." Wetness—not that of the spray—trickled down Lodvar's face. He'd learned long ago not to cry. Not at beatings, and not at injustice. But now his heart had been torn from him. No way to halt the tears.

Magnus crouched down beside his sister. For the first time, he released the bloodied axe, placing it on the stones. "That was a berserker's fit, I know. She took the fit."

"Ja."

"A woman."

"A berserker's daughter." Who would have thought the gift—the curse—could travel down the female line? Lodvar had never heard the like, not even in legend.

"The desire to defend us sent her over. It was love." Magnus touched Gyda's cheek. "Shaman, talk to your gods. Tell them they cannot take her yet."

Lodvar would, if he could. He would bargain away his own life in exchange for hers, if the gods agreed to it. The prospect of remaining in the world without her frightened him far more than death.

He took her hand in both of his. Perhaps if he poured his strength and his will into her, spending all of what he was to bring her to life again...

Behind him, the ocean quieted. With the fringes of his attention, he noticed that people—Tolljur's people—came in from the edge of the water and down from the cliff to stand around him, both Tolljur and Eadha among them.

The berserker loomed above his daughter, and Eadha threw herself down on the rocks. She reached for Gyda, but halted when she saw that Lodvar held her hand.

"What happened?" Tolljur wheezed.

"Fadir, she took a fit. The berserker's fit."

Tolljur stared. "Nei. It is not possible."

"It is." Eadha's pain sounded in her voice. "She is a warrior—like you, Tolljur—to her heart."

Tolljur bent and pressed his fingers beneath Gyda's ear. "Her heart still beats. Wife—call her. Speak to your gods. Bid them send our lass back to us."

Turning her head, Eadha gazed into Lodvar's eyes. "I do not have that power. But I know who does."

Lodvar shook his head. "My power is all spent."

"Perhaps," Eadha replied. "But your love, I think, is not. Tell me, Shaman, is your love for Gyda not deep enough?"

Deep it was, deep as his life, as his breath, as his will to live. For an instant, he continued to gaze into Eadha's eyes, bright with golden light. Clutching

Gyda's fingers, he bent his head. Seeking, seeking...

He might ask the gods, ja. He might seek to bargain with them once again, beg them to take his life in exchange for Gyda's. Would the gods, though, consider that a fair exchange? A shaman for a warrior destined for the halls of Valhalla? He had no doubt she was destined to be there one day.

Not yet.

Better, he thought, to ask the voice that had been so long in his mind, in his heart. She who had accompanied him always on some level, from boyhood, through every difficulty, and whom he'd encountered here, of all places, on these stark rocks amid the blue sea.

Heed me, my love. Be with me. Let us walk together for a time in this world. Return to me and be my bride.

Abruptly, Gyda's fingers jerked in his. Magnus gasped, and a sob broke from Eadha's throat. When Lodvar opened his eyes, he encountered Gyda's gaze, bright and lucid.

"Forgive me," she croaked.

"Forgive you?" Lodvar repeated the words through wooden lips. "For what?"

"I think I lost your knife. In the sea."

****

Bitter liquid dribbled into Gyda's mouth and found its way into the back of her throat, making her choke and spit.

"Ugh! What is this? Do you try to poison me?"

Calmly, her father responded, "Nei, Dottir. This will help restore your strength. Trust me."

Opening her eyes, she pushed the cup away and struggled to sit up.

She was home, in Fadir's house. The familiar furnishings of the dwelling fell into their assigned places all round her, just as the pieces of memory began to reassemble in her mind.

The battle. The struggle aboard Friti's boat. The terrible rage that had fired inside her.

Gunnar.

She hurt all over, as if she'd been thrashed from head to toe. Indeed, she felt as if she'd been pounded against the rocks of the shore as with a giant flail. Even her skin hurt.

But the longhouse looked dim and quiet—as if a struggle for survival had never taken place. The fire burned low, and she sensed—

She sensed that the darkness, which had swept in so fiercely across the water, had gone.

Seeking her father's eyes, she struggled to form words. Her tongue felt too big for her mouth, and her lips ached. "That tastes terrible."

Fadir chuckled. "I know. It will help, though, so I do assure you."

She reached out, and he took her hand. He sat beside her with his back to the fire, making a large silhouette. She could not see what lay in his eyes, but she felt his strength, solid as bedrock.

"What happened?"

"You fell into a berserker's rage."

"Ja." Gyda grappled with it. Not something that ever happened to women. Not something she'd ever expected to happen to her. "Like you."

"Ja."

"Like—like Magnus."

For an instant, Fadir said nothing. Then he grunted.

"All my life, I dreaded begetting another like myself. I did not want the responsibility for bringing into the world a child who would have to carry my burden. Then you were born—a lass—and my fears calmed. When Magnus arrived scarcely a year later, a boy—" He shook his head. "How I worried for him! But he took so strongly after his mother, even as you took after me." Tenderly, he touched Gyda's cheek. "Your mother said he looked much like her father, even as you look like my søstir. The years passed and never—never a hint of anything."

"Until now."

"Until now."

Wonder filled Gyda, along with regret. Having experienced the sting and bite, the helpless rage of the fit, she understood why this man—so gentle at his heart—would choose to spare her from it, if he could.

She whispered, "I think we never had cause to experience our rage before this. You were always there, standing strong to defend us. When the time came, could we do anything but stand, also, in defense of those we love?"

"Love." Tolljur repeated it softly. "That is something your mother taught me. There is no greater power in this world nor, so I believe, the next. It alone can defeat pain and fear. It alone can reach beyond the boundaries of death."

"Magnus—has he recovered?"

"Magnus has the strength of ten bulls. He will be fine."

"And you?"

"Likewise, I will be fine. Have I not faced one of my worst nightmares, and seen my children come through the torment I would spare them? Another lesson learned. I need to trust in your strength, the both of you."

Gyda drew a breath. "Lodvar—where is he?"

"He sleeps. Exhausted by what he demanded of himself. Never have I seen anyone, not even Kaddi, call up such power in such a short span of time. I promised him I would sit with you, in order to persuade him to rest."

"And Modir?"

"She helps prepare Kaddi's body for the funeral rite. Dottir, Kaddi spent his strength helping Lodvar, and perished in the doing."

Gyda closed her eyes against the pain of it. An image of the old man appeared bright in her mind. "He is not gone. A part of him—a part of him will remain with us."

"Ja. A spirit so strong as that cannot be vanquished."

"And—and Gunnar?"

"Do you not remember?"

The pounding of her rage, and terror. Hot blood flowing over her hands. "I killed him."

"Ja, Dottir."

"What happened to the rest of them?"

"Friti's body washed ashore when the eddy overturned the second vessel. Our defenders killed or captured the rest of Friti's men. Both his ships are wrecked, and mine sustained a lot of damage." He smoothed her hair back from her face with a scarred hand. "Not that I mind the cost."

"It is done?"

"So it would seem." The darkness banished, ja, and

life forever changed. They would have to pick up the pieces, heal their wounds, and go on.

"Fadir," she whispered, "about Lodvar—"

"What about him?"

"I want you to know, I am his bride. We swore ourselves to one another, before ever that final battle took place. I hope you will not object, because I need him. I do not think I can explain—"

Tolljur smiled slightly. "Dottir, you do not have to. That is one need I can fully understand."

Chapter Thirty-Eight

In the clear morning light, the shore lay littered and stained, as with rubble cast by the hand of a giant. Wreckage from Friti's boat which had broken apart in the final eddy, its back shattered like that of a fragile bird, strewed the stones. Bodies and cargo alike floated far and wide, even though Tolljur's people had been working to gather it in since dawn.

It made a sight such as Lodvar had never seen and hoped never to see again. Neither of Friti's ships would sail home to Husavik.

Would he?

Leaning heavily on Kaddi's twisted staff, he marveled at his weakness. He should not try to make any decisions now. His mind, like his strength, had been scorched during the battle. His heart...

His heart longed to see his mother in Husavik, and feared for her. But much like Tolljur's two ships that, anchored, had managed to survive the waves, it now belonged here.

Or wherever Gyda might be. Anchored to her in body and spirit.

Upon that thought he felt her—felt her—and turned around. She approached along the clifftop, leaning as heavily on the arm of her brother, who came at her side, as Lodvar did on Kaddi's staff. Ja, they all leaned on one another. The strength—it flowed from the gods to each of them, and to the land itself. Uniting all into one.

Instinctive as breathing, Lodvar sent out his thoughts, his being, to touch with hers. He could sense her weakness, her devastation, her anxiety. And beneath it all, a certainty that steadied him.

Here was his bedrock. Here, his life.

"Well, Shaman," Magnus spoke as soon as they reached him. "Surveying what you have wrought?"

"Me?" Lodvar stared. "I am no warrior."

A rueful smile curled one side of Magnus's mouth. "Are you not? I might differ, but I will not waste my breath."

Lodvar looked at Gyda. Pale, cut, bruised, and bandaged, with dark shadows beneath her eyes, the sight of her nevertheless caused his heart to bound.

My love.

Which of them spoke the words? Cursed if he knew.

Aloud, he asked, "Where are your parents?"

Magnus answered, "Preparing for the funeral rite." He gestured toward the bay. "Gunnar's boat will become the funeral pyre. Kaddi, and others of our honored dead, will take their final voyage out to sea."

"And the other dead? Those of Husavik?"

Magnus's nostrils flared. "They are being collected. What do we owe them, Shaman?"

Lodvar contemplated it. He had viewed Friti's body after Tolljur's folk carried it in from the tide—all that anger and desire for vengeance flown.

"Perhaps," he told Magnus, "it is more a matter of what we owe ourselves. What manner of folk are we? Do we spit upon our vanquished enemies?"

Magnus looked thoughtful. He nodded. "You make

a good point. We, who carry the blood of berserkers, especially, must learn to rise above."

"So we should." Gyda looked at him. "Life is long, and filled with wondrous magic."

Magnus shrugged and took himself off without a backward look. Gyda reached for Lodvar blindly. Their hands connected and held tight.

"Ach," she said, "now I can breathe. Now I will grow well."

"Gyda—"

"I do not wish to speak of it." Her eyes met his. "I wish to speak only of the future. I want my future to be spent with you. Tell me you will stay here, in Sorvagur."

"Truthfully, I cannot imagine being anywhere else, save with you."

She stepped into his arms. "I am sorry I lost the knife you gave me."

"I am not. The man from whom I received it—he never loved me. Even though he married Modir later, when it suited him, it was not for her sake, or mine. Just a convenience. Let the knife, like the past, be gone."

"Your mother—"

"Ja. I will need to find a way to rescue her. To bring her here to Sorvagur."

"Will she leave your father? After all this time, would she be willing to abandon him?"

"I think so."

"Then ja, we will find a way. What will happen at Husavik, now that both Friti and Gunnar are dead?"

"The gods only know. Friti has other children. I suppose they will fight things out among themselves."

"And us? What will happen between us?"

Lodvar drew her close against him. He inhaled the incomparable scent of her—woodsmoke, soap, and woman.

"I am not worthy of you, Gyda Tolljursdottir. A slave—"

She snorted. "A man who speaks to the gods. A powerful shaman."

"Still—"

"The man who speaks to my heart."

"Gyda, might I dare to hope—"

"Dare." She leaned into him. "Am I not already your bride? And who could stand before such a union—of berserker and shaman?"

Before he could answer, a cry came across the clifftop. They turned as one to see Eadha and Tolljur appear, the latter limping as he came. Eadha carried what looked like a black cloud in her hands.

Gyda breathed, "What on earth?"

Both her parents were breathless when they arrived. Puffing, Eadha said, "I wanted to catch you before—well, before you make any decisions."

Fixing her bright hazel eyes upon Lodvar, she hurried on, "Young man, Tolljur and I have something to say to you." She glanced at her husband, who smiled slightly.

"Well, Wife, say it."

"I do not speak for you."

He threw back his head and laughed. "By my heart, Eadha, you do."

She smiled back at him and shook her head. "Lodvar, your mother was one of my closest friends, When I arrived as a slave at Husavik—well, she saved me."

"As I heard it, you saved each other."

"I tried to help her." Tears filled Eadha's eyes. "I could not bring her away with me to freedom. Now you are here, and I—we—want you to know you are welcome."

"Thank you, Mistress."

"Tolljur and I have been going through Kaddi's things, preparing him for his final voyage."

She shook out the bundle in her hands. Unfolded, it proved to be Kaddi's black cloak made of raven feathers. "We want you to have this."

Lodvar's throat promptly closed. "Ach, I could not. He should wear that on his final journey."

"No," Tolljur said. "He should pass it—and the power it represents—to the next generation. To you."

Taking the cloak from his wife's hands, Tolljur placed it carefully around Lodvar's shoulders. "Look there. The fit is just right."

Indeed, so it was. Even though Lodvar stood a head taller than the wizened Kaddi, the cloak seemed to lengthen to fit him.

"Will you stay and fill Kaddi's place? We are in need of a shaman."

Straightening his spine, Lodvar looked Tolljur in the eye. "I am honored, Jarl Tolljur. There is naught I would like better. First, I must away to assure that my mother, back in Husavik, is safe—with Gunnar and Friti both gone, I hope she may be persuaded to return here with me."

"That would also be my dearest wish," Eadha agreed.

"Ja," Tolljur agreed. "She will be most welcome."

"And now, Husband, come." Eadha took Tolljur by

the arm. "These two have things to say to one another." She reached out and touched the raven feathers of the cloak softly, before laying her fingers against Lodvar's cheek. "It suits you."

They went off, and Gyda turned to Lodvar, a smile in her eyes. "You see, you have received all the acceptance you could wish."

"I am humbled."

"Well, it is certain I am not the bride of a boastful man! Some who had successfully raised wind and fire, and commanded the seas, might begin to think highly of themselves."

"That I will never do."

She leaned closer. "Perhaps you should. It is not every man worthy of being husband to the daughter of a jarl and a berserker besides."

"Gyda..." Lodvar searched for the words he needed. They must come from his heart, from the deep place in his spirit where he'd carried her so long. "I loved you before I met you—all my life, it seems. You were always there, calling to me. You gave me a reason to go on, even in the darkest times. I never dreamed—" He paused abruptly, unable to express his feelings.

She curled her fingers around his wrists. "Ja? You never dreamed what?"

"You would be beautiful, as well."

"As well as what?"

"The better part of me." Lodvar drew a breath and bowed his head over their joined hands. "Will you do me the great honor of spending the rest of your life with me?"

Her fingers contracted painfully on his wrists before she slipped her hands into his, palms to palms.

Her voice sounded unsteady when she spoke. "The honor—the honor will be mine. But, Lodvar, it is you who might wish to reconsider." Her gray eyes sought his. "Do you truly wish to tie yourself to a woman with berserker blood in her veins, who has proven she can, at any time, slip into the berserker's rage?"

"I do. Are you sure you wish to tie yourself to a shaman? It is not an easy life either."

"I do." Radiance ignited in her eyes. Before the brightness of it, all doubt fled.

She brushed her lips across his. "It seems, Shaman, the vows have truly been spoken. You know what comes next?"

"The honeymoon."

"Ja." She kissed him, her mouth molding to his just as her spirit and his melded into one. "But I tell you now, Lodvar Haraldsson, one month—and one lifetime with you—will never be enough."

A word about the author...

Multi-award-winning author Laura Strickland delights in time traveling to the past and searching out settings for her books, be they Historical Romance, Steampunk, or something in between. Her first Scottish Historical hero, Devil Black, battled his way onto the publishing scene in 2013, and the author has never looked back.

Nor has she tapped the limits of her imagination. Venturing beyond Historical and Contemporary Romance, she created a new world with her ground-breaking Buffalo Steampunk Adventure series set in her native city in Western New York.

Married and the parent of one grown daughter, Laura has also been privileged to mother a number of very special rescue dogs, and is intensely interested in animal welfare. Her love of dogs, and her lifelong interest in Celtic history, magic, and music, are all reflected in her writing. Laura's mantra is Lore, Legend, Love, and she wouldn't have it any other way.